It looked like love.
It felt like love.
But this isn't a love story.

The Places I've Cried in Public *is a work*
of fiction but it deals with many real issues including
controlling behaviour and sexual assault.

Links to advice and support can be found
at the back of the book.

First published in the UK in 2019 by Usborne Publishing Ltd., Usborne House,
83-85 Saffron Hill, London EC1N 8RT, England. usborne.com

Text © Holly Bourne, 2019

Author photo © L. Bourne, 2017

Cover and inside artwork by Jan Bielecki © Usborne Publishing, 2019

The right of Holly Bourne to be identified as the author of this work has been asserted
by her in accordance with the Copyright, Designs and Patents Act, 1988.

The name Usborne and the Balloon logo are Trade Marks of
Usborne Publishing Ltd.

A CIP catalogue record for this book is available from the British Library.

ISBN 9781474949521   JFMAMJJ SOND/20   04918/7

Printed in the UK.

HOLLY BOURNE

The PLACES I'VE CRIED IN PUBLIC

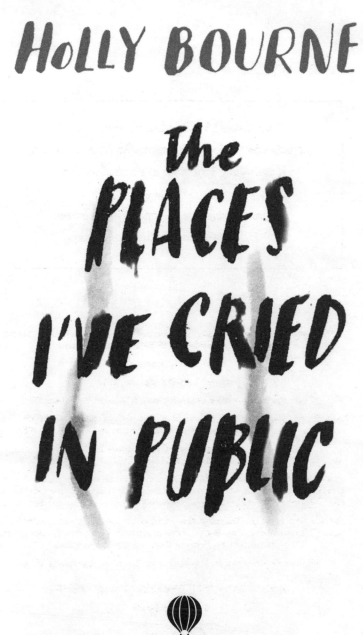

USBORNE

Can you see the girl crying?

She's not always easy to spot. She may have her head down, pretending to be on her phone, using her hair to cover her blotchy face. Or she may be leaning against the bus window, turning into the glass so you can't see her tears.

There are telltale signs though – the odd gasp for air, her back jolting with a suppressed sob, or she'll wipe under her eyes, catching the tears and smearing them into her skirt before they give her away.

Girls cry on park benches. Girls cry in train station waiting-rooms. They cry on the dance floor of clubs. Girls cry at the bus stop. Girls cry at the back of lessons. They sit on the pavement and cry on cold concrete at two a.m., their shoes held in their hands. Girls cry in school bathrooms. Girls cry on bridges. They cry on the stairs of house parties.

This is the story of one.

What keeps making her cry?

Or is a better question: *Who?*

A Bench by the
Railway Bridge

It's half two in the morning and I'm back here where it started.

Yes, of course it's cold. It's half two in the morning, mid February, and I'm not dressed properly. I just bunged my coat on over my pyjamas and ran here in my slippers. I'm sat on this bench, shivering violently under the useless faux fur of my coat and I'm not sure why.

You see, I was in bed, doing my usual *not-sleeping* and *trying-to-figure-out-what-the-hell-happened* and *thinking-it's-all-my-fault* and *huddling-into-a-ball-and-disintegrating*, and then, tonight – half an hour ago, to be precise – it became clear.

I needed to come here.

My breath escapes in short puffs of crystallized fog that float down to the dormant railway tracks. It's so quiet in this alleyway. It feels like the whole world is asleep. Apart from me and my broken heart.

I've used up so many tears on you already and it's not helping me get over this any better. So I'm sat here in the freezing cold, my jaw shaking, and I'm trying to connect the dots.

This bench may not look like much. It's got a plank missing, a grey mossy finish from years of weather, and it's plastered in offensive graffiti. But this nondescript bench is significant, because this bench is where I first cried.

Not my first *ever* cry, but the first cry I can link back to you. To the story of us. Though you and I were more of a scribble than a story.

If I can untangle the messy line of biro, if I can trace back the scribble, it might finally make sense.

Here's the starting point. I'm sat right on it.

I pull my coat tighter around myself. I close my eyes, and I remember.

"Don't worry," Mum said, watching me not eat my cornflakes. "*Everyone* will be new."

She gave me that smile. The one that begged me not to make her feel guilty about it all.

"Everyone will know at least someone, whereas I know literally no one."

"You will, by the end of the day."

I didn't finish my cereal, so I had to fish the orange pulp out with my fingers before I could pour the leftover milk down the sink. "I hope so," I said, before going back to the bedroom that didn't feel remotely like mine yet. I'd not finished unpacking, which didn't help. Boxes of my life were still piled around the space, waiting for me to admit this was my life now and actually open them. I'd only removed my clothes, record player and vinyl, and, most importantly, my guitar.

I didn't have time to play it but I picked it up anyway, shrugging the strap over my shoulder and perching on the end of my bed. I strummed a chord, feeling instantly calmer. I sang softly.

"Come on, Amelie, or we'll be late," Mum called down the hallway. I still couldn't get used to us not having stairs.

I unwrapped my guitar from around myself and reluctantly put it down. "I'm coming."

I piled into the front seat of our hot car and it was like climbing into an uncomfortable hug. My legs smudged sweat onto the leather. Summer was reluctantly holding on, apparently missing the memo that it was now September. We pulled out of the communal car park and I turned the radio up.

Mum turned it down again. "Are you sure you're going to be okay walking home? Call me if you get lost."

"Mum, there are these things called phones. They have maps on them now and everything."

"Well, you can still call."

We drove along streets I didn't know, rounded corners I didn't know, drove past students I didn't know, who were on the way to the same college as me that I didn't know. They walked in clumps, while I shrank into my seat. We got stuck in traffic as cars struggled to find parking spaces. Exhaust smoke fugged its way through the car's air conditioning, making it smell of pollution.

"I may have to spit you out here," Mum said. "Are you going to be okay?"

I nodded, even though it wasn't the truth. It wasn't her fault any of this was happening. It wasn't Dad's either, not really. Having no one to blame for being ripped out of my old life almost made it worse.

"Hang on." She indicated and yanked the car into a space. I opened the door, readying myself for the big unknown, when Mum reached over and put her hand on my shoulder. "Are you *really* going to be okay?" she asked for the third time, in her posh accent that wasn't an accent since we'd moved down here. "I'm sorry, Amelie. I know you didn't want this."

I smiled for her and nodded for her. "I'll be fine."

She left me on the pavement in a cloud of fumes, and I watched her weave away through the thrumming cars. I wasn't entirely sure where to go so I followed the scatterings of people my age, all walking in the same direction. My skin prickled as my shyness rash erupted across my chest. Great, just what I needed on my first day in a brand-new college in a brand-new part of the country – to be Blotchy Shy Girl.

I fell into step behind two other girls and, despite the heat, did up my denim jacket to hide the worst of my red chest.

My skin got itchier as I imagined the potential hell awaiting me that day.

- Having to nervously stand around, begging people to come and talk to me with my eyes.

- Not knowing where I was going or what I was doing, and feeling insecure about how crap I was at basic human functioning.

- As a result of my shyness, probably attracting some kind of weirdo who I don't like, because they're the only one who talks to me, and then spending the rest of my life being their friend out of duty.

- Freaking about where to sit at lunchtime and ending up in the corner, alone, watching everyone else be the friendly, extroverted person I wish I could be.

- Having to introduce myself and stumbling over my words and my voice going all croaky and my rash getting rashier and everyone thinking I'm a weirdo.

The girls in front chatted excitedly, wisps of their conversation floating over their shoulders.

"*Did you see Laura on results day? She's gone full-on goth. Do you think her new boyfriend knows she loves Taylor Swift? Should we tell him?*" They giggled and my stomach twisted. I forgot how mean girls could be. Back in Sheffield, I had my own little bubble of nice people who I loved and trusted. It had taken sixteen years to find friends who got me and I them. I couldn't believe I had to start again. The girls turned left and I copied, finding myself face-to-face with my new college, freshly painted for the new year. Streams of students trickled in through various entrances and everyone seemed to know at least someone. They launched themselves into hello hugs, asking one another how their summers had been. They were all laughing and chatting too loudly and excitedly – showing off on this fresh start of a new day. This was a small town. The most they could hope for was to "rebrand" slightly over the summer. Whereas I was entirely new. There was not one known face within this compound I stomped into, in my too-hot tan cowboy boots. And maybe that could be liberating – this chance to start over – except I didn't want to start over. I wanted to be back in Sheffield with Jessa and Alfie.

Alfie...

I almost cried then, in broad daylight, before my first day had even started. Tears prickled the backs of my eyelids and sadness welled up in my intestines. And, because he knew me, because he knew me and loved me so well and so hard, Alfie sensed it.

My phone buzzed, right on time.

Alfie: I'm thinking of you today. Just be you –
blotchy shyness rash and all. You WILL make friends.
Remember, only two years x x

I stood to one side. A smile twitched across my face, though it was a bittersweet one.

Amelie: HOW DID YOU KNOW THAT THE RASH HAD COME OUT? X

A sharp bell rang out and I checked the time on my phone – 8.55 a.m. I only had five minutes to try and find room D24 and meet my new form group. I rummaged in my satchel for my map of campus. The paper shook in my hands as I managed to locate the refectory right in front of me, and, apparently D24 was in the media block to the right of it.

There, I thought. *That wasn't so bad. You are coping.*

My phone buzzed again.

Alfie: I miss that rash. You'll be amazing today x x

I found myself closing my eyes. Standing there with the sun warm on my eyelids, the last dregs of late arrivers striding past me, I could picture every contour of Alfie's face. The mole just next to his left eye, every tuft of his misbehaving hair. Instinctively, I typed out a reply.

Amelie: I love you

I stared at my screen, watching the cursor flash next to the "u". Another surge of emotions ran through me and I deleted what I'd written. I watched the screen erase the truth, one letter of it vanishing at a time. The bell rang again. I was now late for my first day of whatever the hell my life was now.

Amelie: I miss you

I sent that one.
It wasn't a lie, but it wasn't the whole truth.

I shake my head. Here, now, on this cold bench at almost three o'clock in the morning. My breath comes out as more of a pant. My body's so freezing I can't imagine ever being warm again. That warm day, not so very long ago, couldn't feel further from this cold witching hour of *everyone-else-is-asleep* o'clock.

What would've happened if I'd sent that first message?

That is one of the Big Ifs I've been turning over. What if I *had* told Alfie I loved him? What if I hadn't deleted that truth? What if I'd gone with my gut instinct, the primal part of me that typed out the words *I love you* – even though we had that stupid agreement? If I'd sent that first message, would it have stopped what came afterwards?

I will never know.

Because I didn't tell Alfie I loved him. I only told him I missed him. I pressed *send* and watched one tick turn into two ticks. Then I put my phone back into my bag and ran to the media block.

If you're shy, trust me when I say there's nothing worse than entering a room late. I opened the door to D24 in a flustered sweaty heap and everyone turned around like meerkats. I tugged at my denim jacket as my rash bloomed further across my body.

"Sorry I'm late," I stuttered to my new form tutor.

"Don't worry. You're not even the last to arrive. Lots of you get lost on the first day." He gestured to an empty chair in the circle. I sank into it and avoided eye contact with the people sat opposite. "As I was saying," he continued, "my name's Alistair and I'm your form tutor for the next two years." He looked young, with ginger hair and a pink shirt. "You're lucky, I'm pretty damn awesome."

The circle laughed self-consciously and I looked up to take everyone in. I just KNEW they'd all spent ages picking out today's *this-is-me* outfit and the room reeked of *trying-too-hard*. One guy sitting opposite had a political slogan emblazoned across his chest and held a leather-bound journal so we knew he Cared About The World and Wrote Things In This Special Journal. The girl next to him showed off freshly dyed pink hair, wearing large cupped headphones like a necklace and a denim pinafore over yellow tights. Not that I could judge. I'd agonized over exactly which granny dress to wear and couldn't handle the fact it was too hot for my usual cardigan. "Even if you went to war, you'd go in an oversized cardigan," Alfie had once said, before removing my cardigan and looking at my shoulders like they were the best pair of shoulders in the whole goddamned world. My fashion style is essentially, *If some old person has recently died in a dress, that's the dress I want to wear.* I don't even own a pair of jeans.

The door burst open and a girl with red hair and a perfect fringe appeared on the threshold. "Is this D24?" she asked, not seeming to care how everyone's heads had craned in her direction.

"It is indeed," Alistair said. "Sit down, sit down."

She walked over in her own time and smiled before sitting next to me.

"Hi," she whispered to me, just like that. "I'm Hannah."

I felt words catch in my throat but managed a "Hi" back.

Alistair made us wait five minutes for the last latecomer, but they didn't show. He proceeded to welcome us to college and explain how it was different to our secondary schools. We were allowed to wear our own clothes. We wouldn't get detentions. We didn't even have to turn up to class, though we'd get kicked out if we got less than eighty per cent attendance. Today all our lessons would be introductory, before the real timetable started the next day.

"Now, you're organized into forms based on your subjects and you guys are all specializing in the performing arts in some way," he explained. "I'm head of PA. That's why I'm your tutor." He then unexpectedly jumped onto the table and started cancan-ing and doing jazz hands while we all laughed and looked at one another in disbelief. "*Therefore I'm expecting all of you to sign up to this term's talent show,*" he sang like an old-fashioned crooner. Alistair twirled, jumped off the desk, and landed back onto the grey carpet. "Right, let's all get to know each other."

The following hour was hell's teeth. Actually, you know what? I think maybe that's making too light of it. Alistair made us stand up and freakin' *sing* three facts about ourselves. I squirmed in my chair, my rash spreading down and itching my stomach as no one else seemed that embarrassed. I guess performing arts students aren't natural introverts – in fact, I'm the only singer I've met with significant social anxiety.

"*I'm Darla,*" sang the girl with pink hair. "*I love writing songs, taking photos of sunsets, and living every day like it's my last.*"

"*Hello, Darla,*" we were forced to sing back.

Leather Notebook Boy, to be fair, was not a happy bunny. "I'm George," he said gruffly. "I like books, and football, and politics, and I think I may be in the wrong form because I'm not studying any performing arts."

Alistair burst out laughing. "*Oh no, George,*" he sang, all dramatically like we'd suddenly walked into a musical. "*You may very well be in the wrong room. Let me check my notes!*" He twirled again and picked up his clipboard. "*No, your name isn't on here,*" he sang again. "*I'm so sorry, but you don't belong heeeeeeeere.*"

"Bollocks," George said.

Alistair skipped over and peered at George's welcome sheet. "*You're in B24, not D24,*" he sang out.

"Double bollocks."

"*Please do not swear in my classroooooom…*"

George collected his stuff, still cradling his leather notebook. "Let's sing him out," Alistair suggested, before bursting into "So Long, Farewell" from *The Sound of Music*. Everyone joined in, like this was a totally normal occurrence. Apart from Hannah, who rolled her eyes at me and mimed shooting the side of her head.

When it was her turn, she stood up, and said, "I do drama, not music. I'm not singing."

"*As you wish.*"

"I am Hannah." Her voice demanded to be listened to, in a quiet, assured way. "I like drama but I hate musicals, and this, this…" She paused for effect. "This is my idea of hell on earth."

The room gasped but Alistair was totally unbothered by her criticism. "I can't believe someone in my form doesn't like musicals," he muttered. "There must be some kind of mistake."

Hannah shrugged and sat back down. It was my turn. Everyone twisted towards me and my chest tightened, my lungs drawing in on themselves.

Pretend it's a gig, pretend it's a gig, I told myself as I scrambled out of my seat. *How am I supposed to sing when I can't breathe? Okay, pretend it's a gig. You get through enough of them somehow. Breathe…breathe…*

"*My name's Amelie.*" My voice cracked but I recovered as I sang. "*I just moved here from Sheffield. And I like songwriting and singing and playing the guitar."*

As always, like with my gigs, the world hadn't ended. People were vaguely smiling, hardly interested.

Alistair grinned as I sat down. "You have a lovely singing voice, Amelie," he commented. Everyone turned towards me again and I essentially became just a shyness rash. I hated him for a moment – for singling me out and making me the centre of attention, even though it was a nice compliment. I slunk down in my chair and hid behind my hair until the exercise was finished.

Things didn't improve in the public-humiliation Olympics. Alistair then made us play "hilarious" ice-breaking activities. One was a game called Zip Zap Boing where we had to pass "a ball of energy" around the circle, using a series of ridiculous sounds and actions. I only zipped, which meant saying the word "zip" and passing the "energy" from one side of myself to another. Hannah only zipped too, and muttered under her breath, "This is awful and I want to die." I smiled at her widely to try and show her we were the SAME and we could BE FRIENDS. Then we were given bingo cards with things like *Favourite colour is pink* and *Likes to run* on them, and were instructed to find people with these traits. I almost considered dropping out of college right there and then, and telling my parents it wasn't for me. However, a bingo square said *Comes from another place* and everyone flocked to me right away and I didn't have to approach anyone or say anything apart from "Yes, Sheffield" multiple times. Once everyone had ticked me off, they started chatting to each other like it was the simplest thing in the world. I stood on the edges, clutching my bingo card, my armpits sweating, missing my old life and my old friends. Then I heard Hannah's voice behind me.

"Can you pretend to like pink for me?" she asked.

I spun and smiled goofily at her. "I mean, it's *always* been my favourite colour."

"Great. Wow. What a coincidence." She marked it down on her sheet. "And, do you have any pets?"

I nodded. "Yep. A unicorn."

"Me too!"

Both our smiles grew wider and I wrote down her name in that square. "It's Hannah, right?" I asked.

"Yep. And I can pretend to have broken a bone, if you want?"

"Brilliant. Which one?"

"All of them." She shrugged. "I jumped down an elevator shaft in protest against this ice-breaker game. Broke every bone in my body. I'm a miracle of science."

We both giggled and our bonding continued.

"Do you have curly hair?" I asked her.

"I mean, when I curl it. Yes, yes I do."

"Are you left-handed?"

"Sometimes I put out my left hand to look for the L shape, because I forget my left from right. Does that count?"

"Totally counts."

"Right, my turn to tick some off. Have you ever been abroad?"

"I lived in Sheffield," I replied.

"Totally is abroad."

Darla interrupted us by yelling "BINGO!" We all clapped her and she did an actual faux Oscar acceptance speech.

Alistair then talked us through the campus, and how the timetable worked, and said we could come to him any time we needed. Despite his extrovertness, I kind of liked him. Form time would definitely never be boring. He dismissed us and everyone trickled out of the door, chatting like they were friends already.

I dawdled with my bag, taking a bit too long to fit my notepad in. Hannah was fiddling with hers and I hoped we might talk more. She zipped hers up and raised an eyebrow at me. "Well, we survived. Do you feel inducted?"

"I feel like I may need therapy for the rest of my life."

She laughed. "What have you got next?" We fell into step and pushed our way out of the media block into the sunshine. Hundreds of students hurried from A to B, stopping to check their own maps to figure out where exactly "B" was.

"English language," I said.

She pulled a pair of mirrored aviators down onto her nose. "Oh no, I'm doing lit. Otherwise we might've been in the same class. We're heading to the same block though. Have you got a map?"

I walked with Hannah all the way to my next lesson. She told me she'd chosen to come to college rather than stay at her secondary school. "It was a religious school and they banned sixth-form girls from wearing vest tops, even in the summer. I ain't staying somewhere like that." She was one of only five students who didn't stay on. We stopped outside my classroom door, and I checked the number to ensure I was in the right place. "Some of us are meeting for coffee actually," Hannah said, adjusting the strap on her rucksack. "There's this place in town called BoJangles. You can come if you like? At lunchtime?"

I could've hugged her. Because, had it been up to me, I'd never have mentioned seeing her ever again even though I was desperate to. I bleated out yes and asked where BoJangles was.

She showed me on her phone. "It's so cute you don't know your way around our tiny town," she said. "Don't worry, it takes about five minutes to get the hang of it. Anyway," she took her sunglasses off and waved goodbye. "See you at lunch."

"Bye," I called after her, watching her red hair merge into the chaos of new students getting lost in the corridors. "Thank you," I said quietly, almost to myself.

It's *so* cold, I'm going to have to leave soon. There's a thin layer of ice creeping closer towards my arse. I bow my head, pull my legs up, and push my knees into my eye sockets.

Hannah isn't my friend any more.

I don't really have friends any more.

The rest of that first day went as well as it could. I managed to find all my rooms. I met my teachers. They told us how much harder A levels were compared to GCSEs. My music teacher, Mrs Clarke, seemed cool and she was the most important one. I went to BoJangles and I sat quietly as Hannah introduced me to Jack and Liv. We bonded over how the North is different to the South.

"So you say 'bAth', whereas we say 'bARth'."

"Gravy? On chips? That's the most disgusting thing I've ever heard."

"So, where exactly is Sheffield? Oh, okay. And what's the Midlands? I thought Sheffield was up north?"

"You play guitar?" they asked, once we'd exhausted all the words I say differently. "And you write your own songs? Wow."

On the whole, as first days go, it was okay. These guys all knew each other better than they knew me, but they'd gone to college to meet new people and I was a new person. Hannah clearly led this little group of defectors from their religious school, and Jack clearly fancied Hannah. He stared adoringly while she described how naff the drama facilities were at their old school. "So, why have you moved all the way down here?" Hannah asked, checking her perfect fringe in a hand mirror.

"My dad got made redundant. He couldn't find another job up north."

Hannah put her mirror away and looked at me with genuine sympathy. "Wow, that sucks." The rest of the table made supportive noises over the foam of their coffee.

"It's okay," I lied. "My mum grew up near here, so I've been down south a few times before."

"Well, just in case you don't know," she said. "We put ketchup on our chips, not gravy."

"Heathen."

And we smiled the smiles of new friends being made.

I hadn't met you yet, of course. This was still Before You. Maybe I sensed you though – on that very first day – walking home in the sun, to the place that wasn't yet home.

All I know is that I just about felt okay as I walked back to the new flat. My phone led me down this alleyway as a shortcut, past the backs of people's gardens.

I'd have two hours to play guitar before my parents got back and snatches of new lyrics drifted into my head as I walked through the speckles of sunshine. The alleyway curved left and I emerged onto a rickety railway bridge. My phone told me to cross it, so I did, stopping in the middle to look out at the train tracks vanishing into the point of a triangle. My brain got all quiet and a lyric wiggled its way through my subconscious.

I've got a horizon either side of me... I've got your love

etched deep inside of me... I want to go back, but life has
other plans...

I knew right away it was a keeper. The start of a song. I bashed the lines out on my phone as a memo note, keen to get it down before it vanished back into the ether. I'd just finished typing when my phone started vibrating in my hand.

My heart twisted over as I held it to my ear.

"Hello?" I said, even though every singing, sad part of my body knew who it was.

"Ammy! How did it go?"

Alfie's voice was the sound of safety. The sound of comfort and home. And yet it sounded so far away from this bridge.

I tried to ignore my lurching stomach. "It went okay actually. I met this drama girl, Hannah, who was pretty friendly and cool. The mixing equipment at college is good."

He laughed and I could picture him doing it – the way he always held his hand up to his chin, the way one eye closed up a little bit more than the other. "Well, that's the important thing," he said. "And I'm glad not all southern fairies are too awful."

My phone tucked between my shoulder and my ear, I walked towards this bench at the far end of the bridge, sitting down right where I'm sat now.

"I don't think I'll make any friends if I refer to everyone as southern fairies."

He laughed again. "True! But you can secretly think it at all times. In fact, we won't let you back into Yorkshire if you don't."

"You better let me back me into Yorkshire!"

Laughing in the background, the noise of a scuffle, Alfie called "HEY" and then Jessa's voice boomed into my ear. "AMELIE, WE MISS YOUUUUUUUUUUU. COME BACK UP NORTH, YOU TWAT."

My smile split my face in half. "I miss you too."

"School was SO weird without you today. I even considered putting a cardigan around a balloon and pretending it was you."

"I'm not currently wearing a cardigan," I told her. "It's too warm down here."

"OH MY GOD, GUYS," she shouted away from the speaker. "SHE SAYS IT'S SO HOT DOWN SOUTH SHE ISN'T EVEN WEARING A CARDIGAN!"

There were sounds of disbelief from my old friends. "Pics or I won't believe it," Kimmy shouted. Then laughter and more disturbance and I found myself bent over, pressing my hand to my guts.

"Give me the phone back, Jessa. Jessa?" I heard Alfie negotiate. "I'll let you have a chip. Okay, three chips. That's more than three! Okay…hang on… Sorry, Ammy, you still there?"

"I'm still here."

"Hang on. I'll let them walk in front so we can talk properly."

I heard the crunch of Alfie walking across gravel. "Where are you guys?" I asked, trying to keep my voice from squeaking.

"Oh, the Botanical Gardens – same old, same old." I could

picture them. I knew exactly which chip shop they'd gone to, and I knew exactly which bench they'd sit on.

"What have you got on your chips?" Though I already knew the answer.

"Gravy, cheese and mayonnaise – the secret ingredient!"

"It's the mayonnaise that makes it so wrong."

"I'm before my time, Ammy, you know that…" There was a pause down the line. "I miss you," he said, eventually. "Today was weird and horrible."

I gulped and blinked up at the blue of the sky. "Two years will go quickly enough."

"That's what we keep saying." Another pause. "But, you're okay? I was thinking about you – sending you happy thoughts. Did you get them?"

One tear escaped. The beginning of this. I collected it with the tip of my finger and flicked it off. "I did. Thank you."

We both sighed, not saying it. We'd said it all before I left. "How did your first A level chemistry lesson go?" I tried to steer the conversation towards upbeat. "Were you allowed to use the Bunsen burner?"

"How many times do I have to tell you there's more to it than Bunsen burners?"

"They're the only reason you like science, and you need to stop lying to yourself."

Alfie laughed, but it was a sad one. I could hear Kimmy and Jessa arguing somewhere near him. "I'd better go," he said, "they're eating all my chips."

I did not want the phone conversation to end. I did not

want to lose the sound of his voice. But we'd agreed to get on with this, we'd agreed to accept the shitty situation for what it was. We'd agreed to put us on ice.

"It's only two years," Alfie had said, clutching my face the night before I left, my entire sixteen years of life packed into cardboard boxes. "Then we'll both be at Manchester and we can be together again."

"What if you can't wait for me that long?"

"You know I will."

"I don't want you to feel tied to me and resent me," I'd said, crying and not sure I really meant it.

"I won't. And neither will you. We agreed, remember? We're free to do anything with anyone, apart from falling in love."

"It's literally impossible for me to fall in love with someone who isn't you."

I'd certainly meant it at the time.

We'd kissed and both cried and had sex for only the eighth time, and it was bittersweet and clumsy and a bit snotty, but still lovely. Afterwards, we stayed up all night, whispering about how amazing Manchester would be.

"Okay," I said, only two weeks later – feeling like every centimetre of distance between us was an individual knife in my stomach. "Thanks for calling. I really appreciate it." Another tear splashed onto my dress before I had a chance to catch it.

"I'm so glad your first day went okay."

"Me too...thanks again."

He rang off and I looked at my phone for a very long time as a wave of grief hit. My phone wobbled in my shaking hands and a teardrop splashed onto the screen. That was all it took, visual confirmation of my sadness. On this bench, this very bench, all those months ago – when the sun was shining and I hadn't met you yet – I dropped my head onto my lap and I cried. Anyone could've walked past and seen me. The grief was too raw for me to care. My back shuddered, my dress splattered with salty tears and trails of snot.

I am on this same bench now, my bum numb from the cold. I'm sat in exactly the same place and I want to reach through a wormhole in time and comfort myself, pat my own back. I reach out with my gloved hand, like I can touch my former self. Like I can wipe away her tears. Like I can pull her hair back from her ear and whisper into it, urging me not to do all the things I was about to do. The things that led to the me I am now. This empty husk, this confused mess.

It started here.

I don't understand what happened yet, but I know it started here.

If I can join the dots, maybe I can begin to understand. Because I don't understand any of it. Nothing about the last six months makes any sense. Not how I behaved or what I've lost and how much it hurts. It's a mess within a mess.

This bench is Dot Number One. This is the first place I ever cried in public.

I close my eyes against the freezing night air. I feel Past Me rise up, like I'm sitting on my own ghost. I feel the tears on her face, the shudders of her back. I reach through time and I whisper to her:

"Oh, Amelie, you haven't seen anything yet."

The words turn to frost and float out over the railway tracks.

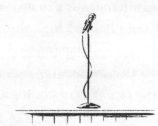

The College Refectory

I've had a week away from seeing you and half-term has lowered my tolerance to be around you. It feels like there's no oxygen in here. Maybe because it's pissing it down outside so everyone's sheltering from the rain. Or maybe it's because the heating is cranked up to maximum and all the windows are steamy. Or maybe it's the scent of mass-produced spag bol wafting over from the kitchen. Or maybe, just maybe, it's because you are here. With her. In the corner.

I can't believe you're here and you're kissing her and I feel like I could die right now.

I'm alone, as always. Exhausted from being up so late last night, sat in the opposite corner, my knees hunched up, the hood of my hoodie popped, curling up like a snail that doesn't want to get smushed. I don't really come in here any more. I hide away in the music room, or fold myself into a silent cubicle of the library. I look through the mass of sweaty bodies – of people laughing and eating spaghetti and not thinking about how heartbroken they are – and I stupidly pick out your face. You're smiling at her from under your trilby hat. You're looking at her how you used to look at me. It hurts in such a profound way there almost isn't room for it in my body.

Why am I doing this to myself? I think, for the millionth time since I got here.

I see Jack and Hannah cuddled up at a table near the door, doing a very good job of pretending not to notice me. My stomach's heavy with bile and the smell of lunch makes it worse. I've hardly been eating and my parents are worried, and I've hardly played guitar and Mrs Clarke is worried, but the only person I want to notice all this and worry is you.

And you're not worried, Reese. In fact, you don't see me at all.

Which is so dumb, because it was here that I first met you. And you more than noticed me that day.

Of course, this sweaty canteen didn't look like this back then...

"Whoa, for a shitty college talent show, they've really gone all out," Hannah said, as we pushed through the doors of the refectory.

The three of us stopped and looked around to marvel at the transformation. A professional stage had been erected where the jukebox usually sat. A makeshift bar had popped up in the kitchen. A proper lighting rig hung from the ceiling, and the whole place sparkled with some intergalactic projection, casting Milky Ways across the walls. The place was packed, like the whole college had decided to come. We were two weeks into term and everyone was still keen to mingle and bond.

"How did the stoned music-tech people have the energy to do all this?" Jack joked, making Hannah laugh. I smiled as I looked between them. I had the bonus of knowing they liked each other before they did – a front row seat for the Jack and Hannah Show. It made me very happy for them but also made me miss Alfie so much it hurt to breathe.

He'd not messaged me in a week.

Not that he was supposed to. Alfie was free, I was free. That was the plan. But that didn't stop me from freaking out that he'd met someone else and forgotten about me and Manchester. This just about distracted me from my IMPENDING STAGE FRIGHT OF ABSOLUTE HELL.

"Where do we put our stuff?" I asked, hoisting my guitar onto my other shoulder.

"I don't know," Hannah said. "I don't need anything for my slot. In one of the classrooms, I guess?"

I took a deep breath, because this meant I had to separate from them, and go talk to other people to figure it out. This made me very nervous and I was already very nervous because I was about to sing my soul out in front of a whole new college of people. Back in Sheffield, I had a little following, which took the weensiest edge off my stage fright. But here, I had no idea if my music would land whatsoever. "I'll go find out."

"Cool. We'll get some drinks," Jack replied, opening his blazer like a swaggery gangster and tapping his nose. "What mixer do you want? Coke, or lemonade?" He had a small water bottle filled with vodka, hidden in his inside pocket.

"Coke, please."

"Meet you near the stage," Hannah called as Jack steered her through the gathering crowd. They vanished into the swell of people – some of whom I was starting to recognize now I'd been here two weeks. Carolyn, a girl from my English class, walked past and said "Hey". I waved back and blushed, hating myself for being so socially awkward. More people trickled in, creating a bottleneck by the doors as they stopped to take in the transformed cafeteria.

You have to sing in front of all these people.

I willed my brain to shut up, trying to focus instead on the right now and working out where to dump my guitar. I spotted Darla and her new green pigtails.

"Darla," I shouted over.

"Hi, Amelie, you alright?"

I pushed through the crowd, bashing someone with my guitar in the process. "I'm good," I said. "I just need to get rid of my guitar. You're playing tonight, right?" She nodded.

"Do you know where we're supposed to put our stuff?"

"Everyone's taking it to the music block," she answered.

"That makes sense. Thanks. So, when you on?" I asked, forcing myself to be friendly.

"Third. You?"

"Second to last."

Darla raised her eyebrows. "Ouch. So you have the whole evening to worry before you go on?"

Her comment hit home like a throw by a professional pitcher. I laughed and it sounded like someone treading on a mouse. "Hahahahah, I know. It sucks. Thanks again."

I said goodbye, squeezed my way out of the bottleneck, and emerged into the balmy black night. It was almost too hot in my cardigan – my grey one, with handmade thumbholes in the cuffs. I was wearing it over a light-blue tea dress and I'd plaited my hair in random sections. My phone buzzed and I couldn't open the message fast enough. Alfie! It must be him.

Jessa: Good luck for the talent show, Granny Cardigan. Have fun freaking out beforehand and pretending to yourself you're not going to win. That's always been so fun to watch x

The smile I smiled was only half of one. Love her as I did, Jessa wasn't Alfie, and that's who I really wanted to hear from. But I sent a reply and did feel less alone and freaked out after I'd done so.

Amelie: I'm not going to win... Seriously though, thanks so much for your message. I wish you were here. Well, no, I wish I was THERE.

I lugged my guitar through the dark to the music block, where a paper sign on the entrance said *Leave your instruments here.*

I pushed through the door, my guitar clattering against the frame, and that's when I first saw him.

Such a handsome face, that was the first thing I noticed. I always thought the word was only used by Disney princesses, or my gran, but that was my initial thought the second I saw Reese Davies.

Cor, he's handsome.

He was standing with his band, but I only really noticed him as he turned to see who'd caused the clatter. His eyes clocked mine and he smiled the smile that would turn out to be the undoing of me.

"Umm, hi," I squeaked. "Is this where I leave my guitar?"

He was tall, and his face was all angles and chin all strong with a dimple right in the middle. He was wearing a hat, indoors, but he was so handsome I didn't even think he was a dick for doing that.

He opened his mouth to reply but Mrs Clarke appeared, looking wilty and a bit stressed. "Amelie, hi! Yes, you're in the right place." She reached out for my case and I handed it to her gratefully. "How are you feeling?"

"Very nervous," I admitted.

"Don't be. You're going to be great."

"I hope so."

We hadn't spoken yet but I was already super aware of Reese's presence, like he was radiating a magnetic force field.

"What are you opening with?" Mrs Clarke asked me, and I talked her through my ten-minute slot while also craning to hear this boy in a hat discuss his.

He'd turned back to his band. "I still think we should open on 'Welcome To Nowhere'," he said, with that quiet authority that would turn out to be the undoing of me.

"Yeah, but, Reese, we agreed on—"

He smiled as he cut his band mate off with his hand. "Dude, we're supposed to be rock 'n' roll, chill the hell out. We can mix up the set list. We've got ten whole minutes to play with, and it's not like we're going to get detention." The rest of them laughed reluctantly and I watched his smile, before Mrs Clarke distracted me again with enthusiastic questions about my own songwriting process.

Now how I wish I'd just walked out of that room and kept walking, walking, walking. But I didn't. Instead I made my way back into the refectory, found Jack and Hannah, let Jack pour a hefty amount of vodka into my Coke, and continued down this path of destruction.

You never know at the time, do you? You can never know if a moment is going to make your life better or rip it apart and piss on the pieces. What scares me most of all, Reese, is that now, back in this stuffy refectory, with my soul sucked dry and my heart beyond repair...I...I...

I still worry I'd do it all over again.

What have you done to me, Reese?

The talent show opened with a beatboxer who went on a bit too long. We found Liv in the crush – she was with a bunch of new friends from her photography class. I'd instantly found Liv to be a bit on the "intimidating" side of "intimidatingly cool" – with her cropped hair and artsy disposition – but she was friendly enough and acted pleased to see me. We all waved hello and yelled into each other's ears to try and be heard above the dude gargling down the microphone. I let the others take on the burden of conversation-making while I stood at the back, nodding and trying not to freak out about my slot.

"It seems like such an unfair combination," Alfie had said before my last gig up in Sheffield, kissing my shaking fingers. "That you're so incredibly talented and yet find being on stage so incredibly awful."

"What if I vomit?" I asked him.

"As I've said many times before, I'll still fancy you," he confirmed.

Vomiting is one of my stage-fright fears – that I will just projectile hurl all down myself. This is closely followed by a fear of peeing myself. This is closely followed by forgetting all my words and just standing there like an idiot. This is closely followed by remembering my words, but singing out of tune. This was my first gig in years without Alfie's gentle reassurance, without him standing in the front row and nodding me along.

Why hadn't he sent a message?

"You okay, Amelie?" Jack yelled over. "You look a bit green. Want some more lubrication?" He held out his water bottle of vodka.

I knew it wasn't a marvellous idea, but I said yes anyway and let him tip more into my cup. When I took a sip, it tasted of almost pure vodka.

The beatboxer finished, to mild applause. The teachers judging held up scorecards of rather-generous fives and sixes. There was a dance act up next. A group of long and lean girls in Lycra hot pants leaped around the stage waving ribbons to some rap mix-up song. The night found its groove. I had another top-up from Jack. Hannah got up and performed an amazing sketch from *The Vagina Monologues*, which won her a few eights. I watched Jack watch her and knew my suspicions were right. I nudged him with my elbow.

"So, you and Hannah?" The vodka had made me able to initiate conversations.

He smiled blearily. "Am I that obvious?" he asked.

"Maybe just to me. I'm more of a watcher than a participant."

"I've noticed."

"I think she likes you too, for what it's worth."

"Really?" His face lit up for a millisecond before dropping into a confused grimace. "But she spent the whole of our school-leaving ball kissing this dickwad from the football team."

"Maybe she was just…"

But I was interrupted by a band coming up onstage. Everyone whooped and cheered louder than ever. I glanced up to see what all the ado was about, and it was hat boy from the music room and his band. *Reese.* He clutched the microphone and flicked the brim of his trilby. "Hi, everyone, we're That Band," he announced, self-confidence lacing his every word. They launched into "Welcome To Nowhere" and it was pretty seamless. The song was tight, the melody catchy. It rose and fell in the right bits. Charisma hurtled out of Reese's voice and crackled through the mike. It was impossible not to look at him. He didn't have the best singing voice, but his air of arrogance carried the song so perfectly I was surprised he didn't spit up lightning.

Hannah found us among the dancing smush. "How did I do?" she yelled.

I reluctantly looked away from the stage. "You were great! When can I vote for you to be prime minister?"

We all hugged – her, Jack, Liv and me. As we broke apart, Hannah looked up at the stage.

"Oh god," she groaned. "All aboard the Dickhead Express."

That.

That was my first red flag. Right there. There's a whole long line of them, punctuated through the mess that was us. Every single one ignored.

Did I stop at this flag and think, *Oh, I wonder why it's so red and flaggy?*

No, I did not.

I leaned in, excited she knew who he was. "Who are you talking about?"

She pointed him out. "Reese fucking Davies. The singer. Otherwise known as King Of The Bell-ends. He went to the other school but we were in the same Stagecoach growing up."

"Why is he such a bell-end?" I asked.

The band skidded into a slow song and it was hard to talk over it without being overheard. The slow song wasn't as good as the opener and I edited it in my head as I listened. They didn't drop the chorus soon enough and some of the lyrics were slightly clichéd, but still, with the way he sang it, I think every girl there fell a little bit in love with him. Apart from Hannah.

The rest of the set whizzed past in a haze of me staring at him too much. The lights went up. The judges awarded them some nines while everyone clapped, and suddenly it was almost my turn.

"You're up next," Hannah called as my eyes followed him offstage. "You'd better go get ready."

Liv and Jack cried "GOOD LUCK, YOU'LL BE AWESOME!" down my ear. I wobbled my way to the side of the stage, where Alistair was waiting.

"Amelie!" he exclaimed, reaching out to high-five me. His face was flushed pink, clashing with his hair. "I'm excited to hear what you're going to do for us." A stand-up comic was on, currently pacing the stage in a suit.

"Have you ever noticed how long people take at cash machines?" he asked, to no laughter at all.

I involuntarily screwed up my face. "I'm a bit nervous," I told Alistair. Understatement of the entire kingdom. A musi-tech student handed me my guitar and I swung it on, feeling slightly more confident – it acted as a wall between me and the world.

Alistair smiled kindly. "I have to say, I was surprised when I saw your name on the sign-up sheet. You barely speak in form time."

"Everyone's surprised when they find out I sing," I admitted. "I don't know why I do it to myself."

An awkward ripple of polite laughter ran through the crowd.

"Uh-oh, someone's flatlining out there," Alistair said, before noticing the stress on my face. "Don't worry! From what I've heard, you're going to smash it. Mrs Clarke says you're very talented."

I tried to let the compliment dissolve in to give me strength, but it didn't work. All the vodka was making me whirry, and the lack of a message from Alfie was making me anxious, and the sound of the comedian dying was making me sick, and… *Why the hell do I do this to myself?* Before every single gig, I ask myself that question. Much too quickly, there was lacklustre applause and the comedian climbed down the steps leading off the stage.

"You're on." Alistair gave me a double thumbs up as all the usual horrid thoughts rushed in. *You're going to be rubbish. You're going to humiliate yourself. Everyone's going to hate it. Why didn't you go to the toilet beforehand? What if you're sick?*

I still found myself climbing the steps, wobbling in my cowboy boots, and pulling my cardigan further over my dress. I sat down on my stool and was so terrified it took me for ever to hook up my guitar.

"Wooo, go, Amelie!" Hannah called out to punctuate the terrible silence, and that tiny act of friendship was enough to get me together.

"Thanks for that," I murmured into the microphone to titters of laughter. The crowd relaxed, helping me relax enough to get my tech sorted. Then, before I had time to think about what the hell I was doing, I leaned into the mike again. "I'd like to sing you a song I wrote called 'Worth The Risk'.

"If we do this,
we can't undo,
what it does,
to me and you…"

I went straight into the piece I'd written for Alfie – my favourite song. The room around me hushed as my music caught them and landed. I closed my eyes and felt the meaning of each word, the story I was telling.

"Only time knows if this is a mistake,
if we are worth the risk we're about to take."

My voice climbed and hit the notes it needed to, and I could tell it was good. *I* was good. I opened my eyes and saw a crowd transfixed. I held them all inside my heart, my song, my story. A surge of euphoria took me over. I was here. I was doing it. I was singing my songs and people were enjoying them, and moments like that make the nerves worth it.

I sang about Alfie and me. About how we'd tiptoed around our feelings for so long, both of us terrified of losing our friendship. Both convinced the other only thought of them platonically. I sang about all the almost-moments and only managing to finally get it together a few months ago, not realizing that we didn't have much time left to be together.

This is the first time I've sung this without him in the audience, I thought. My voice caught and I blinked hard, thinking of the lack of Alfie in the crowd and the lack of a message from him on my phone. It was almost a relief when the song finished.

The audience stood patiently, captivated. I checked my tuning before launching into an easier song. This one was my crowd-pleaser – "Ain't That The Way It Goes" –

an upbeat folk number with a catchy chorus. I felt my confidence regrow as people smiled, a few of them dancing and twirling one another around. I smiled back and even managed to lose myself in the song a bit, tapping my foot, laughing at the funnier lines. Everyone applauded hard when I was done.

"This is my last song," I told everyone. The song I'd started to write overlooking the railway track. "It's new, so I hope you like it. It's called...'Home'."

Just the word *home* set me off a little. Saying it out loud felt like being kicked in the stomach – the part of my stomach that used to feel safe and good whenever I walked through my old front door. Into the home that was snatched from me.

"My heart is where the steel is," I sang, and all my favourite bits of Sheffield flooded back. The water fountains outside the town hall, which I ran through on a rare, hot summer's day; the looming skyscraper of the university arts tower you used as a guiding beacon; the surrounding heather-laden cliffs of the Peak District. *"My heart is steel since I left."* I choked. Oh god, I was losing it. I couldn't lose it, not up here. Not with a whole new college of people watching.

I managed to make it through the first verse and chorus but, halfway through the second verse, I came to the line, *"And I can't go back because home isn't even home any more."*

I started crying, right there onstage. The tears couldn't fall quick enough. My voice wavered. My hands shook on the mike. I couldn't believe it. I was crying openly onstage while trying to win a talent show. I was hijacked by humiliation. Yet somehow I kept singing. I tried to put all my emotion into the song, which was pretty easy what with all the bawling. I allowed myself to remember how awful it was saying goodbye to Alfie, to remember standing in my empty bedroom, looking around and knowing I'd never set foot in there again. I remembered the choking feeling in my throat on the drive down the M1, where all the overhead signs said *THE SOUTH* in aggressive block capitals and how I couldn't even comment because it would make Dad feel even more guilty. I pumped it all into my singing, and the tears fell and fell until I finished on a large sob and a D minor chord.

There was total silence. I wiped under my eyes and looked out at the mass of people, feeling that surreal jolt back to reality I always get when I finish a set. The silence stayed silent for five whole terrible seconds, and then the applause started.

It was louder than it had been for anyone else. I blinked and my mouth fell open and my astonishment spurred everyone to clap harder. I stumbled off the stage, almost crying again at the response, where Alistair greeted me with a grin carved through his freckles. "You're not supposed to come offstage yet," he told me. "You've not even waited for your score!"

"Oh...whoops."

I whipped back to the judges just as they revealed their cards. Two nines and two tens. *I was winning!* I'd just publicly burst into tears, but somehow that had put me in the lead.

I wasn't sure the winning was worth the humiliation of crying, but still. Alistair clapped me on the back, ecstatic. "I've got my eye on you, Miss Talented. She's in my form, everyone. MINE!" he called out to no one. I was almost too embarrassed to return to the crowd. I rubbed my eyes, glad I wasn't wearing any make-up to smudge, handed back my guitar and tried to find my friends. People congratulated me on the way back to them. Darla ran up and gave me a giant hug like we were besties.

"That was amazing," she screeched. "Wow, it's always the quiet ones, isn't it?"

"Thank you," I muttered, desperately searching for the security of Jack and Hannah and Liv. I found them at the back and they all greeted me like I was a war hero – piling onto me for a hug.

"Oh my god," Hannah kept saying. "I'm just in shock. You're so...timid usually. Oh my god. You were amazing."

"I cried!" I replied – still wishing the universe would delete me. "I'm so embarrassed. I literally just cried in public."

"That's what made it so good," she reassured me, pulling me in for another hug. "It was so moving. Sorry you're so homesick, Amelie. I can't imagine how hard it's been."

The next half-hour was a bit of a blur, to be honest. The last act – some gymnasts – finished, and, when their scores were revealed, everyone worked out pretty quickly that I'd won. My name got called and everyone cheered, and I wanted to die but also savour every moment because *I won I won I won!* I think people expected me to do a speech but I could hardly even walk. I took the little metal trophy and went to leave the stage as fast as I could. I stopped as I spotted him at the bottom of the stairs with his band, waiting to pick up his award for second place.

"Here, let me help you," he said, holding out his hand to help me down. I met his eyes and I swear to god something very strange and powerful happened. The rest of the refectory turned to smudge. I became aware of every pinprick of my skin. I took his hand and the surge of chemistry was so potent that I couldn't even say thank you. I just sort of let him gently pull me down. He didn't break eye contact and we just stared at one another in a weird, shared chemical wonder. My body felt like it had released a thousand opera singers shooting into my blood.

"You're amazing," Reese Davies whispered into my plaited hair, before dropping my hand and beckoning the rest of his band onstage.

And I was left standing there, breathless, wondering what the hell had just happened.

You've not made eye contact once since I've been sat here – your eyes are only for her. The jealousy is like nothing I've ever known before. I feel like I could actually vomit with envy and it would come out cartoon-green. Why don't you look at me like that any more? You used to stare at my face like it was the only thing in your life you trusted to give you the answers. And now, nothing. Like none of it happened, or mattered. I'm sat only metres from where you first touched my hand to help me offstage, and it wasn't long after you whispered to me, "That was the moment I knew you were the one, Amelie."

Were you lying? I mean, you can't have more than one "one", so what the hell was I?

This is just one of the many, many questions I don't think I'll ever have the answer to.

There was much more blur after Reese helped me offstage. Some of it was the vodka catching up on me, some of it was the overwhelmingness of everyone trying to talk to me. Most of it was down to him. I was trying to figure out where he'd gone, because even though I had no idea who he really was, I suddenly felt like every face that wasn't his was a waste. I lost Hannah and Jack in the crush of congratulations. Everyone patted my back and called "Go, Amelie!" and I had no one to absorb the attention. My chest started to tighten and so I muttered my excuses about looking for them and backed out of the refectory.

My new college glowed orange against the blue of the falling night. I walked around a corner and leaned against the wall, feeling the coldness of the brick seep through my cardigan. I closed my eyes to recharge – on full introvert burnout by this point. I decided to pick up my guitar and maturely run away home and hope no one noticed. I took a few deep breaths and pictured collapsing in the brilliant emptiness of my bedroom. I smiled at the simple pleasure of the thought, and opened my eyes, expecting to find nothing but the start of my route home. But when they flickered open, I jumped in shock. Reese was standing right in front of me.

"What are you doing all on your own out here?" he asked, tilting his hat-bedecked head.

We locked eyes again and breath deserted my body. It seemed to run out of his too. The pull to this stranger was instantaneous, the chemistry fizzing.

"Just…um…getting some air," I said. "I need to get my guitar."

"I'm heading to the music block too. Will you walk me?"

My need to be alone vanished right away. You hear about romantic moments like this, where two people are tugged together, like God is aggressively knitting your wool into the same jumper. Walking with him to the music block was the most exciting journey I could ever imagine. J. R. R. Tolkien couldn't even dream up a quest more enticing than going to the music block with Reese Davies. I unpeeled myself from the wall and we fell into step naturally, already weirdly attuned.

"I like your hat." The words tumbled out and I shook my head as I said them, blushing.

"Cheers, it's one of my favourites. I call him Old Faithful."
He flicked the brim with his finger and we laughed together.
I kept sneaking glances at him as we walked over, taking tiny
gulps of him in. I liked everything about the way Reese
dressed – like an old-fashioned British dandy. His hat matched
his waistcoat, which finished just on the top of tight black
trousers. He looked like he'd walked out of a different period
of history. Everything about it should have been wrong, but it
was so very right somehow.

"Were you hiding?" he asked. "Sick of people telling you
how absolutely incredible you are already?"

"I wasn't hiding. I was just…" I blushed again. "…hiding."

He really laughed at that. "Shouldn't you be lapping up all
the glory, rather than running from it?"

"I'm shy," I admitted. "Attention is my hell."

"You wouldn't be able to tell from that set. You *are*
incredible though." He laughed again as he watched me
struggling to accept the compliment. "I'm Reese," he added.
"I've seen you around. I've always wanted to say hello.
So, hello." He waved almost goofily.

"Oh, okay. Hello." I was so freaked out by the charged
atmosphere between us that it was impressive I managed
even that.

He grinned. "Hello yourself! It's Amelie, right?"

I nodded, dumbfounded. How did he know my name?
How had he seen me around? I hadn't noticed him. Surely I
would've clocked the hat?

We reached the music block and stood there, just staring

at each other under the orange light. I kept giggling to punctuate the loaded silence, though Reese seemed more comfortable with it than me. "Where's your band?" I asked. "I liked your set, by the way."

"Thank you, and god knows. I saw you leave and I followed you out here." He scratched his neck, which had a hint of a blush creeping up it. "Sorry…" he stammered. "I sound like a stalker now. This is going well, isn't it?"

"What's going well?" I asked.

"Trying to get to know you."

A wave of overwhelm crashed into me and I was suddenly unable to handle what he'd just said. "We should probably get our stuff."

Reese ignored what I'd said. "What are you doing now?"

"Umm, going home?"

"Carrying that guitar all by yourself?"

"I've been doing it for years."

"Yes, but you're probably exhausted from being worshipped all evening. You should let me walk you home." He grinned in a way that said he knew I wasn't going to say anything other than yes. Which I wasn't. He held open the music-block door like a gentleman, and I giggled for about the trillionth time as I walked in. Mrs Clarke was surrounded by piles of instruments and dumped bags, trying to sort them into proper piles. She looked wrung out, but perked up when she saw us step through the door.

"Amelie! Congratulations, you were amazing. Just amazing," she said. "I watched from the back and it blew me away." Then she spotted him behind me. "And you too, Reese. Was that a new song you opened on?"

"It was," he confirmed. "The others didn't think it was ready, but I overruled."

She raised both eyebrows. "Well, I'm a very proud music teacher tonight, that's for sure. You two come for your stuff?"

I picked my way through to my guitar, keen to give myself something to do that wasn't getting static shocks from the sparks flying between us. I picked up my case with an *oomph*. Alfie's bumper sticker was still plastered across the top:

I'M NOT SHY, I'M JUST HOLDING BACK MY AWESOMENESS SO I DON'T INTIMIDATE YOU.

The room faded out as I stroked the edge of the sticker and touched my heart. Then I remembered the total lack of a message from him on my phone, stood up, and hoicked my case over my shoulder.

"You all set?" Reese asked, nodding at me like we knew each other really well already.

"You not taking your guitar?"

"I'm leaving mine here. I've got music first thing on Monday, and it frees me up to help you with yours."

I wrinkled my nose for a second, thinking *I don't need help*, but also simultaneously thinking *Please help me so we can continue standing near each other.*

"Bye, Mrs Clarke." I waved goodbye to my teacher and scuttled after him.

"Bye, Amelie. Congratulations again. Make sure she gets home okay, Reese."

He saluted.

"Where do you live?" he asked once we were outside again.

"Umm. Cherry Hill Gardens." The words still sounded foreign on my tongue. That wasn't where I lived. I lived at number twenty-six Turners Hill, Sheffield. Well, I used to...

"Yep. I know it. This town is so tiny it's pretty easy to navigate." He took my guitar off me without even asking, swinging it over his shoulder, then guided us out of college and towards my house.

It should've felt weirder than it did – walking home with a complete stranger in a waistcoat and hat. And yet there was something about him that made it feel weirdly right. Oddly normal, like Fate had drawn a line along the ground and I knew I had to follow it.

"So, you're not from around here, are you?" Reese asked, as we left the aftermath of the talent show behind.

"Is my accent really that strong?"

He laughed. "Yes. It is. But also everyone knows everyone here. I can probably tell you at what age every single person in college got chickenpox." I watched him roll his eyes. "Where *are* you from?"

"Sheffield."

"That explains your musical talent then," he said. "Home of the Arctic Monkeys, Pulp, The Long Blondes. And now you, Amelie."

I smiled and shook my head, impressed. Most people didn't know where Sheffield was on the map, let alone our home-grown music talent. I told him as much.

"If there's one thing I know, it's music," he said. "Who are you into?"

"Oh my GOD, that's always the hardest question ever!"

His grin was lit up as he walked under a streetlight. "Okay, I'll narrow it down. Songwriter you most wish you could be."

"Laura Marling." The answer came out instinctively. How else would I have developed a full-blown obsession with cardigans?

"I knew you were going to say her," Reese said. "You're so like her! I was thinking that throughout your set."

As compliments go, it doesn't get much better than that. I shook my head and denied it almost automatically.

"It's true. I'm not a liar. I wouldn't lie about something like that."

"Do *you* like her?" I asked.

"Like her? I'm obsessed with her! In fact, I judge anyone who isn't. It's a very good way of measuring a person." And we lost half a mile comparing favourite songs and albums and lyrics and bridges of her music, my mouth wide in astonishment that I'd met someone who could match my Marling knowledge. "Right, next question," Reese continued as we plunged into the darkness of the alleyway. He took out his phone to use as a torch. "Favourite musician that not enough people know about."

Again, my answer came instantly. "Aldous Harding."

"No way. You know her?"

"YOU know her?"

Reese shook his head in equal disbelief. "This is weird. This is too weird."

It got weirder. As we talked about music, it was like I'd met my musical soulmate.

"Yes, Taylor Swift isn't taken as seriously as she should be," he agreed. Reese fired questions at me and practically every answer was "Me too, me too", and we'd grin at one another like loons. "So, when did you start writing songs?" he asked. "What grade are you up to on the guitar? Where do you get your inspiration? What's your writing process? Seriously? Yeah, me too. Me too."

We walked through the dark and I talked about myself more than I'd ever done before. Whenever I answered a question, he threw me a new one. That never usually happens with boys. So often boys just talk *at* you, wanting a pretty nodding dog to mirror their supposedly brilliant opinions. Even Alfie could get self-absorbed sometimes, especially if he went off on one about GM foods or noble gases or something. But not Reese. And he seemed so bewitched by my every reply, genuinely interested in what I had to say, that it felt oddly intoxicating. I let my guard down without even realizing, gesticulating and laughing at myself as we walked through blodges of orange streetlight.

"I've always written songs...since I was tiny... I was that clichéd kid who demanded a musical instrument before I could even talk... That song was about being homesick... I mean, it's not terrible here, but I hardly know anyone. I had to leave so many people behind... My favourite colour? Green.

Why? What's yours? You too? Seriously? You're not just saying that? Yeah, my parents are still together…just. It's been tough, what with Dad losing his job and all… Yes, that's why we moved down here." We stepped out onto the railway bridge and, self-conscious that I'd been talking about myself too much, I tried to fire some questions back.

"So, how long have you lived here?" I asked him.

He sighed. "My entire goddamned life."

"And your band, how long have you been together?"

He rolled his eyes again. "My entire life. We've been friends since primary school."

"You guys were good. Really tight."

"Thank you." He didn't dodge the compliment, just accepted it. "We've been playing together since Year Seven. It's brilliant, but I don't know…" He trailed off and we stopped right in the middle of the bridge.

"What is it?"

It was hard to make out his face in the dark but I could catch glimpses when the moonlight hit. He had a really strong jaw and way more stubble than most boys at college. Way more than Alfie, who was always insecure about his distinct lack of beard. "I just… I don't know… Sometimes I feel like I want to go solo, you know?" he said. "Being in a band is great but it can also hold you back. I mean, look at you tonight. It was all you. You won because you didn't have to compromise what song to sing and in what order. That's why it came across so beautifully. Whereas we were arguing beforehand about our set list… Sorry." He turned to me and smiled, shrugging off his monologue. "I shouldn't be grumpy when I'm trying really hard to impress you."

I blinked several times to digest what he'd just said. He'd just come right out and said it. He was trying to impress me. Me! I felt drunk on the giddiness of it...

...because I'm a fucking moron.

Let's unpack this now, though, shall we?

Right here, in this stuffy canteen, with you in the corner ignoring me. With my brain rewired so it constantly misfires between hating you and wanting you back, and then hating myself for wanting you back.

What did I miss? That night on the bridge?

I only won because I was a solo artist and you were in a band.

That's right, isn't it, Reese? That's what you meant. Between the compliments and the direct eye contact and you carrying my guitar and walking me home. Which was all part of the plan too, I reckon. Undermine me while telling me I'm beautiful. Which is precisely what you did next.

"You're amazing, you know that, right?" he said, totally out of nowhere.

I laughed. "You don't even know me."

"I really want to get to know you."

He stared at me then in a way that made it impossible not to believe him. And I stared right back, not understanding what was happening but knowing something most certainly was happening. The whole night was too much. I was drunk, and flooded with post-performance hormones, and ecstatic that I'd won, but also homesick and overwhelmed by all the attention.

For a second, I thought he was about to kiss me. We were looking at one another in the way that two people who are about to kiss do. The whole thing was totally nuts. I'd forgotten he was a stranger, that I was in love with Alfie, that things like this don't happen in real life.

"How do you know you want to get to know me if you don't even know me?" I asked, to try and break the tension again.

"I know you feel it too." He leaned in, his eyes so intense. We moved closer and closer in the darkness, searching each other's faces for god-knows-what. Our lips were on the brink of meeting…and then…*WHOOSH!* A train careered under us, whipping my dress up. It honked its horn, like it knew, and I jumped a mile in the air while he just pissed himself laughing, holding onto his hat to stop it falling off.

The moment was gone. Not even Reese's charm could resuscitate it.

"Come on, let's get you home." He put his arm around me and we walked along through the black of the alleyways, my guitar swinging against his back. He was already behaving

59

like my boyfriend or something, even though we'd only known each other for an hour. It felt weird and yet...right? Sort of. I wasn't sure. All I knew was that the night had tumbled completely out of my control.

I managed to ask what subjects he was taking.

"Music, music tech and business studies, so I can learn how to manage the band better," he replied.

"Wow. You're really determined to make it. My parents are making me take psychology and English as 'backup'."

"That's ridiculous. You don't need anything as backup. Not with your talent." He gently put a hand on my shoulder. "You've just got to believe in your music," he said. "The industry is too hard to have even a sliver of doubt that you don't deserve to be singing your songs. I see what I want and I work for it. I believe I can get it. That's why some people make it and others don't."

"I've never heard anyone talk the way you talk," I said, stealing another look at him.

"I've never heard anyone sing the way you sing." He stopped and turned, like he was going to kiss me. And I would've let him this time. A million trains could've charged past and I wouldn't have moved a muscle, as long as it ensured he actually kissed me. But he didn't. Instead, he reached out and took a plait from my hair, wrapping it around his finger. "God, you're pretty."

I stood there, waiting for the kiss. Totally confused as to why I wanted this complete stranger to kiss me, especially with Alfie back in Sheffield. My hair rippled in the breeze and

I started to shiver as I waited. He still didn't kiss me though. He turned and carried on walking out of the alleyway.

"Tell me about your parents," he asked, like we hadn't just shared the moment of all moments. "What do they do again?" And I had to scuttle to keep up with him as we carried on our way home.

"This is me," I said, when we arrived outside my new block of flats.

He pulled my guitar off and handed it back in a way that made our hands deliberately brush.

"Can I take you out?" he asked. Again, just like that. Everything about him was just like that.

"I don't know," I stumbled. "There's someone…back home." I'd eventually remembered Alfie.

"You have a boyfriend?"

"No…well, yes. I did…"

"So you've broken up?"

"Yes, only a few weeks ago." I nodded, feeling the grief arrive, though it wasn't as stabbing as it usually was. Because I was already interested in Reese. A tiny piece of my heart had already been chipped off, ready to have his name carved into it, leaving a little bit less of it to hurt about Alfie.

"It doesn't have to be a date," he pressed. "We could just get to know each other? At the very least, I'd love to write songs with you." He smiled and it was the sort of smile that could be printed onto posters and sold to hysterical girls to pin over their beds. "I thought I should get to you first, after tonight," he continued. "You're going to be inundated with requests now. But I get dibs, right? I noticed you first."

Casual ownership of me. Another humdinger of a red flag. A flag so red a bull would freaking *eat* it.

"I'm not sure," I said, which was the truth.

"Then think about it."

"Thanks for walking me home." Out of nowhere I felt a strong urge to be alone. An urge to go inside and give myself space to think, away from this boy and everything that was going on.

"So…are you going to think about it?" he pressed.

I laughed again. "You're very persistent, aren't you?"

He raised both hands. "Look, no pressure. I only want to get to know you."

I thought he'd lean in then, maybe at least give me a peck on the cheek, but instead he just left, with a flick of a wave and a "See you on Monday" called over his shoulder. He didn't even ask for my number. I stood open-mouthed, watching him walk away, staying like that for a while. I could sense his presence in the air – it hung around like strong aftershave. I crossed my arms, sat on the wall, and I smiled.

I let myself start to absorb the night, shaking my head, pondering in disbelief how life can be so drastically altered any time you leave the house.

My phone went.

Alfie: Hey. How's things? Hope it's going OK down south

Alfie's message arrived too late and too *not-like-Alfie* to save me. There was no kiss, no in-jokes, nothing personal. He could've safely sent that to his gran. There was no apology or even acknowledgement that he'd not messaged in over a week. My heart twinged with sharp pain as I realized what this message meant... Alfie had begun the severance. I read it and read it again, looking for hidden meanings that would somehow appear, if only I squinted harder. But there was no other meaning than the one I'd instinctively come to. *We need to let go a bit more, Amelie. We need to not behave like boyfriend and girlfriend any more.*

The timing seemed cosmic. There I was – having met Reese and feeling confused and guilty – and *BAM*, Alfie's message arrives. Letting me off the hook. Setting me free...

...free to completely and utterly annihilate my own life.

You're getting up now, with her. Back in this stuffy room, where I cried onstage all those months ago. You reach for her hand and she takes it. You fold her under your arm and you kiss the top of her head. I huddle up in my chair, retreating into my hood – envy souring my insides.

You're walking past and I hope you don't notice me but I also really hope you do. You come closer, adjusting the buttons on your bottle-green waistcoat. I hate you all of a sudden. The hatred arrives distilled and putrid. *Oh my god, I hate you so much! How have I not realized this?* I can taste how much I hate you on my tongue. All the things you did to me cram into my head – all the ways you wore me away like a picture that needed rubbing out. I look up at you defiantly as you walk past but, of course, you ignore me, you fucking prick.

Defiance metamorphoses into hurt. Tears bubble up. Oh great, I'm going to cry in public *again*, just like I've been doing pretty much permanently since I moved here. I blink up at the ceiling and then, once I'm sure the tears won't fall, I make myself look around as a distraction. There are people eating and talking and laughing and not falling apart and not publicly humiliating themselves. I blink and blink and concentrate and concentrate and it takes a moment for me to realize you are standing right in front of me. I jerk backwards.

"Reese?"

"Woah, I didn't mean to scare you." You tilt your head, your eyes filled with caring. "Are you okay? You look…not okay."

I can't breathe. I can't believe you're here, talking to me

like you care, like I'm worth your time again. I look around. She's standing by the door, waiting for you, looking at me like I'm pathetic, which I certainly am.

"I'm fine," I stammer. "Why wouldn't I be fine?"

You pull up a chair and sit on it backwards. You're looking at me like you're you again, the you I've not seen in so long. "Come on," you say.

We both know why I'm not fine. You just kissed the top of the head of the reason I'm not fine. "Shouldn't you be with her?"

I sound bitter. It was supposed to come out as enquiring yet mildly disinterested, but it comes out so bitter I'm surprised I don't cough up a lemon.

You make a pained face. "In a sec. I just wanted to check that you're alright."

I nod as defiantly as I can. "Right as rain."

It comes out surprisingly convincing and you look shocked for a moment. You lean back. You breathe out. "Well, if you're going to be like this." You roll your eyes, you unwrap your legs from the chair, and you stand and adjust your hat. I feel like I've won a point. I'm almost smiling. You're about to leave and I want you to stay but I don't show it. I will hold onto this point. This one whole point I've somehow managed to score.

And then…

Then…

You lean over, so close I think you're going to kiss me again.

"I do miss you, Amelie," you whisper into my hair. "I'm worried I've made the biggest mistake of my life."

You are gone before I can compute. You were here and now you're not here. I can still smell your breath in the air. I want to cry and laugh at the same time. The relief of it, oh the relief of it. You miss me! I knew you did!

I miss you so much. I don't hate you. I adore you! I love you! We have to get back together! We must! We are perfect! You are perfect! There's never been two people more perfect.

...But where have you gone?

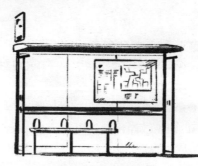

The Number Thirty-Seven Bus Stop

I guess I should tell you what I'm doing.

You've probably not been taking much notice of the special college project going on. You're too busy being infuriating and ruining lives and making me love you and hate you at the same time. But I've been taking notice because I have literally nothing else going on in my life right now, apart from all the despair. Two weeks ago, just before half-term, we got called into some big assembly in the college auditorium, though it was non-compulsory so not many people bothered turning up – you included. Hannah and Jack were there though, holding hands and still ignoring me. I sat in the front row and wondered how long I could go without running to cry in a toilet cubicle.

Our head teacher, Mr Jenkins, got up onstage. I hadn't really seen our head before. He only taught general studies, which literally no one went to.

"Hi, everyone," he said. "Thank you for coming, especially just after lunch. We teachers call this the 'witching hour'."

He laughed extensively at his own joke, as tumbleweed blew across his feet. I wanted to turn to my left and roll my eyes, but nobody had sat on my left because I have no friends now. I may as well have had my own little patch of tumbleweed next to me to keep me company.

"Anyway," Mr Jenkins continued, "I have some very exciting news. I've just found out that our college has been asked to take part in a brand-new project for the Victoria and Albert Museum." He paused to let the excitement that none of us felt sink in. "Riiight. The project is called The Memory Map and it's very interesting…"

And you know what, Reese? It *was* super fucking interesting, even with Mr Jenkins explaining it. The museum wants to collect the memories of spaces. They're starting with our tiny part of the country, our sliver of nowhere.

"Think about it," Mr Jenkins said, pacing the stage with excitement. "Think about all the memories that have been made just in this very auditorium. Think about all the first days of college that have happened here, all the memories created by people sitting in the very seat you are sat on right now. Think of the plays that have been performed here. Right now, right this moment, you are making a memory. You are sat in a chair in this room, and you will always have the memory of this being the place you were when you first found out about memory-mapping."

There are so many memories, Reese, lurking in all the spaces of everywhere. They lie trapped like frozen ghosts, existing only when someone who knows of that memory thinks about that particular time and place and their mind reactivates it. We walk through these ghosts all the time, not knowing we tread the footprints of another person's story. Just one bench on top of a viewpoint could be harbouring so many stories. It could be the bench where a couple broke up, or where another couple had their first kiss. It could be the bench where someone thought about taking their own life, or where they got the phone call that something amazing had happened. Layered in just one bench there's an infinite amount of memories. Multiple people living near one particular bench could all share it as special without even knowing each other. We leave behind echoes of our lives everywhere we go, trapping them into the fabric of the world around us. And that's what the museum wants help collecting. They want us to pick certain points in town and write out the memories anonymously to be in this exhibition.

"Of course the college has agreed to help," Mr Jenkins said, rubbing his hands together with the importance of being asked. "I said lots of students would be willing to contribute their memories of here and the surrounding areas."

Have you guessed it yet? You're clever enough, Reese – well, you always acted like you were. Smarter than me, smarter than your teachers, smarter than anyone. So you've probably figured it out by now. I'm making a memory map. About you and all the places you've made me cry. I reckon it's going to hurt like hell, but it's the only thing I can think of to figure this whole mess out. It's my only hope of getting over this, and I'm grabbing it with both hands and I'm determined to not let go until I can understand. Let's call it "psychogeography", let's call it recovery, let's call it therapy, let's call it closure.

God knows if it's any of those things, but I'm going to retrace all these places and I'm going to see if it helps me figure you out. Because I can't figure you out. You've not called or messaged since you spoke to me in the refectory yesterday. Since you said you missed me. I've been jumping each time I imagine my phone buzzing – which it never does.

I couldn't sleep again last night. I just kept replaying what you'd said in my head, and coming up with all these scenarios of what will happen now. How you'll turn up outside my window and say it's all been a big mistake. How you'll take me in your arms and kiss me and tell me everything's going to be okay. How you'll be so desperate to win me back again you'll shower me with love and affection and promises, and it will go back to how it used to be, but this time it will stay like that for ever. It won't go bad this time.

Because it went *really* bad last time.

So here I am, at spot number three, where I cried after our first date. You don't know I cried that night. I'm only just starting to understand why I did. It seemed so strange at the time, to break down in tears after what was, undoubtedly, the best evening of my entire life. But I did.

I'm supposed to be in a psychology lesson now but I can't bring myself to go. I made it halfway to college and then got all messed up by your lack of message, so I about-turned and came here to sit pathetically at this pathetic number thirty-seven bus stop. The posters are advertising different movies now, alongside a new mouthwash that's supposed to solve all your life problems. But it's the same place – place number three. Where, even after the best night of my life, you still managed to make me cry.

Reese worked so hard for that first date.

College was just as terrible as I imagined it would be when I came in the Monday after the contest. Everyone smiled as I went past, a few people whooped. I was on the radar – my worst nightmare. Luckily, the weather had broken so I hid under my umbrella and pretended I didn't exist as I walked to form room. I arrived slightly late from all the human-dodging, only for the entire class to stand up and applaud me the moment I got through the door.

"There she is, the superstar!" Alistair called as I scuttled to the empty chair next to Hannah.

"I told them not to," she whispered.

I slunk in my chair and the clapping died down but I kept my eyes on the carpet. "Now, it must be a special day today," Alistair said, "because Reese Davies has *finally* managed to find our little form room."

My head snapped up at the mention of his name. And there he was, sat right across from me. He tipped his hat at the class as my mouth dropped open.

"Pleasure to be here," he said to Alistair, while looking me right in the eye.

"We appreciate you taking the time to come to this compulsory part of your education," Alistair laughed. And I realized *he* must've been the guy who never showed on our first day. "Now, everyone, speaking of non-optional," Alistair continued, "we need to talk about General Studies. Mainly because it's not even October and yet loads of you aren't going."

Reese smiled at me throughout the next twenty minutes, showcasing a giant cornucopia of smiles. Sometimes it was only a lingering smoulder-smile of hotness, one was a sheepish grin, and one a smug smirk at knowing he'd surprised me. At one point he crossed his eyes and stuck out his tongue. Whenever I dared look up, I met his eyes. He didn't once stop staring at me. My heart beat ten-trillion times a minute, and my stomach turned cartwheels under his scrutiny. I was aware of how every muscle in my body was arranged. My shyness rash bloomed and itched under my scratchy cardigan. I built myself up for our inevitable conversation when the bell rang, practising opening phrases in my head. *"Fancy seeing you here"? Or maybe I should go with a joke about him following me?* Therefore it was a total shock when he dashed out of the classroom the second form time was over, swinging his bag onto his back and practically running out the door. I shook my head, wondering if I'd just imagined the whole thing.

"Where did you go the other night?" Hannah asked me as we packed up our bags. "You said you got home safe, but you've not told me how."

"Where were *you*?" I dodged the question, her comment about Reese being King of the Bell-ends still singing between my ears. "You and Jack vanished."

She sighed and flicked her hair back. "God, yeah, about that. We've both got a free next, haven't we? Wanna go for a coffee? It would be useful to get your opinion actually. You know, as an outsider?"

I nodded and pretended it didn't hurt like hell that she'd just referred to me as an outsider. We walked briskly to BoJangles, hardly able to talk through the sleeting rain and ensuing umbrella wars. When we arrived, there was only one table left, at the front, by the steamed window.

"You bagsy the table, I'll get the caffeine," Hannah ordered.

I squeezed onto the chair and claimed the table with my bag just before a mum with a toddler. I shot her an *I'm sorry* look and tried not to think about Reese as I stared out into the rain. *Did I imagine him looking at me the whole time? Why did he just walk out?* I felt a pull in my stomach, a weird anxiety I couldn't describe. I yearned for it to be obvious he liked me, like it was the other night – even though I wasn't sure I even liked him yet. Even though I was supposed to be madly in love with Alfie. I *was* still madly in love with Alfie. I was just being stupid, flattered by the attention.

"Oh my god, I needed this coffee." Hannah clattered two steaming mugs in front of me. "I'm so glad you were up for this. Thank you."

I picked up a spoon to stir in the foam of my latte. "It's fine."

I waited for her to tell me what was going on. That's something you learn from being a quiet person – if you just sit there, stuff comes out. People are so desperate to fill the silence that you end up being told things you wouldn't be normally. Hannah took a big slurp from her cup, checked her phone, and took another slurp. Then she put the cup down and said, "So after the talent show, Jack told me he liked me."

I stayed silent, knowing she'd soon reveal if she thought this to be a good or bad thing.

Hannah analysed my face for information, and I must've given something away because she said, "You *know*? Oh my god! What did he tell you?"

I panicked, not wanting to betray Jack. Sensing it, she reached out and patted my hand. "Look, he's already told me he likes me. He just came out and said it, so you're not betraying his confidence."

I picked up my drink. "Well then, you know all I know. I just didn't think he was going to tell you, that's all." I examined her over the rim of my cup. "Do you like him?"

She let out a huge puff of air. "I don't know!"

"Oh, okay then… I mean that's okay if you're unsure but—"

"I think I do," she interrupted. "But, like…it's Jack, you know? Jack!"

I nodded. "He is Jack. That is correct."

She giggled and gave me a look of genuine warmth. "I don't know what I feel. I'm confused and a bit scared. That's why I wanted to talk to you about it. Because, like, you didn't go to school with us, so don't have all the backstories we think are important but probably aren't. You're new and neutral, and if your songwriting is anything to go by, you're wise." I blushed and she saw. "God, you're literally the hardest person to compliment in the UNIVERSE. I feel like I'm punishing you."

"Sorry."

"Don't apologize. Just help me. What do I do?"

I leaned back in my chair. "Well, *do* you really like him?"

She spluttered out another giant sigh. "Yes, no. I don't know. We've been friends for forever."

"So…?"

"Well, what if it ruins the friendship? What if I don't fancy him enough because we're too close as friends?"

All the memories of Alfie poured in like water from a broken hydrant. I remembered all those exact same agonies. The preciousness of the friendship, the worry it wouldn't be worth the risk, the freaking out that kissing him would feel wrong. "You won't know if you fancy him until you've kissed him," I told her expertly. "That's how you'll be able to tell. You'll either be thinking *Oh god, stop, you're like my brother* or *Please never remove your tongue from my throat, I don't care if we die of starvation!*"

She burst out laughing and threw her head forward, her auburn hair spilling all over the table, getting a strand in her drink. Then she giggled herself out and raised her head, looking at me seriously. "But what if I kiss him and it's not good. Then what? The friendship will be all weird."

I bit my lip. "If the kiss is weird for you, chances are it will be weird for him too. Then you can just laugh and say, 'That was weird', and you'll get over it."

She narrowed her eyes. "How are you so knowledgeable about this?"

It was my turn to let out a sigh. "I've been there," I admitted. "There was a guy. Back in Sheffield. He was my best friend and then we got together."

Hannah's eyes widened. "And then…"

I gulped. "And then I moved down here and we decided it was best to leave things."

She reached over and took my hand again, giving it a good squeeze. "Shit, I'm sorry, Amelie. I mean, I figured it was tough enough having to move away, I didn't know you had to leave your boyfriend behind too."

All my feelings for Alfie rushed in, jumbling my brain, making me want to cry. I squeezed her hand back. "We've got a plan," I told her. Suddenly I wanted to talk, wanted to tell someone everything. About the pain I'd been carrying, between just me and him, and not being able to talk to him about it. "We're both going to try and get into Manchester. They've got a good music course for me, and they've got a good chemistry course for him. So we just need to be apart for these two years, otherwise we'll ruin it with the long distance. But, it's not like we're going to fall in love with anyone else. So I just need to hold tight..." I trailed off, wondering how the hell Reese slotted into all this, and the way his smile had made me feel that morning. "Well, I thought that was the plan," I added. "I've not heard from him in ages. He's probably moved on already. I think we may've been kidding ourselves."

"I'm so sorry, Amelie," Hannah said with true sympathy. "I can't imagine how hard it's been."

"Don't, or I'll cry again. And I'm still recovering from the humiliation of doing that in front of the entire college."

"Don't worry about that. Literally no one remembers that already, apart from you." Hannah turned to look out at the pouring rain and her face was serious again when she spoke next. "Was it worth it? With Alfie, I mean? Like, if you hadn't got together maybe it would've been easier for you to move here."

I knew she was mainly asking to help her make her mind up about Jack, but the question still burrowed right into me. I didn't reply for almost a whole minute, staring into the rising steam of my drink instead. *Is any broken heart ever worth it?*

"Of course it was worth it," I eventually got out. Remembering the amazing moments with Alfie, the delight at realizing we had the same feelings, those tentative first kisses that felt so safe and right, the way I had a best friend who would always be on my side, who I also got to make out with. "But it hurts now. Anyway, you and Jack aren't about to be separated by two hundred miles."

Hannah nodded. "True. Though, we'll both be going to uni in two years…"

I smiled. "So you're thinking about the logistics already. You DO like him."

The way she blushed confirmed it.

"Just kiss him," I said. "See what happens from there."

"Okay, I will." She put her coffee down resolutely and I knew she'd follow through on it. I'd not known her long but I could tell Hannah was the kind of person who always did what she said she was going to do. I felt happy for her, and yet also sad for me. She and Jack were essentially my only new friends and now I'd be playing Queen Gooseberry of Gooseberryland. Especially as Liv had clicked off with her new photography gang and spent all her time in the darkroom developing pictures of her belly button.

Hannah swerved into a topic change. "So, what's going

on with you and Dickhead Extraordinaire, Reese Davies?" she asked, as I almost choked on my slurp of coffee.

"What?"

"Rumour has it you left with him on Friday night. Then he stared at you all through form time."

"What?" I repeated, to buy myself time.

"So, the official story," Hannah leaned over the table, her lip curling in disapproval she didn't even try to hide, "is that the moment you were onstage, Reese told everyone you were amazing and he had to get to know you. Then someone saw you both leave college together, with him carrying your guitar. Please tell me nothing happened! He's not a nice person, Amelie."

I shook my head and tried to digest the huge hunk of news that had just dropped into my stomach. Did he really say that? It made my insides go all loopy. "What's wrong with him?"

"He's just so up himself! Like, he thinks his band are going to be The Next Big Thing. And he's had loads of girlfriends before, never seems to treat them well. He always refers to them as 'psychos' afterwards."

"Really?"

"Seriously. Be careful. I mean, I know he's good looking and everything, but come on, that ridiculous hat tells you everything you need to know."

"I quite like his hat."

"Oh god...come on. Please, Amelie. The reason I wanted to hang with you was because I thought you had some sense."

"I only said I like his hat! Anyway, nothing happened.

He only walked me home. I've got Alfie to think about…"

"Good girl. Now, how do I go about kissing Jack?"

We laughed until our drinks were drunk and lessons beckoned. The rain was even heavier on the walk back into college and we squealed as water soaked through our tights and the hole in my left cowboy boot. I pushed through the doors to the music block, shaking out my umbrella and wringing out my dress. There's something giddy-making about walking through heavy rain, and I felt utterly joyful as I sloshed my way to my music lesson, leaving a trail of puddles behind me.

Reese, you were waiting outside my music lesson, you will recall.

He tipped his hat again, leaning against the wall, one knee bent, looking so damn cool.

"You again." I smiled, the giddiness giving me confidence.

"Are you going to go out with me then?" he asked, ignoring the students squeezing past him to get through the door.

"I have to go to my music lesson," I laughed, feeling even giddier now that I'd somehow managed to magically become the sort of girl who has boys like Reese wait for them outside lessons. Hannah's warning hummed quietly in the back of my head though, killing the buzz a little.

"I told you, no pressure, I just want to get to know you."

"I said I'll think about it." I went to push open the door.

"Just a coffee?"

My smile grew fatter. "I said I'll think about it."

I couldn't concentrate all through music. I drummed my pen against the table and thought about Reese and Alfie, and Jack and Hannah, and how life can change very quickly indeed. I hardly concentrated on Mrs Clarke's lesson about composition but instead ran over Hannah's words, wondering if I should trust her judgement. I had no reason not to. But I also had no reason to distrust Reese. And the problem was, I didn't feel this weird animal magnetism to Hannah, whereas just being in the same room as Reese made me feel like I was wearing chainmail and he was a giant sexy magnet.

"Amelie? A quick one?" Mrs Clarke asked me when the bell rang.

I squeezed the still slightly damp sleeves of my cardigan as I made my way over to her desk. "Yes?"

"Congratulations again, for Friday night."

My face did its usual response of turning a mixture of pink, red and blue – which I guess is just purple.

"You're really going to have to get better at taking compliments" – she smiled – "because, I've had quite a few requests come through over the weekend."

My stomach flipped. "Requests for what?"

Her smile grew wider, her peach lipstick stretching across her pale face. "Well, two students have asked if you're interested in having a writing partner. And we also had a talent scout in the audience. She's interested in setting you up with some local gigs. Getting your name out there?"

My hands curled into themselves and hid up my damp sleeves. "Really?" I stuttered. "Wow." My body did the usual rip-in-two it does whenever my music goes well. Half of me wanted to leap in the air and praise the good lord and dance a merry jig. But the other half just heard *DOOOOOOOOOOOM* in a booming voice because I'd have to perform more and face my stage fright again and it'd be so much easier to just stay at home for ever, curled up in a blanket.

"I can send you the details, I just wanted to check it was okay first to pass on your email. Exciting, huh? I knew from our first lesson how talented you were."

The bell rang again, and a jostle at the door signalled her next batch of students had arrived. I only had a minute to get across campus to English.

"Anyway, sorry for making you late. If you want any extra help preparing, or deciding what to do, that's what I'm here for."

I stuttered out a thank you and wobbled my way out of the classroom.

Gigs.

Writing partners.

A smile tickled the corners of my mouth. My love for

singing always won over everything else eventually.

Well, back then it did.

I didn't see Reese for the rest of the day. I felt twitchy and too aware of myself travelling between lessons, wondering if he'd be waiting outside my class again, and then anxiety was replaced by odd disappointment when he wasn't. I'd start to worry I'd blown it by not giving him an answer right away. I mean, if Hannah's stories were anything to go by, he wasn't short of options. I wouldn't be able to keep him hanging too long. Then I'd remind myself of Alfie and our promise, and wonder what the hell had got into me.

It went like this:

Anxiety...

Excitement...

Disappointment...

Relief...

Worry...

Guilt...

Anxiety...

...all the damned day long. I zoned out during lunch, as Hannah stared at Jack but pretended she wasn't, and Jack stared back and pretended he wasn't.

The day ended and I hadn't seen Reese again. I tried telling myself it was a relief, yet my heart still got in a huge strop about it.

This is good, I kept telling myself. *You don't need this.*

What about Alfie? You don't want to date someone who wears a stupid hat anyway.

I imagined what Alfie would make of him. God, he'd hate the hat. Alfie's only outfit was: jeans, T-shirt and trainers. He considered wearing shorts in summer the most stressful thing ever.

I hugged Hannah goodbye at the college gate, whispered "set up a kissable opportunity" in her ear, and left her blushing. I hoicked my bag over my shoulder, nodded to all the people who smiled and wished me congratulations, and walked back towards the flat.

There he was. At the entrance to the alleyway. Hat tipped, smile beaming, leaning casually on the railing. I juddered to a halt, like a cartoon character who just about saves themselves from falling off a cliff.

"Well, fancy seeing you here," he said, stealing my line.

I giggled, like the stupid idiot that I am.

"Are you following me?" I asked, dumbly.

"Only in a romantic way, not a creepy way."

"Don't I get to be the one who decides that?"

"Sorry, I'll go." He went to walk off. Properly, not even as a joke. So, of course, I called "Wait", just like I'm sure he knew I would.

"So you *do* want me to walk you home?"

I giggled again and uselessly tried to maintain the power. "I guess you can walk me home." I sighed like the idea was awful.

"Here, I'll take your bag." He reached out for my heavy tote and I honestly found it romantic rather than patronizing

84

and archaic, because we've established already that I'm a giant idiot.

"Are you really homesick?" he asked, out of the blue, as we fell into step, skidding on slippy leaves from the earlier rain.

"Why do you ask that?"

"It's just, whenever I look at you, which is a lot...in a romantic way, not a creepy way, of course...you always look like you're wishing yourself away."

I touched my face self-consciously, surprised I was giving myself away so obviously.

Or maybe he just really gets you, I thought. *Maybe you have a connection.*

"I *am* homesick. Everything is so different here. It's like being in a different country."

"How is it different?"

I found myself telling him all of it. All the way home, right up to the wall outside my flat, where we sat down, our bums getting increasingly damp as the wetness from the brick seeped through. I told him how it wasn't just the accent that was different here, but so many other things. How much less space there was down south. How there were queues for everything – in the coffee shop and at traffic junctions. And though queuing *seems* very polite, everyone down south seemed to use manners as a defensive shield, to cover up their chronic unfriendliness. "In Sheffield, you chat to anyone," I told him, swinging my legs. "If you ring to book a taxi, as you wait for your fish and chips, you chat to the lady down

85

the phone, or the person serving you, or whoever else in the queue. It's all *duck* and *pet,* and it's lovely, really it is. You feel like everyone is a friend. But down here, nobody talks to anyone...and everyone bumps into each other." I sighed. "Up north, if someone walks towards you on the pavement, you both move to make way. But down here it's like pavement Hunger Games! I've got actual bruises on my arms from being knocked into so much."

He listened and he agreed. He said he'd noticed all those things too but no one had ever put it like that before.

"You're so good with words," Reese told me. "I thought it was just your songs, but hearing you talk... You just say things in such a wise way. It's like this is your eighth life or something."

I swelled under the compliment and he looked at me with such wonder that I found myself believing him. *Maybe I do have a way with words. Maybe I am wise for my years...* There's nothing more intoxicating than seeing your best self through the lens of someone's adoring eyes. It's potent and heady, and how amazing it felt to bathe in the glow Reese projected onto me. I could practically tan in it.

I shook off the compliments though, blushing and bashful. "Well, if that's true, it's a bit of a waste on someone as shy as me," I said.

He reached out, like he was about to tuck a strand of hair behind my ear, but then he stopped himself and just smiled. "I like that you're shy. I'm shy too, you know..."

I burst out laughing.

"I am! Really!"

"The lead singer of a band? Who stands around waiting outside a girl's classroom? *Shy?*"

"Yes! I could say the same about you," he argued. "You did a solo set all by yourself. That's not so shy, is it?"

"Yeah, but I almost died doing it."

"Well, I almost died too. And I almost died trying to chat you up the other night. And I almost died waiting outside your classroom earlier. And I almost died waiting for you to bump into me on your walk home. And..." He reached out again, and this time he did tuck my hair back. I closed my eyes for a second, savouring how it felt. "...and I'm almost dying right now. Just talking to you. I can't explain it. You make me really nervous, Amelie. But knowing you better is worth the nerves."

This is mental.

That was the one rational thought that popped into my head, before it flitted right back out again.

It was *mental*. He was acting like he was falling in love with me, yet he didn't know me. We'd only had two conversations.

Did I listen to that little thought though? That burp of rationality? The little voice that kept quietly putting its hand up at the back of the classroom, whispering truths like *This is a bit full-on, isn't it?* and *He doesn't even know you* and *Do you even like him, Amelie? Or do you just like how much he likes you?*

Clearly, I did not listen.

Because otherwise I wouldn't be sat here at this manky bus stop when I should be in college. Otherwise I wouldn't be checking my phone like a twitchy rescue dog.

Instead I stayed sitting on that wall and we talked about the universe and everything in it. And, the next day, after college, he was there leaning on the fence by the alleyway again and I smiled and we fell into step, just like that. And, every lunchtime for the next week, when Reese reigned supreme over the cafeteria, joking with his band and taking it in turns to mess up Rob's hair, he'd always catch my eye and grin. Or he'd faux bump into me in the corridors and hold his hands up and say "Sorry" while Hannah growled. The first time this happened he slipped me another note. I pretended I needed a wee, locked myself in a cubicle, and opened up the folded paper, feeling so nervous I did end up doing a wee.

When can I take you out?

I laughed and felt my stomach flip-flop and held the paper to my chest, shaking my head and grinning. I kept the note in my purse, folded up with the other one he'd handed me outside my music lesson, which simply read: *I can't stop thinking about you.*

I found, not so very gradually, my thoughts weren't always with Alfie and how much I missed him, and instead Reese merged into my head. I'd reread his notes and feel the smile unfurl in my stomach. The words never lost their potency. Each time it was like reading them anew.

He wants to go out with me

He can't stop thinking about me.

This guy. This gorgeous, sensitive, popular, talented guy who could have any girl he wants…he wants you, Amelie. Isn't that funny? Isn't that the most compelling of thoughts? Isn't that what every girl wants but never gets? It's happening to you, Amelie. You must be special after all. Because he's pretty special and he thinks you're special. If you agree to see him, this could very well be the start of something incredible, because he can really, really, look into your soul.

I held out for only five days.

We walked home together on Friday, exactly a week after the talent show, really taking our time. We stopped to admire the pretty leaves tinged with the first autumn colours, and we pointed at the fat squirrels and shared our favourite things about winter.

"Coming home soaking wet and standing next to the fire," Reese said.

"Tree branches lined with Christmas lights."

"Christmas! Oh my god, The Pogues. 'Fairytale of New York' is my favourite song ever! I listen to it all year round."

"Me too!"

Reese took my hand. He finally touched me properly – holding my hand, our fingers entwined all the way. When we arrived at mine, he turned and took my other hand, so we were a fused circle.

"So?"

"So…?"

"A little bird told me you've been booked to play the Cube," he said.

My nerves jangled like a door with a bell that rang when you opened it. "Yes." Mrs Clarke had ran up to me breathlessly with the news that morning. "We've never got a student in before," she'd panted.

"What's the Cube?" was all I'd been able to ask, not realizing what a huge big deal it was in this town. It was apparently the biggest local music hall.

"It's incredible," Reese said with admiration.

"I'm only opening for the Contenders. I'm the first support act so I'll be playing to, like, five whole people who have no idea who I am and are only tolerating me so they can bagsy the front row."

He smiled. "I love how you're so modest."

I looked down, embarrassed. "Not modest, just honest."

When I looked back up, he was staring at me so intensely, I swear to god I felt naked. "Please go on a date with me," he begged softly. "We both know this is something. Give this a chance."

And I found myself leaning in, my mouth whispering a reply with no cognitive functioning beforehand. "Okay," I sighed. "I'll go on a date with you."

His eyes crinkled so much with his smile that they almost

disappeared into his face. "I'm away seeing my dad this weekend, but next Monday? That's the quickest I can do."

"Monday it is."

"You seem very twitchy," Mum commented, half an hour before Reese was due to pick me up. She folded herself into a kitchen chair and sighed as she took off one of her high heels.

"She's been like that since she got home from college," Dad replied for me. "She won't tell me why though. Why would she? It's not like we created her and fed her and nursed her and gave her everything in life." He was cooking dinner and left the pan momentarily to affectionately grip my shoulders. I turned my head up and smiled at him.

"I'm just meeting some friends for food," I lied. "You know I get nervous going out and chatting to people."

"And yet we can never shut you and your guitar up in this flat. Lucky us."

I rolled my eyes and held back a remark. My music practice had suddenly become an issue, after a lifetime of it never being an issue. Back in Sheffield, I'd had this cute little shed at the back of the garden. Dad had even stuck loads of egg boxes inside it for soundproofing and made a sign that said *Where the Magic Happens!* I'd lived in that shed. I used to sneak my friends into the shed late at night. Alfie and I even lost our virginity in that shed. He'd made a naff joke afterwards about it being "Where the magic happens" before I thumped him, and he caught my hand, and then we rolled up in a tatty blanket and took it in turns to say "I love you" into the early hours of the morning. Now, my parents were exposed to just how much time I spent playing guitar. I'd tried to be careful, strumming as lightly as I could and whispering more than singing, but I'd still get Dad knocking on the flimsy flat wall, asking me to "Keep it down, love".

Mum took off her other shoe and groaned, rubbing the arch of her foot. "Well, I hope you have fun tonight," she said. "You look very nice. New dress?"

I nodded and went red. The charity shops around here were amazing. It was like nobody bought ANYTHING second-hand. I'd found the dress in Cats Protection and it was more daring than usual. It was red with small white polka dots. None of my granny cardigans matched it, so I'd teamed it with a leather jacket and I'd even blodged on a bit of tinted lip balm too, one I'd got for Christmas last year and never used.

"You're wearing make-up," Dad marvelled, like I'd drawn all over my face with a Sharpie.

"Just tinted lip balm." My face was now the same colour as my dress and lips.

"Ooooh, is there a *boy* going tonight?" He said in a girly voice as he dipped the wooden spoon into his sauce to taste it.

"Of course there's not," Mum replied for me. "She's still head-over-heels for Alfie."

I stood up, almost knocking over my chair as her comment unleashed a fresh tsunami of Alfie-related guilt I'd been trying to run from. Was this cheating on him? How could I miss him terribly and also want to go on a date with Reese at the same time? What did it mean? How would I feel if I knew Alfie was about to go on a date with someone else? Fucking sick – that's how I'd feel. So why the hell was I doing this to him? But he'd not messaged me in over a week...so maybe he was totally over me? And if he could do it, then so could I...and oh god, I missed him. I missed him so much. I should cancel. Why was I going on this stupid date with someone I hardly knew? But I also really wanted to go on it...

I made myself smile and caught the chair before it clattered over. "Yep. Still head-over-heels for Alfie."

I went to my room to check my appearance again. Yep. I looked exactly the same as I did five minutes ago.

Alfie Alfie Alfie.

Reese Reese Reese.

"What should I do?" I asked the mirror. "What the hell should I do?"

Just then my phone buzzed in my bag, and I made an instant decision. If it was Alfie, then I'd cancel the date. It would be a sign from the universe, and you have to trust signs from the universe, even if you're the only person who's decided they're a sign or not. If it was Reese, then I'd go on the date and see where it took me, guilt-free.

I reached into my bag and pulled out my phone.

Jessa: Granny Cardigan, Granny Cardigan, oh Granny Granny. Granny Cardigan, Granny Cardigan, oh Granny Granny – I MISS YOU

I smiled, but I had no idea what the universe was trying to tell me with that one.

I waited for Reese on the wall outside, so my parents wouldn't see him. I went out five minutes early and kept checking the time on my phone, staring at the top of my road, preparing myself for the sight of him appearing. I went through all the different ways we might greet each other. Would we hug? Or kiss on the cheek? Or just half-wave? What if he was late? Would I pretend I didn't mind?

I didn't need to worry though, because the moment he turned up, it was like I'd fallen down a rabbit hole called Perfect First Date.

He was on time. He smelled fantastic. He grinned at me the moment he turned the corner, and, when he reached me, he very gently brushed his lips against mine.

"You look amazing," he said.

"I look freezing," I replied dumbly, my body melting despite the cold.

"It's okay, where I'm taking you is warm."

He took my hand as we walked into town and my entire arm felt like a shaken-up Coke bottle. I stopped noticing the cold, I stopped noticing where we were even heading. My whole body was focused solely on the contact between our meshed fingers.

"How's the band?" I asked, as he stroked the inside of my thumb.

"Annoyed I'm missing band rehearsal tonight."

"Oh no! I didn't know. I don't want you to—"

"Relax, Amelie. I'd much rather be here with you. They'll get over it."

A sliver of anxiety knotted my intestine. I didn't want his band mates to resent me. Nobody wants to be Yoko.

"Where are we going anyway?" I asked, after we'd passed through the main strip of town, past all the obvious first-date places like Pizza Express and ASK.

"Patience, little one. You didn't think I was going to take you to Pizza Express, did you? Not when I've got a chance with the most talented and beautiful girl in college."

I giggled and simpered like I'm sure he knew I would, as we turned down a quiet side road and stopped outside a tiny yellow door, with a sign that read *JETSON RECORDING STUDIO*.

"Voila." Reese bowed, with a flourish of his hand.

"There's a recording studio *here*?" I stared at it in disbelief.

"Miracles happen." He fiddled in his skinny jeans and produced a key, waving it in the air. "It's not huge, but all the local bands record their demos here. And it's ours for the whole evening." He unlocked the door, pushed it open, and gestured for me to go in first. "After you, gorgeous."

My hand went to my mouth as I stepped into a grotto of fairy lights rather than a grotty recording studio. They hung from the ceiling like it was raining stars, snaking around the reception area.

Reese stood right behind me, his breath on my neck

"Do you like what I've done with the place?"

My body seeped back into him and I turned my head to look up at his very handsome face. "You mean, it's not always like this?" I joked to try and hide how overwhelmed I was.

"Umm, no, Amelie," he deadpanned. "It's not always decorated with fairy lights. I did this for you."

"It's beautiful," I said. It really was.

"Come on, let's eat. Then we can lay down some tracks."

He led me through to the studio, which was further adorned in a sea of light. It was like a very tasteful version of those houses that make the papers at Christmas because they've overdecorated. I'd never been in a real recording studio before, but it looked a lot like the ones I'd seen in documentaries – two rooms separated by soundproof glass – though recording studios aren't normally covered in fairy lights with a picnic blanket laid out on the floor.

I stopped in the doorway. "How did you…?" I took in the feast he'd laid out on the gingham blanket: a box of strawberries, mini pizzas and a bottle of wine.

He wrapped his arms around my waist from behind and removed my hair from one shoulder. "That's for me to know, and for you to enjoy." His mouth was so close he was almost kissing my neck. My eyes closed as my body exploded. "Now," Reese said, stepping forward and picking up a strawberry to hold out. "Please say you're hungry?"

My stomach was in such knots, I didn't feel I could eat – not even macaroni cheese, which is my favourite food in the universe. But I didn't want to be rude, so I folded myself down onto the picnic blanket and picked at strawberries and got caught up in our riptide. Reese was so perfect. He poured wine, and asked me more questions.

"What does it feel like, to you, when you play music?" He held eye contact over his wine glass.

I smiled to myself. "I'm always terrified beforehand," I started. "Like, almost physically ill. I hate myself for booking a gig, I hate myself for thinking I'm good enough to play. I'm convinced I'm going to humiliate myself and get laughed out of town...and then... Well, the moment I strum the chord, everything just sort of melts away, you know?"

He nodded. He knew. Once again, there was no need for explanation.

"...And when it's over, it's like waking up from a dream. Except one that everyone else has been allowed to see."

Reese nodded. "It makes you so vulnerable, doesn't it? Making music?" he agreed. "People think it's an ego thing, but it isn't. Because you have to let go of your ego to really create. You have to let go of what other people might think, or how it's going to be received, and just stay true to the song you want to write."

I put down my uneaten strawberry. "That's exactly it! That's why I think I can do it, even though I'm so shy. Because confidence has nothing to do with it."

We beamed at one another and a word floated into my head.

Connecting.

We were connecting.

Fusing like sparking wires, attracting one another like magnets, slotting in together like two puzzle pieces. I felt like I knew him already. That we were on exactly the same wavelength, the same page of the same book. I remembered trying to explain songwriting to Alfie. He'd always been so supportive, but he'd never really got it. "I just don't get those kinds of thoughts," Alfie had once said, when I explained how songwriting felt like releasing poison.

"So, you never, just, *torture* yourself with things you've said, or stuff that's happened, or everything that's wrong with the world?" I'd asked him, shocked and feeling like something was wrong with me.

Alfie had shaken his head. "Not really, no. Not unless something really terrible has happened."

I'd laughed it off and told him he was "such a scientist" while he'd nodded proudly. At the time I'd found it endearing, but it had also made me feel slightly disconnected from him. One moment, I'd feel jealous of him for having such a quiet brain, one that never bothered him with *what-if*s and *if-only*s and *why-the-hell-did-I-do-that*s. At other times I felt sorry for him – like he was missing out on a huge part of the human experience.

Not Reese. He got it, he totally got it.

Here's another word for how I felt all that evening, though. *Overwhelmed.*

The giant waves of his charm kept crashing over my head, dragging me under before I'd had a chance to draw breath. "You're so gorgeous," he'd say, out of the blue, while we finished the wine. "I don't think you realize how stunning you are." I would just about recover from one compliment, and then another one would land. "I can't stop looking at you," he admitted.

Once we'd finished not-eating, he gathered up the wasted food and shoved it all into a bin liner. "Let's lay down some tracks."

"What? Here?"

"Yes. That's why I brought you here. I've been dying to hear you sing again since the talent show."

He held out his hand to pull me up off the blanket, then pushed me to the little room with the microphone.

"But I don't have my guitar…" My mouth fell open as he pulled it out from under the desk. "How did you…?" I could hardly breathe I was in so much shock.

He grinned like a magician who'd just pulled off the biggest magic trick of their entire life. "You leave it in college overnight on Mondays," he said, "because you have music last thing, and first thing on a Tuesday. I told Mrs Clarke we were songwriting partners now and that you'd asked me to get it."

I shook my head, flabbergasted but delighted. It didn't occur to me as weird that he knew my timetable because… well, we've explained the whole idiot thing. I just laughed and thought it was romantic, put my guitar strap over my head, and perched on the stool. "So, now what?" I asked into the microphone.

"Now you sing, my canary."

He waved goodbye and shut me in, before reappearing on the other side of the glass. He muddled with buttons while I watched and marvelled from the other side of the partition. How did he even get permission to take over a recording studio for the night? Where did he get all the fairy lights from? How did he know how to use a mixing deck? And finally, *How can such a marvellous, spectacular, golden star of a person be interested in me?* It felt like someone else's life. Someone special, someone not like me.

His voice crackled into my headphones and I jumped a little.

"Alright. I'm ready for you. Sing that 'Worth The Risk' song from the show. It was brilliant."

I felt the kick of betrayal before I'd even done anything. That was my Alfie song. Yet I found myself strumming the opening chord and I started singing somehow, and the guilt evaporated as I set eyes on Reese through the glass. He had his headphones on, both of us tuned into our own private frequency, and we watched each other as I sang, and I swear it was the most intense, intimate thing that had ever happened to me. If I could have paused that moment, I would have. I'd have paused it, and climbed into it and wrapped myself up in it like it was a blanket, pulling it over my shoulders.

I sang out to Reese – betraying the boy I swore I'd never betray – hardly even thinking about it. When I was done, he was suddenly not on the other side of the glass. He flung the doors open and strode into my booth before cupping my face with his hands and kissing me. I kissed him right back, no control over my instinct to respond. I dug my hands under his hat, running my fingers through his hair. He pulled away, smiling, and lifted my guitar over my head like it was a dress. Then he kissed me again. It was all tongue and tasting and gasping and his hands clawing at my back like kissing me would never be enough.

I'd never had a kiss like that.

I hadn't been sure if they were even real. My first kisses with Alfie were lovely but they were also tentative and unsure. We'd clunked heads a few times, laughed and apologized. It took us a while to get the hang of one another. It was safe and cute and, as I said…lovely…but it wasn't like this kiss in the recording booth. When I kissed Reese, I felt like a mammal. Like instinct was taking over as my body melted into his. He pushed the stool back and half folded himself on top of me, and I remember thinking, *God, Alfie would never have the confidence to do anything like this*, and feeling guilty for thinking it.

Our fusing wasn't all physical though – the emotions were just as full-throttle.

Just when it veered into way-too-much-for-a-first-date, Reese gently pulled away. He stared into my eyes with complete wonder and leaned his forehead against mine, letting out a sigh of relief.

"I've wanted to do that since the moment I saw you sing." He drew back and stared at me some more. "There's something about you, Amelie… I can't describe it."

I laughed, because I didn't know what else to do. I'd never

taken drugs before but I guessed this was what they felt like – heady and racing towards euphoric, and like you were running too fast for your legs.

"This is some first date, Reese, I have to say."

His eyes intensified. I could almost see flames flickering behind his retinas. "Well, I knew I had to bring out the big guns. Everyone at college is after you."

I laughed so hard I almost fell off my stool, and he reached out to catch me.

"Steady now. What is it? What's so funny?" he asked, stroking my cheek. I felt so powerful in that moment. So high on how into me he was. I felt that whatever I did or said, it would still be intoxicating to him. Even if I farted, he'd probably cradle my face and whisper, "That's the most incredible fart I've ever smelled."

I didn't fart though. I just told him he was being ridiculous, and he swore he wasn't. Then we kissed again and the second kiss was even better than the first.

We never listened to my song.

Instead we just kissed and kissed and kissed until my mouth was sore and my head was swimming and I was giddy and so happy but also confused and just stuffed with emotions, like I'd eaten an eight-course meal of them. Time passed faster than a roadrunner on steroids, and, after my phone went off for the third time, I had to extract myself and pick it up.

Mum: Hi Amelie. Just checking what time you'll be back? x

Mum: I hope you're having fun, poppet, but it is getting late.
Mum: Where are you, Amelie? It's a school night remember.

I checked the time at the top of my phone. "Shit," I said. "It's almost ten o'clock. When did that happen?"

Reese wiggled his eyebrows in response and I laughed, shaking my head as I jabbed out a reply.

Amelie: Sorry! Got caught up. About to head home now. Won't be long.

He watched me put my phone back in my bag. "I really have to go."

"Stay," he said simply.

"I can't."

"The world won't end."

"But my mum will worry."

He shrugged. "So, let her worry."

I carried on collecting my stuff – readjusting my dress, which was very much no longer on my shoulders, pulling up my bra strap. Reese followed me around the room like a puppy, undoing all my efforts. He slid my straps back down and kissed my bare shoulders, wrapping his hands around my waist. "Right, I'm ready to go…"

He twisted me around and started kissing me again. I resisted for a whole millisecond before we staggered backwards and collapsed onto the floor.

"I have to go," I kept saying.

"I know," he kept replying, as he kept kissing me.

It wasn't just the kissing that made it so hard to leave. It was everything. It was the fairy lights and the thoughtful picnic and the way he'd pull away to stroke my face and look at me like I'd fallen from heaven. This time we were interrupted by my phone ringing. I twisted out of his grip. "Hello?"

"Amelie? Where the hell are you? It's almost eleven!"

"Sorry, sorry. I'm almost home," I lied. "The bill at the restaurant took for ever to come." I sensed Mum about to explode and counter-attacked. "It's been such a great night and everyone lost track of time. It's so nice to feel like I've finally made friends down here." I closed my eyes to block out the guilt and there was a pause as her own guilt sank in.

Her tone changed entirely. "It's lovely you're making friends," she said sadly.

"I'm so sorry, Mum. I'll be back as soon as possible."

"Well, we're going to bed now. I just wanted to know where you were. Don't be much later, honey. And be quiet when you come in."

We said goodnight and I hung up. Reese, who'd been kissing my shoulder the whole time, moved up to my neck. "Did I hear they're going to bed?" he whispered.

"I really have to go now, Reese."

I thought he'd fight it but instead he went stiff and straightened up. "Alrighty." He instantly switched into ultra-efficient leaving mode – scurrying about, snatching down the fairy lights, and hardly speaking to me as he did so. I stood there awkwardly, crossing my arms and worried I'd somehow hurt his feelings.

"Do you need any help?"

He shook his head and spent a further ten minutes removing all the romantic touches in silence, until we were stood in just a normal recording studio again. Me with my bag, him with a pile of stuff – and the whole length of the room between us.

Are you mad at me? I thought. The first time of many times I would think that. It felt like he was angry I wouldn't stay out, even though it was late when my mum rang and a school night. The woozy good feelings from the perfect evening drained out of me, replaced with anxiety that somehow I'd messed everything up.

"Ready?" he asked curtly, picking up my guitar. Or maybe I was imagining he was curt? But he didn't hold my hand on the walk home – he hardly spoke to me. And he walked a tiny bit too fast, so I had to scuttle to keep up. I worried and panicked and fretted the whole journey back, wondering what the hell I'd done to undo such a perfect evening. Nausea curdled inside me, until we reached the bus stop at the end of my road. He stopped and I stopped alongside him, watching him turn towards me.

"What is it?" I asked.

"Would it scare you if I told you tonight was the best night of my entire life?" Reese said, putting my guitar down. He reached out for my face to stroke my cheek. A complete one-eighty. The anxiety dispersed – totally forgotten – and love rushed in. Yes, love. I could feel it already, pulsing through both of us. Too soon, too powerful, too unstoppable.

"It wouldn't scare me." I leaned into his hand.

The moon was bright and the sky was cold and, to most people, it was just 11.45 p.m. on a regular Monday night – but not to us, as we stood there, staring at each other in utter wonder.

"So you had a good time?"

I burst out laughing. "I had an amazing time."

He looked so proud of himself. He reached down and squeezed my fingers so tight. "Will you...will you be my girlfriend, Amelie?"

I nodded. I nodded so hard and so furiously – confirming the inevitable. What we already knew to be true, since the moment our eyes first met.

"Yes. Of course."

Reese's dimples practically jumped into his hat as his face ripped into an open grin. "This really is the best night of my life," he said.

"Mine too."

I giggled into his mouth and then he hugged me so hard. The hug was even better. The feeling of his arms tight around me, the scent of his neck. The sheer force of it, like he was trying to squeeze me into him so we moulded into one piece of clay. "See you at college tomorrow, girlfriend." Then he was gone – leaving me standing there, touching my lips and giggling.

It was so perfect. I was so happy, so giddily happy. I couldn't believe what had just happened. And it felt so amazing to have something here, down here in this strange town where I knew hardly anyone. I mean, Hannah was great but she was inevitably going to get all-consumed with Jack. But now I had someone too. A person with a life I could slip into. A person as brilliant as Reese. How incredible it was, how Hollywood, that we'd just met like this. How great and beautif—

Then I remembered Alfie.

Then, I broke.

My knees buckled and I found myself bent over, hardly able to draw breath through my grief. I staggered into the plastic bench of the bus stop, and that's when the sobs arrived. They ripped through me so strong and I felt so faint I had to put my head between my legs. Alfie's face swarmed behind my closed eyes and every good thing, everything I loved about him, bubbled up and frothed over and spilled out of me.

Because here was the undeniable truth.

Things were over between Alfie and me.

They had to be. I'd just severed something I never thought I'd sever. So quickly, so easily, and yet so drastically. I cried for us, I cried for Manchester, I cried for the guilt I felt. I cried in anger that it had come to this. The thing about undeniable truths is that the truth is never set in stone, so their undeniability always has a sell-by date. What is true morphs and changes as we turn the pages of our lives, morphing and changing ourselves as we inevitably lose control of what happens to us and the impact it will have. It was an undeniable truth that I had loved Alfie, with all my heart and soul and toenails, and was going to wait two years to be together with him again. I hadn't lied to him when I promised that. It was true at the time. But time changes the truth. And, at this very bus stop, an undeniable truth was replaced with a new one. The new truth was: *I could not still love Alfie if I felt the way I felt about Reese.*

It hurt. It hurt so much and I cried so very hard for so very long – ignoring the empty night buses that hissed to a stop every twenty-two minutes.

Another thing I learned that night was that it's entirely possible to feel powerful-yet-contradictory emotions at the same time. After my first date with Reese, I felt complete joy, and yet complete heartbreak. The first causing the second, the second ruining the first. The emotions battled in my brain, fighting to be the winner. I imagined telling Alfie about meeting Reese and hiccups of grief spasmed through my body and I sobbed like a guttural pig. Then, like the wind changing, I remembered the fairy lights and the taste of Reese in my mouth, and a smile of pure joy laced through my sadness.

It would be a while until Alfie *did* find out, of course. But that part of this wretched trip down Miserable Memory Lane will come later. Right now, I'm just sat here at this bus stop, looking out at the drizzle that's just started, missing college and watching buses come and go. I'm not sure how to fill the rest of the day. I guess I could go home and stare at the ceiling some more – I'm getting really good at that…

I shake my head as it strikes me just how…*naff* my crying locations are. My memory map is the most underwhelming collection of compass points ever. But, I guess, isn't that always the way with dramatic moments? They don't play out like in the films, with stunning backdrops that reflect the drama of your life. Your heart can break at a regular bus stop, or on a grotty train, or on some crap patch of grass near your house. You don't need dramatic settings to experience dramatic emotions.

I stare out at the drizzle and relive my memories from the rest of that night.

I stayed out too late, my sobs refusing to subside for so long and I didn't want to wake my parents when I got in. Whenever I thought I'd got all my crying out of my system, I pulled out my phone and reread every lovely message Alfie had ever sent, and just set myself off again.

My phone vibrated with a message at one a.m.

Reese: Goodnight girlfriend xxx

There were three kisses. No build-up to the kisses. No *One, if I'm lucky, after a certain number of dates.* Building to maybe *Two, in time, if things are still going well.* To *Three, after months of worrying they don't feel the same way.* Nope, Reese went straight into three kisses. I stared at that row of "x"s and smiled so hard, but then that set me off about Alfie again.

A mess. That's what I was, at this lonely number thirty-seven bus stop.

And, here I am, *still* a mess.

A mess with no messages on her phone. Let alone a message with three kisses.

The Good Places

What's more painful – torturing yourself with happy memories, or torturing yourself with bad ones? I guess I'm about to find out, because it's Saturday and I'm taking myself for an unexpected detour. It's sunny in that bright, wintery way that makes every bare branch glow gold and flirts with the idea of spring. I've packed myself a little lunch – a cheese sandwich, a packet of salt and vinegar crisps, an apple and a bottle of Diet Coke – and I'm taking myself on an excursion.

Oh, by the way, when I say "excursion", what I really mean is "an exercise in ritualistic masochism" – because what better way of mending a spurned heart than ruining yourself with memories of the good times?

"You're going out?" Mum can't contain the disbelief in her voice. She takes in my coat being on and my hair being brushed and the bag over my shoulder. Very rare occurrences for me on a weekend, these days.

"Just for a few hours," I say.

Her face melts into the sort of smile that would break your heart if it wasn't already a pulpy mess. "That's great, Amelie. Really great. You meeting up with Hannah? Going into town or something?"

I nod ever so slightly, and her smile stretches wider. Her shoulders drop a centimetre as she releases the subconscious tension she's been carrying about how dysfunctional her daughter is.

"Well, have a great time. It's lovely out there. I saw a few snowdrops coming up yesterday. It's March now and spring is on its way."

I nod again and try to smile back, before calling goodbye to Dad, who's still eating toast in the kitchen. I emerge from the flat, blinking into the low sunshine, and I start walking towards all the Good Places.

Here I am, outside the closed college gates, staring into the empty grounds, which are usually spilling over with students. I grab hold of the railings, and the metal's so cold I can feel it through my gloves. I can see hundreds of imprints of me, trapped in the memories of all the days I have spent behind these gates. The good days, the amazing days, and the days where I felt like my universe had fallen out. This is a nice memory though.

I was so nervous walking into college the day after our first date. The previous evening had felt like someone else's life and I didn't trust any of it had actually happened. I was exhausted, my eyes red and sore, from both the lack of sleep and crying about Alfie. My hands shook beneath the pulled-down sleeves of my cardigan as I wobbled into college, scanning for a sight of Reese's trilby. There was fifteen minutes before the first bell, so I wound my way through the refectory for a coffee, thinking I just about had time. I smiled back as people smiled at me, still slightly recognized from the talent show. My varnish was fading though. Everyone was too worried about coursework that had been set and realizing the friends they'd made in those fearful first few weeks maybe weren't their people after all, or reflecting on the depressing realization that, despite their reinventions and wardrobe full of new clothes, they were still themselves.

I spotted Hannah just as she spotted me. She and Jack were in deep conversation in the corner table, but she waved me over. I waved back and waited for my coffee to sludge its way out of the crappy college machine. Then Reese's hands were around my waist, and his mouth was on my neck, and the brim of his hat dug into my head.

"Good morning, gorgeous," he whispered into my skin, tripping the wire on all my senses. "I couldn't sleep last night, I was thinking about you so much. Come and meet my friends."

"I was just going to say hi to Han—"

But he took my hand, and I was so overwhelmed that I left my coffee behind as I was taken to his table and was introduced to Johnnie, Mark and Rob – his band mates.

"Oi, you lot," Reese said. "This is my girlfriend, Amelie."

"Hey, nice to meet you." Rob stood up and waved. "Congrats on the talent show, you were great. And commiserations on going out with Reese." They all laughed, just as I caught Hannah's eye across the canteen. She made a *What the hell?* gesture at me, and I shrugged helplessly. I'd fill her in later, once I had planned how to handle her disapproval.

But everything to do with Hannah is a bad memory, and I'm not in the mood to focus on the bad things today. And, that morning, with my left-behind coffee I honestly didn't mind about and how proud you looked as you introduced me to your friends, was a good memory. A happy memory.

So many good memories lie behind these closed gates.

How you walked me lesson to lesson, being late to your own classes, because you couldn't stand a minute of not being with me. We'd hold hands and feel everyone's envy seep out as we passed, giggling and nuzzling our way from English literature to psychology before you rushed off to business studies. There were the lunches spent with your band, being the loudest table in the refectory – laughing, and hiding Rob's drumsticks while Jack and Hannah watched on from the corner. I tried to get you to sit with them sometimes, but you'd always have a good reason not to. "But the guys have got us the best table" or "In a minute, I just need to chat to Rob about our coursework. Tomorrow?" But tomorrow never came, and I was so distracted by your arm constantly around me, your eyes constantly watching my face as I spoke, like each word that tumbled out was a golden spool of thread, that I never really pushed it.

There were those lazy afternoons in the last gasps of the year's sunshine. We'd spread out on the college grass after lessons. I'd use your stomach as a pillow and we'd think up song lyrics together. Words spilled out of me back then. I wrote about ten songs in that first month – all of them about you, of course. I went from not knowing you existed, to feeling like I couldn't exist without you. What was so wonderful was knowing you felt exactly the same.

Well, so you kept telling me.

I leave college behind me and walk the short distance to BoJangles. The streets are busy with people enjoying the novelty March sun. They bury their red noses into scarves but smile as they walk from shop to shop, pushing buggies full of toddlers wrapped in so many layers they resemble a pass-the-parcel. There's only one seat left in BoJangles, the window seat. I order a latte and sit facing inwards, looking at the groups of mothers jiggling babies on their laps, or grown-up couples ignoring one another as they slurp from giant cups and scroll through their phones. I inhale the scent of my coffee and let the good memories fill me up. The times you and I spent in here together, physically unable to tear ourselves apart. We just stared into one another's eyes – finding it painful even to unclasp our fingers to pick up our coffee cups. You once reached over and pulled my ponytail loose. "You look so pretty with your hair around your shoulders." I'd blushed and soon stopped wearing it in a ponytail at all. Anything to please you, to get that hit of adoration.

"When did coffee become such a big deal?" I said once, after hearing another college student order a soy flat-white. "When did your order become intrinsically linked to your identity?"

"That's a rather deep thought for a latte drinker," Reese said, and I headbutted his shoulder in affectionate protest.

"I think you're secretly DYING to add milk to your Americano. But your masculinity is too fragile."

He puffed his chest out. "My masculinity? *Fragile?*" He kissed up my arm. "Maybe when I'm around you." His kisses led up to my ear. "You make me feel completely helpless, Amelie," he whispered, before we tasted the coffee in each other's mouths and got dirty looks from people around us.

I slurp at my latte and it hits my stomach hard, the caffeine turning it into slosh. I've not eaten breakfast again, but I'm not hungry. Your stomach needs to not resemble an accomplished knotting badge entry in order to feel hunger. Two mums loiter beside me, eyeing up my empty mug and sending *please leave* vibes to me, so I screech back my chair.

"It's all yours," I say, dodging past the one with the double buggy.

They don't even say thank you, just rush to claim it with their giant toddler-transporters.

I push out into the winter sunshine and wander to the end of this tiny, nothing town. I turn left, and I'm outside the yellow door of the recording studio. I relive that perfect first date for the eight millionth time, until it's too painful to stay.

I turn back towards town and walk to the local park – scene of many more good times. I eat my cheese sandwich on the bench where you finally agreed to take off your hat so I could see what you looked like without it, and I gurgled with laughter as you tried to snatch it back. I walk to the sludgy concrete pond and remember when we decided to skip form time to feed the ducks instead. We made up little names and storylines for each duck.

"Look, that duck has a different beak from all the other ducks and they won't hang out with him," I said, trying to throw my bread just towards him.

"Poor Beaky." Reese made his hands into a trumpet.

"HE'S JUST BEFORE HIS TIME, YOU BULLYING, DUCKISH TWATS," he called at the other ducks, who scattered from the noise while we giggled.

"It's okay, Beaky. Your time will come." I threw him my last piece of bread. We invented Beaky's whole tragic backstory and planned his dramatic duckish coming-of-age.

"Even feeding the ducks with you is the best thing ever," Reese said, before plunging his hands into my coat pockets to warm them up, groping me a little through the fur, while I squealed, "Not when Beaky is watching."

I look for Beaky now, but I can't see him anywhere. Maybe he didn't look *that* different to the other ducks. Maybe we just conjured him up, because we were cute and falling in love and that makes the whole world feel magical. I shiver, pull out my Coke bottle, take a sip and think about happy memories.

You never know if happy memories are going to become sad ones. They glow and shine in the vast realms of our subconscious, making that part of our brain feel like it's filled with glitter. We pick them up and cradle them like expensive cats, or wriggle into them like they are jumpers we've left to warm on a radiator. Until the day when, for one reason or another, life can suddenly make this happy memory into a sad memory instead. Good memories exist in the naivety of not knowing any better. Those perfect first weeks I shared with you – I didn't know they were numbered. I couldn't imagine it. They wouldn't have been *happy* memories if I'd been worrying it could all go as tits-up as it did. I guess a happy memory is only logged and labelled accordingly if you can live in a moment without fear of it going wrong. In the moments when true happiness is so overwhelming that you forget to be scared of it ending.

But, in time, those moments can easily become bittersweet.

Or, in my case, maybe just bitter.

It's getting dark – the afternoon still glooming its way into evening far too early. I'm not sure how I'm going to get through spring, not even with the snowdrops. I can see no light on any horizon, no reason to get out of my warm bed in the mornings. I wave goodbye to probably-not-Beaky and make my way home. There's only one spot left on this happy memory detour and I'm heading straight towards it.

"Amelie, you're back." Dad greets me at the door with a ruffle of my hair. "Did you have a nice time out?"

I nod as I peel off my coat and dump my bag on the shoe rack.

"That's great. Now, are you ready for my cooking tonight? Your mother has let me make a northern feast! Pie and mash and gravy and all things Yorkshire. You up for it?"

I nod again, keen to get into my room and finish this.

"I'll call you when it's ready."

I wave hello to Mum as I walk past the living room, taking off my mittens, scarf and hat. I drop them onto the carpet when I get to my room, and flop down onto my unmade bed and cry quietly into my bed sheets – pretty much what I do whenever I get home. This whole memory map may be about all the places I cried publicly, but there's been a whole lot of private crying going on too. I do my usual twenty minutes until I almost can't breathe any more, then I sit up, rubbing my nose with the back of my arm. I look around the walls of my bedroom, which are white and bare because the landlord won't let me paint it or Blu-tack anything up.

I then plunge myself into the final batch of happy memories.

The good times I had with you. Here in this room. This bed...

I know this all hurts but I have to do it.

Because Mum and Dad didn't get home till late most evenings and college finished at three, after only four dates with Reese – each one more perfect than the last – I took him up to my flat.

We stood on opposite sides of my room, suddenly nervous, like we hadn't been solidly kissing in any spare moment for the previous two weeks. Neither of us knew where to look. Till he stepped towards me and we catapulted at each other and kissed like we were about to die in a plane crash. We fell backwards onto my bed, and all we did was kiss but our legs were tangled and it took so much effort to stop.

We finally unwound our bodies and Reese laughed at my hair all messed up.

"You're so stunning," he said, mesmerized by my bird's-nest head. Then he put his hat back on and went over to examine my vinyl collection. "So, what do we have here then? You have a record player, that means you've passed the brilliant-girlfriend test."

"Of course I have a record player! What do you want to listen to?"

It got dark as we pulled out sleeve after sleeve and Reese told me things I hadn't known about some songs and also told me lots I already did know, but I didn't mind pretending that I didn't because it made him so happy to teach me.

There are so many smidgens of happiness that dance in the memories of my bedroom. Little smiles Reese made, the way I'd notice him looking when he didn't think I'd notice, that time he threw his head back with laughter at one of my silly jokes.

Then, after less than a month, we slept together for the first time. So early, so quickly, yet it had felt like we'd waited so long. I remember I was sad that day, because Hannah and I had argued about Reese for the first time.

"You're kind of...disappearing into him, Amelie," she said over coffee and English notes at BoJangles. "It's weird. Why don't you hang out with Jack and Liv and me tonight? We're going to the cinema."

"Sorry, we've just been so lost in songwriting, that's all. The cinema sounds good. I'll ask Reese if he's up for it."

Reese and I walked home together that day after college, hand in hand, stopping every five feet to kiss. "Shall we hang out at yours and write some songs?" he asked between kisses, both of us knowing that songs would not get written.

"Hannah and that lot have invited us to the cinema."

He screwed up his nose like I thought he would. "No way. Not tonight. They're probably watching some shite with loads of boring acting in it."

"I don't think so. Even if they are, it would still be nice if we hung out with them."

"But they don't like me!"

"What? Yes they do." It wasn't true but I said it anyway.

"Amelie, come on. They never come sit with us at lunch, do they?" It was true. I had offered but Hannah just pulled a pained face. "You can go with them tonight if you want, but I won't feel comfortable going."

"But you're away the rest of the weekend, at your dad's."

"I know. But if you'd rather go to the cinema…" He pulled me into the nook of his armpit. "Don't you fancy spending some time alone? Just us?"

He may as well have said to a junkie, "Do you fancy some drugs?" I was already dreading our separation that weekend, missing him before he'd even left. Hating his dad for being a cheating arsehole and leaving Reese and his mum when he was a baby. I mean, didn't his dad think about how that would impact our weekend plans? I nodded and nodded and laughed as he kissed me too much for a public place. I sent Hannah yet another apologetic message as we climbed the steps to my flat, and I didn't even feel guilty because I was so, so obsessed with the idea of us alone.

Amelie: Can't come tonight but can do tomorrow???
Hannah: Yeah, sure. Shame not to see you tonight though. I reckon you'd really like Sofia Coppola.

"See?" Reese said, reading the message over my shoulder. "Told you they'd be watching weird art shit."

When we got in, we did that clichéd thing of kissing the second the door was closed, staggering backwards to my bed, attached by the mouth. We had sex. Just like that. Like it wasn't a big deal, like we'd known each other longer than we had.

Sex with you…oh god. I'm in my bed, clutching my arms, and I almost can't think about it. I have never felt more connected to a human being than I did doing that with you. You stopped, halfway through, Reese, and just stared into my eyes. I…

I…

I shouldn't be doing this.

Why am I doing this?!

Why am I lying here and crying again and torturing myself with all the good things?

It's like I can't help myself. I CAN'T. Focusing on the good is not good, it only makes the pain worse. Now I'm not sure if any of it was real, if any of it really happened.

Because how could you look at me that way, Reese, and then do what you did to us? Those two things cannot coexist. It literally makes no sense. Why did you say you missed me if you didn't?

Dad's clattering in the kitchen. Soon dinner will be ready, and I need my face to de-blotch by the time I drag my pathetic arse to the kitchen table. My parents can't bear to see me sad any more. I've used up my break-up sympathy quota. We were only together four months. I know my levels of misery are not appropriate to the length of our relationship, but try telling my feelings that. I'm sour, like curdled cream. It's been over a month now. Why am I still so broken?

I can still almost smell you on my pillow.

I watched you nap after we finished, and smiled in such a deep way it was like I was tattooing contentment onto my insides…and…

Stop it! Stop it! Stop it!

I smack the side of my own head. I let out a grunt of pained exasperation.

"Your Yorkshire feast is almost ready," Dad calls from the kitchen, interrupting my mental freefall. "I've made so much gravy you could drown a cow in it."

I take a deep breath in, filling myself with enough faux enthusiasm to reply without my voice shaking.

"Can't wait," I call back. "I'll be out in a second."

The Cube

I dragged myself into college today and dragged myself into my music lesson. Surely that deserves some kind of medal? I've been feeling pretty damn proud for getting through till eleven a.m., especially as you still haven't messaged since you told me you missed me last week. I mean, I've not listened to a word Mrs Clarke has said for the last hour, but I turned up. That counts for something, right? However, just as the bell goes and I'm wrapping myself in multiple layers, Mrs Clarke interferes.

"Amelie?" she calls my name gently, just as I'm stepping past her.

I stop rather than say yes.

"Do you have a lesson now?"

I shake my head, regretting it instantly because I sense a Chat brewing.

"Neither do I." She gestures to the empty chair opposite her desk. "Sit down? It would be good to talk to you about your coursework."

Coursework.

The word bulldozes into one ear and zings right back out the other, producing no emotional response in me whatsoever. She may as well have said the word *potato* or *brick*. She must pick up on my complete lack of caring because, as I slump down, she says, "It's already two weeks late."

"What's two weeks late?"

Her eyes widen slightly behind her glasses. "The first draft of your music coursework."

"Oh yeah, of course." I try to laugh but it comes out hollow. "D'uh, you were just saying."

Mrs Clarke picks up a pen and taps it on her desk in a perfect music-teacher rhythm. "Ideally I like my students to have two go-arounds with their composition before we submit for marking. The way it's going, you're only going to have time for one. You're so talented, it *shouldn't* be a problem." She smiles kindly. "So…umm…Amelie, where's your coursework? How far have you got with it?"

My throat closes. "I've not started it."

There's an unsurprised silence. "That's what I was worried you would say."

I just stare at her, because I'm not sure what else to do. There's no room for worrying about music coursework, or any other part of my life. Reese, you've blacked out the sun.

You've made me pathetic, and uncaring about anything that isn't you. I take another deep breath and prepare for a bollocking. But Mrs Clarke doesn't bollock me. Instead she takes off her glasses and rubs her make-up-free eyes wearily, looking all weird and naked and shrewlike without them. She plops them back onto her nose, becoming Mrs Clarke again, then she looks me right in the eye.

"I've been a sixth-form teacher for over fifteen years, Amelie," she tells me. "Do you really think you're the first student who's let boyfriend trouble completely fuck up their A levels?"

Her swearing jolts me into the room a little. She swore?! She's a teacher and she swore?!

"I know this is a sixth-form college," she continues. "Therefore we're a little less pastoral here. But, Amelie, and I'm being totally unprofessional here…it would break my actual heart if you, of all people, messed up your music A level. I simply can't allow it." She crosses her arms. "So, can we please talk about what the hell happened between you and Reese Davies, and work out how we're going to get you back on track?"

I jerk my head up at the mention of your name.

She notices my response. "So, this *is* all about him?" I see a very small eye-roll. "I assumed as much. You two were quite obviously a couple, alongside being writing partners. What's happened? Have you split up?"

She's the first person who's asked this with genuine caring in their voice. It's too much. The dam breaks, yet again. I lean forward and my shoulders heave as I cry. All I am is crying. The only emotion I have is grief.

"He...he...he ended it," I get out. Such an ill-fitting choice of words for the severity of the mess. Yet it's enough for Mrs Clarke to push back her chair and crouch next to me, her hand awkwardly patting my shoulder. She lets me get it out, this new batch of crying. After ten minutes or so, it runs out of energy. (Worry not though, there's plenty more where that came from.)

"Is this your first break-up?" she asks. "Sometimes the end of first love can feel like the end of the world."

I shake my head and wipe my snuffly nose. "I had a boyfriend before." I sniff. "This break-up feels different. I feel like part of me has died. I don't understand what's happening to me." It feels so good to talk, to let out all these thoughts that have been crammed into my skull. My parents hate you, Reese, so I've not felt able to talk to them about you. I forget she's my music teacher and that this is all probably an overshare and just find myself stuttering it all out.

"Mrs Clarke, I don't know where I've gone. Does that make sense? I mean, I'm here. I know I'm here. But it's like I'm not, too. Do you understand? And I hate myself. I hate myself so much for ruining everyt—"

"Hang on, why do you hate yourself, Amelie?"

Oh, here comes the crying again. Reese, I've run out of words to use that mean "crying", and we're not even at the Cube yet. I'm going to have to *thesaurus.com* the word.

By the end of this, I'm going to be *bewailing* and *lamenting* just so I don't bore you with the word *cry*. "Because I messed it up," I bewail. "I was too much for him. I should've been better, but I screwed it up because I'm too egotistical and wasn't considerate enough of his music and…" I break off for more lamenting, and I feel Mrs Clarke's hand tighten on my shoulder.

"It's okay," she keeps saying. "It's okay."

She lets me cry myself out again, and part of me feels like this is a really, really, good way of dodging the bollocking about my coursework. Though I don't think anyone could act the way I cry, not even an Academy Award winner. Eventually, I calm down and wipe my nose on my cardigan sleeve until it's sodden with snot.

"And there I was," Mrs Clarke deadpans, "thinking, *Brilliant! Amelie has a broken heart. She'll be able to write a break-up album that tops* Rumours *by Fleetwood Mac.*"

I giggle, which is a huge breakthrough, I have to say. "I've not been able to write," I admit. "I can't play. I can't do anything. I've never felt this empty before."

Then she asks a question, Reese. One that nobody has thought to ask before.

"Reese. Was he…did he…I mean, was he *nice* to you, Amelie?"

The rooms feels very small all of a sudden, the walls flexing and boxing me in as I consider my answer. And my immediate response isn't "Yes".

"He loved me," I say.

Because that's what you always said, after you did anything bad.

Mrs Clarke is quiet, and already I'm worried I've said too much. I don't want her to hate you. She teaches you! She can't be thinking you're bad news. You're not. Are you? Are you, Reese? I start to panic. The thought of Mrs Clarke thinking badly of you is unendurable, like the itch of chickenpox.

"He was a great boyfriend," I start to gabble. "Sorry, I don't know why I didn't just say yes. Of *course* he was nice to me. I mean, I wouldn't be so sad about the break-up if he wasn't, would I? I'll do my coursework. Sorry. I'm just finding it hard to write, like I said. But if you give me an extension, I promise I'll stick to it. Please don't hate Reese. I'm sorry. It's all my fault, you see. I don't think I explained it properly. All of it was my fault."

"All of what, Amelie?"

"*It.*"

The "it" that I'm working through now. The messy line of biro. The dots on a map where you made me cry – I'm sure it's all my fault somehow. If only I'd done things differently. Been...less me, then I wouldn't have driven you away.

Mrs Clarke is talking all slowly now, like she's panicking she'll say the wrong thing. "If someone we love is unkind to us, Amelie, it's never our fault. You get that?"

I nod, but I've stopped listening properly. My brain for some reason is yelling *REJECT, REJECT, THAT'S NOT RIGHT*, but I nod because I know she wants me to. Mrs Clarke stands up, telling me all sorts of things I should probably be listening to. She's saying she can give me an extension, but I am very behind on everything. She's saying she's spoken to my other teachers and I'm also behind on my other subjects. They are concerned. They do not want this to get to the point where my parents have to come in.

"Now, you don't have to answer straight away," Mrs Clarke says. "Have a think about it. We can catch up after our next lesson?"

I jolt out from the nothing I was lost inside. "Huh?"

"The college counsellor." She looks right at me, her face heaving with concern. "It can't hurt to go there and talk things through."

I wrinkle my nose. "But I'm not, like, mentally ill, am I?"

She smiles gently. "That's not what they're for. Well, that's not only what they're for. Mrs Thomas is really lovely, and she's been here for years. There's no teen drama you can imagine that she hasn't helped with. Break-ups included."

"But…" I stammer, "who needs to see a counsellor about a *break-up*?"

Me. Pathetic me. Pathetic me, who has always been too sensitive and too needy and feels too deeply. If only I'd been less pathetic, maybe you would still love me. If only I wasn't like me. Stupid me. Shitty me. Unloveable me.

"You can see a counsellor about anything, Amelie. And break-ups are painful things. Just ask Fleetwood Mac."

I blink and feel something shift inside my body. When I open my eyes again, there's a tiny light that's been lit. I can feel it, right in the tip of my tiniest toe. There's a flicker of a flame. A spluttering one, one I could blow out without even really trying. But the flame could grow if I protect it from the wind. The flame feels like it could be called hope.

Hope that I won't always feel like this. That I can get past this, get past you.

Hope that someone might understand, might be able to fix it. Fix *me*.

Though I'm still going to carry on with my memory map. Remembering it all hurts, but I know I need to do it. I need to rip off the plaster and let the wound breathe so it can heal. I've got the Cube this afternoon, if I have the strength.

But talking.

Talking to someone.

It could help?

I look up into Mrs Clarke's eyes and there's nothing fake in them. She really, genuinely, cares and really genuinely wants to help me. I can't tell you how it feels to have care radiating off someone onto me. It's been so long since anyone but my increasingly frantic parents have shown me any care at all.

"Okay," I tell her, as the second bell shrills, jerking us out of the moment. "I'll think about it, and let you know next lesson."

I'd like to say that our Kodak moment inspired me not to bunk off my afternoon lessons. That wouldn't be true, however. I'm missing the whole afternoon. I did go to the library though, and actually tried to write some lyrics for my coursework piece.

I managed one whole line.

I've been retracing all the memories, sketching the map of me and you.

Only a snatch of a sentence, but it's better than nothing. And it took me an hour and a half to get it down. It felt right though. For the first time since everything kicked off, I've put pen to paper again and tried to make sense of my feelings the way I used to. It feels good.

I take a bus out of town and towards the Cube. It's grey, drizzly and outside the bus window everyone looks sad and downtrodden and really generally pissed off that spring hasn't showed up yet. An electronic voice announces my stop in a clipped accent, making "cube" sound more like "coob". I step out from the hissing doors into the giant concrete car park, looking up at the Cube and shaking my head. The last time I was here, the sky was black, the air wasn't properly cold yet, and this place...

...this place looked like somewhere dreams came true.

"This is amazing," Hannah said, staring up at the billboard. "I can't believe your name is actually on the sign. At *the Cube.*

This is the most exciting thing that's happened to anyone I know."

Reese stood behind me, arms around my waist, chin resting on the top of my head. "They've not made your name very big," he commented, and Hannah's nose wrinkled.

I was almost too filled with fright to care about them both getting on, though. I'd finally managed to pull them together, to see if they'd be able to get on, and I was hopeful they would. I'd invited Hannah and Jack backstage to try and plaster over the weirdness between us. But mostly all I could see was my name in lights and all I could feel was really, really sick. This was a whole new realm of stage fright – I'd physically vomited twice already that day.

I let out a not-very-calming breath.

"I hope you're all emotionally prepared for me to publicly humiliate myself," I told them and they all sighed – Reese, Hannah and Jack.

"You're going to be fine," Jack reassured me.

"More than fine, you're going to be BRILLIANT," Hannah added.

I stared up at my name again – in lights. Yes, it was very small compared to the headliners, but still – my name, in *lights*. When I'd arrived for soundcheck earlier, I was even led to my own little dressing room with my name on it. It was insane.

"So, you and Jack, huh?" I asked Hannah later, as we both crowded around my dressing room mirror.

She grinned at her reflection and applied a red lipstick that somehow complemented her hair. "What can I say?" she replied. "This northern girl came along and told me to kiss him, and it turns out she gave pretty good advice."

I blushed, not able to handle the compliment on top of all my other terror, and Hannah sensed it. "Jesus, Amelie. You've turned green. I didn't even know that was possible. Are we in a cartoon?"

"Stop it. I don't know how to calm down. I still can't believe I'm doing this."

Everything about the last few weeks had felt like a dream sequence. Getting the gig, Mrs Clarke telling everyone at college and being congratulated wherever I went, rehearsing my set list whenever I got a spare moment from falling madly in love with Reese, telling my parents, and how they wouldn't stop hugging me and saying how proud they were. I'd typed out a message to Alfie and stared at it for a really long time. I'd been on the cusp of sending it earlier that morning, during soundcheck, but Reese turned up to surprise me, so it lay dormant on my phone.

Hannah pulled me in for a quick hug. "You're going to be amazing. That's why you were picked."

"What if I vomit onstage?"

She shrugs. "Then it will be really, really funny for everyone else."

I laughed into her shoulder. "Such reassuring advice."

"I'm not built for such things." She turned back to the mirror and wiped invisible bits of lipstick away from around her mouth. "How do you think Jack and Reese are getting on at the bar? They're not, umm, natural friends, are they?"

I felt a pinprick of upset, even though she was right. I couldn't understand how anyone couldn't like Reese, when he was clearly so very likeable. But getting him and my friends to mix was like trying to combine oil and water.

"They'll be managing," I said. "Reese really likes you both." That statement was a lie.

And Hannah's bullshit detector was on full power. "Yeah, right."

"He does," I protested though I couldn't think of one nice thing he'd said about them to back up my claim. There were plenty of not-nice things. *"I don't know why you hang out with her, she's so up herself, with all that Drama stuff. I'm not being funny or anything, but have you noticed how Jack is like very, very girly? His voice! He can hit notes you can't. Oh, come on. It's just an observation. Do you think they're jealous of us? I do. You can tell they've not even slept together yet..."* I'd squawk and protest and pretend to hit him, and Reese would then catch my hand and promise me he wasn't serious. *"Oh, come on, Amelie. It was a joke! Of course I like your pretentious Drama friends!"*

"How are things between you two anyway?" Hannah asked. "You're, like, literally inseparable."

I saw myself smile in the mirror's reflection, a grin curling up my green face. "It's going really good. I wasn't expecting any of it..." I trailed off. "I know you're not his biggest fan." She opened her mouth to object then closed it again.

"But, I can't tell you how amazing it is when it's just us two."
My stage fright (and face) faded to grey as I got lost in
contemplating how utterly perfect we were.

"You got it bad, girl. And here I was thinking Jack and I
were gross."

Reese's words came into my head. *They are jealous of
us.* I blinked the thought away.

"You two are cute too! It's weird watching you and Jack
together. It reminds me a lot of Alfie."

There was quiet as Hannah recognized this was the
first time I'd brought him up since the coffee shop. I could
hear electric guitars strumming and a macho bloke yelling
in the dressing room next door. The main band, the
Contenders, must've finally turned up again after their very
long break.

"I didn't know whether to ask about him." Hannah fluffed
her fringe. "I mean, I'm assuming you guys are over?"

I watched my throat move in the mirror as I swallowed.
"Well, we'd already broken up before I moved."

Hannah turned to look at me, her backcombed auburn
bob looking all rocky and brilliant. "Yeah, but you mentioned
you were going to get back together at uni. Manchester, or
something? Is that off the cards now?"

Another swallow, this one more of a gulp. "Yes. I thought
Alfie was it, but now I've met Reese I realize it was never
anything really."

She raised both eyebrows. "Whoa, big statement."

I shrugged, like I cared less than I did. Because even

though Reese had eclipsed pretty much everything, there was still a tiny patch of my heart left for Alfie. A patch that wanted to cry whenever I fell further for Reese – that turned black whenever I fell a little deeper.

Hannah laughed nervously. "Now I'm not sure if it's a good thing that Jack and I remind you of Alfie."

I shake my head. "God, no. I didn't mean it like that. Sorry. Things with Alfie were great – it was supposed to be a compliment. Shit. It's just things with Reese are really intense right now, in a good way. I'm sure how you feel about Jack is really intense too, right?"

Hannah bit her lip. "I'm not sure about 'intense'. I really like him. And the more I kiss him and spend time just us two, the more I like him. But, you know. It's a slow build. In a good way."

I nodded. I didn't want to talk about it any more. Not with my set beginning in less than an hour and seventy per cent of college coming to watch me. Not with the Contenders knocking on the door to say hi.

"We've just been hanging out with your boyfriend," Mike, the lead singer, said, bowling in without waiting for me to invite him. I'd met them briefly earlier and they'd loved Reese right away. Within five minutes they were all bumping fists and talking about key changes while I just stood there, feeling like a nervous shy mug.

Hannah transformed into this weird jittering wreck. She held out her hand to shake, like she was a grown-up or something, and stammered out her name. "I'm a huge fan," she told Mike, not letting go of his hand in an appropriate time frame.

"That's great, thank you," Mike said, underwhelmed but friendly. He turned to me. "Hey, so Reese said you're feeling a little nervous? Want to hang in our dressing room? We have whisky?"

Hannah and I looked at each other, knowing the answer was a definite yes. I left my stuff in my dressing room and stepped out into the narrow corridor bustling with pre-gig activity. The moment we did, we bumped into Reese and Jack, who were wearing their guest passes around their necks and literally, actually, laughing together like they had an atom in common.

Reese greeted me with a huge sloppy kiss. "Hey, stage fright, how's it going? Have you heard about our brilliant plan for whisky?"

A love tidal-wave sloshed through me, washing away thoughts of Alfie and guilt.

"I have and I'm in."

His smile crinkled up into his eyes. "That's my girl. Now, where's this dressing room?" he asked Mike, like they were already mates.

"Just to your left."

Reese put his arms around me, kissed my cheek, and steered me into an actual rock star's dressing room. Then he turned back to Mike. "So," he said. "Did Amelie tell you we actually co-wrote some of the songs she's playing tonight?"

It's starting to drizzle – again – like the weather wants to twin with my emotions. Every time I cry, the sky seems to cry with me. I've forgotten my umbrella so I just let my hair go all fuzzy in this car park and my cardigan get heavier with rainwater. I walk around the perimeter to keep warm. There's the stage door. What a feeling it was to walk through that. To be given a lanyard to let me know I belonged. There were so many little nuggets of joy to chew on that evening. Like Mike chatting to me as an equal, or how proud my parents looked in the crowd. None of it compared to the pure wondrous joy of what was about to come next though.

Reese, that was the night you said you loved me.

I smile, despite myself, when I think about the weird rituals and etiquette that surround saying "I love you" to someone for the first time. The invisible barriers a couple has to cross – one being the brave individual for each terrifying step, calling for the other one to follow with no guarantee that they will. You and I didn't dilly-dally around the topic for very long. Compared to most couples, we pounded through the steps. What usually takes months, took only a few weeks.

The Stages of Saying "I love you"

1. Everything's going swimmingly. You really like them, they seem to really like you. You hang out a lot, and it's grand.
2. You find yourself incapable of thinking about anything

other than them. Your favourite thing to do is either stare out the window or go through every message they've sent, smiling from the very depths of your stomach.

3. One day, they'll suddenly do something or say something – usually completely unremarkable – yet you find it totally adorable. You get your first hiccup of love. *I love you,* your brain will whisper.

4. The love hiccups get louder and more frequent, like a delirious form of indigestion. They'll tell a stupid joke and, HICCUP, *I love you!* Or maybe you just watch their face as they're talking and, HICCUP, *I love you!* You try and contain the hiccups, but sometimes they leak out in other ways. You get an urge to just grab their hand and squeeze it hard, or you just stare at them gooily. They start to pick up on it. "*What? What is it?*" they ask. You shake your head and say "*Nothing*". It's the greatest, most brilliant feeling in the whole darn world. Because you're falling in love. YOU are falling in *love!* That magical thing that so many people dream about – it's happening to you! You've found this perfect person, and this is totally, without a doubt, the most amazing thing in the world. Until…until you think…

5. *HOLY MOTHER OF BALLSACKS. WHAT IF THEY DON'T LOVE ME BACK? AM I THE ONLY ONE JUMPING OFF THIS CLIFF?*

6. Every time you're with them, you're now analysing them for signs you're not jumping off the cliff alone. The love

hiccups get worse. They totally get off on this sense the love may be unrequited and it makes you love them harder.

7. There are moments, gorgeous moments, when, sometimes, you'll catch them looking at you all gooey-eyed. "*What?*" you ask. They blush. "*Nothing,*" they say.

8. You take it in turns to say some of the following, on an ascending scale:

   I like you

   I really like you

   You make me really happy

   I think I might be falling for you

   I'm falling for you

   I think I could fall in love with you

   I think I'm falling in love with you

9. None of them are The Big L, however. One of you has got to take the plunge first. It's not even that you're considering it, more that your body is determined to blurt it out. There's a demented troll lurking in your stomach, ripping open your vocal cords, shouting "*I LOVE YOU I LOVE YOU*" up your windpipe, and you keep having to swallow the troll down.

10. ...Because what if they don't say it back? What if this *is* a one-way thing? What if they're still on number one?! They seem chiller than you. Apart from the occasional gooey eye, you're CONVINCED you're more into them than they are into you. And maybe you misinterpreted that gooey eye anyway. Maybe their gooey eye was just

wishful thinking or...I dunno...conjunctivitis or something. Maybe you only *thought* they were thinking *I love you* because that's all *you're* thinking, all the goddamned time.

11. It keeps going, and you feel like you're getting madder and madder, and the anxiety is getting worse and worse, and you swear people say falling in love is supposed to feel good, but this anxiety is INTOLERABLE, but you keep going and they keep going until...one of you goes and finally damn well says it...

And you went first, Reese. Didn't you? Boy, how you went first.

It was pretty surreal, but also pretty damn great, drinking whisky backstage with the Contenders. Well, it was one of those *on-reflection-it-was-great* moments you get when you're anxious. At the time, I was terrified and giddy and hardly spoke. But, now the moment's passed, I can look back and think, *Wow, I sat and drank with the Contenders.* I didn't need to chat much though, as Reese was chatting for all four of us.

"So, where you touring next?" he asked them. "Oh, Brighton? That place has such a great vibe, doesn't it? I've played there a few times. Can't beat it."

Reese's ability to charm just about anyone was madness.

The gigs he'd played in Brighton were teeny compared to where they'd played – the back end of grotty pubs, compared to the sold-out arena. Yet, the way he spoke – with casual arrogance – the entire band nodded, agreeing with him, and they even parroted back things he'd said, like, "great vibe".

I drank my tumbler slowly, marvelling, and not sure if alcohol was my kill or cure. My stomach was tangled in new levels of knots. I couldn't tell if my throat was burning from whisky or from bile.

Hannah was unusually quiet next to me, sipping her drink in equal silence. And Jack, the biggest Contenders fan, was rendered incapable. He just stood next to Reese with his mouth open.

Mike knocked back the rest of his glass, glanced over, and noticed my shaking hands. "You scared?" he asked.

"I'm terrified," I admitted. "I'm going to try really hard not to mess things up for you, but...well..."

"You won't mess things up, girl! We've heard your demo. If anything, worry about showing us up."

Overhearing, Reese nudged closer to me and wrapped an arm around my back, kissing the top of my head. "She always gets such bad stage fright," he told everyone. "I try to convince her she's amazing, but she never listens."

"Stage fright is good though," Mike said, replenishing his glass. "The adrenaline makes you perform better. The day I stop being nervous before a gig, that's the day I really have something to be nervous about."

I can't be sure, but I think I felt Reese's hand squeeze me a bit too hard. "Yeah, of course," he said, leaning back and puffing out his chest a little. "That's what I'm always telling her too."

All the talk of stage fright made it hit harder and my lungs shrivelled in my rib cage and started to to go on strike. A roadie popped his head around the door. "You almost ready?" he asked me. "I'll come and get you in ten. There's a good crowd out there for so early. Lots of friends must've come out to support you."

"Oh god." I ducked out from under Reese's arm, apologized, and then dashed to the loo. I retched up all the whisky – my third puke of the day. When I'd finished, I stared into the murky depths of the toilet bowl, clutching the sides, panicking that this nausea wouldn't pass before I had to go on. As I clutched the porcelain, I got a very small, but very urgent, pang for Alfie. He'd always been so great at handling me and my nerves – wiping my hair away from my damp forehead, lending me his jacket if the nausea made me shivery. Whereas Reese hadn't even checked on me since I ran out the dressing room. I could hear his voice booming from next door, explaining his songs to Mike.

There was a gentle knock at the door and my stomach soared, hoping it was him after all.

"Yes?" I called out, still gripping the toilet bowl.

"It's Hannah. Are you okay in there?"

Disappointment blodged through me. "Sort of."

"Do you want me to come in?"

I stumbled up, fiddled with the lock and held open the door.

"Oh dear," she said upon seeing me. "Let's put some red lipstick on that face to cheer it up a bit."

"Do I look that bad?" I twisted to the mirror above the sink. "Oh...okay. Yikes."

Hannah laughed and she rummaged in her clutch bag. "I do find your combination of talent, ambition and crippling stage fright rather amusing. In a kind sort of way." She uncapped her lipstick, assertively pulled my face to hers and instructed me to spread my bottom lip out. "I mean, you're acting like you're about to get publicly hanged."

"Aren't I?" I asked, only half-joking, and Hannah rolled her eyes.

"No chance. I heard you at the talent show. You're going to be amazing." She leaned away from me and examined her handiwork. "And, like Mike said, nerves are fine. They'll help you perform. Now, make a face like this... Yeah, that's right. I need to fill in your cupid's bow."

There was another knock at the toilet door. Another knock not from Reese. "Five minute warning," the roadie yelled through the wood.

"She's coming," Hannah called back. "There – voila!" She put her lipstick back into her bag. "Now your lips distract from the paleness of your face."

I turned to see what she'd achieved and my eyes bulged out. I never really wore any make-up, let alone a stark red lip. I didn't look like me at all. I felt very aware of my RED lips – like when you're wearing new shoes and they're a bit too

clean. But it did make my face look less ill. In fact, I looked…
good.

Hannah noticed me turning to and fro. "And we're pleased to welcome Amelie as our newest member to the Red Lipstick Convert Club."

"This is so strange," I admitted.

"Strange enough that it's distracted you from your gig for one whole minute."

As if on cue, a final thumping thudded on the door. "Amelie, you're up!"

"Oh god." I started flapping my hands. "Oh Jesus Christ and Gandhi and God and Moses and Ganesh and holy fucking fuckity!"

Hannah burst out laughing. "That's quite the collection of blaspheming."

"I can't do this," I told her.

"You can, you can. Come on, let's get you out of this bathroom." She gave me a quick hug and a shake for good measure.

We pushed out into the corridor to see the sound guy looking a bit panicked. "I was worried you wouldn't come out of there," he said.

"Sorry. I was…vomiting."

He smiled. "Seen it all before, but we do need you now."

Hannah gave me another hard hug. "Jack's just messaged to say he's slipped into the front row. I'm going to go meet him. We'll be cheering you on throughout. See you on the other side."

I squeezed her back, looking over her shoulder to try and spot Reese. No boyfriend to be found. The band's dressing room was empty and quiet. They were probably out for another group smoke, which they'd been doing all afternoon.

"Come on," the sound guy said. "Your audience awaits."

My legs felt all strange as I wobbled behind him to the side of the stage and picked up my guitar. I tried to breathe properly, telling myself that nobody really cared how I did, and using all my other coping strategies – clenching and unclenching my fists, counting to ten and back down again. But it was a bit like using a water pistol to put out a burning inferno. This gig was a bigger deal than other gigs. The stakes were higher.

I imagined Alfie's voice in my head, thinking through what he might say. *"So, the stakes are high, Ammy. So what? Since when did you like steak?"* I smiled as his imaginary words temporarily dissolved some of my nerves, until I remembered he didn't even know about this gig. I'd not even told Jessa back home. I don't know why. I guess I'd been so wrapped up in everything.

"Amelie!"

Reese appeared like magic, like he knew I'd been thinking about my ex. He flung me into his arms. "How are you feeling, little thing?"

"Reese! Where did you go?"

His breath smelled of alcohol and his T-shirt was already sticky from sweat. But I loved the smell of his sweat. I was so obsessed, that if he'd peed on the ground, I'd probably have tried to scoop it up with a mason jar or something.

"I've been looking for you," Reese replied, even though he'd known I was in the loo. "Are you excited?"

"Umm, no. I've just been sick."

"I had a peek around the curtain. It's pretty packed out there, Amelie."

"That's not helping, Reese."

"Amelie?" the sound guy interrupted. "It's time."

"Oh god!"

Reese squeezed me into another hug, and I remember feeling a tiny bit irked that he hadn't really made me feel better. Then he gave me a sloppy kiss on the lips and whispered, "I've got a surprise for you."

I blinked and he'd vanished and I had no time to contemplate what he'd meant. The sound guy put my guitar over me, gave me a thumbs up, and then pushed me – actually pushed me – out onto the stage.

Lights. Heat. Sweat pouring from every gland in my body. I told myself to just worry about walking across the stage to the microphone. Once I made it to the microphone, I worried about getting it adjusted. Little steps – breaking the terror down into digestible chunks. The next chunk was to look up at the audience.

I looked up.

Whoa. There were more people than I expected, and so many faces I recognized from college. I was so scared, that, for a moment, I considered turning and running away. Yet, as always, I strummed the opening chord and I opened my sicky-tasting mouth, and, as always, once I'd started, it was all okay again.

I'm not going to pretend it was cinematically brilliant, that the whole audience were in tears and demanded an encore. I could sense my songs landing though. There were no boos, most importantly, and there was applause between numbers. I started to smile and relax into it and felt energy float off the audience and sink into my soul. Happiness bloomed in my gut and I had that thought you only get in truly brilliant moments. That thought that you know this moment is special and you want to make sure you get it all down properly in your memory – because it will most certainly become a good memory – but then you panic so much about not taking it in enough that you kind of lose the moment anyway. So, that, that happened. Much too soon, I'd sung my last song. There was a hearty amount of applause and I caught my parents' faces in the darkness – Mum literally crying with pride. Relief and joy erupted through me and I grinned and grinned at the crowd. I shrugged off my guitar to more applause. "I hope you enjoy the rest of the show," I said, then...

Then.

I heard the audience react before I saw him.

Reese.

There was a gasp, and I didn't know why everyone was gasping.

"Amelie?"

I turned to his voice, and there – walking onto the stage, holding his own guitar – there was my boyfriend.

"Reese?"

He leaned over and kissed me, our guitars crashing into each other. "*Surprise*," he whispered, wiggling his eyebrows. A chair appeared out of nowhere and he nodded at me to sit on it.

"What's going on?" I asked, struggling to make sense of what was happening.

"Just sit."

My audience, sensing a whiff of romance, started clapping and cheering. And I found when you're onstage and your new boyfriend is telling you to sit down in front of hundreds of people, there's very little else you can do. So I sat down.

Reese pulled the mike up to his height, then he turned, winked at me, tipped his hat and twisted back to the audience.

"Sorry for interrupting, folks," he said, like someone who's never considered having stage fright in their entire lives. "The Contenders will be on shortly. First, can we get another round of applause for my talented girlfriend here?"

Heat shot through every limb of my body. The applause he'd commanded was slightly lacklustre but he didn't seem to notice. I wrapped my arms around myself, not enjoying staying the centre of attention. The good feeling from the gig was trickling into confusion.

What was he doing? What was going on?

"Anyway, you're probably wondering why I'm gatecrashing, but there's something I've been meaning to say and I thought this was the best place to say it. Amelie?"

He turned back to me, and, oh, the way he smiled, it was all forgiven. I stared and smiled back at him.

"...I love you, Amelie," he told a massive audience of people.

There are so many clichés I could use here about how that moment felt. How everything went fuzzy or in slow motion. I could say it was the most perfect moment of my entire life. Or that I got tingles, or I went shaky, or my stomach filled with butterflies, or generally just had "some feels". But I can't remember anything really, apart from crying.

Reese came over to kiss me and the crowd loved it. He wiped the tears from my face, cupped it in his hands, and kissed me as the cheers amplified. My crying made the moment even more dramatic, giving the viewers exactly what they wanted. Giving *Reese* what he wanted. Which was a show. One where he was the star. The best boyfriend of all boyfriends. We kissed tenderly, my tears melting into his face. Then we hugged, clasped together so tight, shaking in one another's arms.

"I really do love you, Amelie," he said again, just to me, into only my ear this time.

A guttural sob worked its way up my throat. "I love you too." And I did. I really, truly, did.

I still do.

He brought me in for another perfect kiss in front of loads of our not-really-closest friends, put his forehead against my forehead, whispered "*I love you*" again, then made his way back to the microphone.

"You hear that, everyone?" Reese told the crowd. "She said it back!"

More cheering. It could've been in a movie, I guess. Apart from all the snot I was producing. People don't tend to snot on one another in romantic scenes in movies.

"And, just to finish things off... Amelie, I've written a song. Just for you."

Reese strummed his acoustic guitar and started to sing.

"It started with a girl, and it's ending with a girl, and the happily-ever-after is you."

He sang beautifully, or maybe that's just how I remember it. I mean, a girl is hardly going to sit through a song written specifically for her and say, *"Hey, Reese, you didn't quite hit that high E."* I cried with joy all the way through, and I can say, with some certainty, it's the most romantic thing that's ever happened to me. In that moment, I really, honestly believed he was The One. I believed his song. I believed his "I love you". I believed I was his happily-ever-after. Everyone politely clapped when Reese finished and he ran over to kiss me once more. Despite being more in love than I ever knew possible, I turned it into a peck, aware of my parents in the audience.

The sound guy had cranked up some background music. We looked up, dazed, and saw a lot of the crowd had dissipated. People were mingling around, queuing at the bar, going out for air before the big gig started. Only a few determined fans remained at the front – one letting out a half-hearted whoop as we left the stage.

The "I love you" had set off a lust bomb though, and we kissed again the moment we were backstage. Reese pushed me against a wall and devoured me with his mouth. I couldn't get close enough to him. I wanted to merge our skin, press myself into him until I imprinted.

"Oh, so now you kiss me properly," he said. "Unlike Little Miss Prude back there."

"I love you and I'm sorry," I gasped, really meaning every word, and kissing him harder so he'd believe me.

We were eventually interrupted by Mike yelling, "GET A ROOM!" We pulled apart to find him beaming at us. "Dude – you pulled it off!" he said to Reese, giving him a triumphant high five.

"Mike was the one who let me gatecrash the stage," Reese explained.

Mike punched his own heart through his chest. "What can I say? I'm a romantic. So…" He turned to me. "You love this guy?"

I nodded, feeling the tears threaten to fall again.

"Well, that's just beautiful. Hold on to it, guys. Never take love for granted. Great set, by the way," he added, giving me my own high five.

I wasn't just on Cloud Nine as we walked back to my dressing room. I was on Clouds Ten, Eleven, Fifty, Gazillion… I had the penthouse apartment of clouds! My cloud had a view of the whole city and a rainforest shower in the en-suite.

We fell back through the door, kissing like it was about to be made illegal. I felt giddy with euphoria. I had to keep pulling away from him to throw my head back with laughter.

"What's so funny?" he kept asking.

"Nothing. I just love you."

"And I love you."

"I, like, *really* love you."

His grin. *God*, his grin. "And I really love you."

"This is crazy. We hardly even know each other," I said.

"When you know, you just know."

We said it back to one another, again and again. Letting all the ones we didn't say before come gurgling up from where they'd been suppressed. I cried again a little bit, and Reese burst out laughing.

"Was my song really that bad?" And I laughed. "Seriously?" he pressed. "Did you like the chord structure? I think the second verse needs a tiny bit more work, but I didn't have much time to write it. I mean, I only got the idea to do this yesterday. And I'd only written half of it by then."

Between kisses, he told me all about how he'd pulled it off, and how Rob had filmed it for YouTube.

"Oh god, please don't let him upload it," I groaned. "I'll die of embarrassment." I also got a twinge of panic that Alfie would see it.

His face hardened, so slightly it was hardly noticeable. "You embarrassed of me?"

"What? No!" I shook my head with full force. "I'm just shy, you know. Can't it just stay our moment?"

"You're not shy. You just sang to a room full of people."

"Yeah, but it almost killed me."

There was a knock at the door, rupturing what felt like the start of a potential argument. Our first ever argument. I felt ill suddenly, like the stage fright had returned.

Don't upset him. Why have you upset him? Don't ruin such an amazing night. What's wrong with you?

"Yes?" I called out.

Dad's Yorkshire accent floated through the door. "It's your proud parents! We're here to undeniably cramp your style." He didn't even wait for me to say "Come in" – he just walked in, with Mum alongside, clutching a bouquet of yellow roses.

"Mum! Dad!" I ran over and they pulled me into a giant hug.

"I'm so proud of you, pet. So proud. I kept telling everyone in the crowd that you're my daughter. Some of them go to college with you."

I broke off the hug to smack my hand to my forehead. "Oh god, because that's not going to cramp my style AT ALL."

Mum crossed her arms, smiling. "Hey, I grew you for nine months and then pushed you out of my body. It hurt. We're allowed to cramp your style whenever the hell we want."

Dad spotted him behind me. "And you must be Reese," he said, striding past to say hello. He was behaving rather normally considering I only revealed Reese's existence the night before, quickly saying, "So, I've got a new boyfriend called Reese down here. He's really nice and he's in a band, and I'm really happy and don't want to talk about it."

Reese took off his hat, like we were in the actual olden times. For a second, I honestly thought he was going to bow. "Nice to meet you." He reached out to shake Dad's hand.

"You too. That was, umm, quite the display you put on tonight."

Dad said it neutrally enough, but my stomach twisted. I knew instantly from his tone that Dad didn't approve of what had just gone down. Grand gestures and simple Yorkshiremen weren't natural allies.

"What can I say? I'm a huge fan of your daughter," Reese said.

"She did very well tonight, didn't she?"

"Oh yes, she did. Brilliant. She was brilliant."

And, you know what? I wonder sometimes. If you'd ever have mentioned how well I did, or even brought up my gig at all, if Dad hadn't said something.

Mum got a full-blown Reese charm offensive. "Lovely to meet you... You must be so proud... I know how much Amelie adores you both... Didn't she do well?... So you grew up around here, did you? Whereabouts?... Oh, my auntie lives near there... It's got that weird clock, hasn't it?... Yep, that's the one...such a charming area."

I love you, I thought, watching him speak. *I love you, I love you, I love you. And you love me back.*

There was yet another knock at the door and Hannah and Jack appeared on the threshold. "YOU WERE SO GOOD!" she screamed, running over and flinging herself at me, while Jack nodded.

"Yeah, excellent show, Amelie," he added.

"You couldn't tell you were nervous at all!" Hannah said. "I was telling Jack about all your vomming, and he couldn't believe it because you came across so confident."

"You're making me blush." I pulled her in for another hug. "But thank you. And thank you for being my shrink earlier."

"Happy to help."

I beckoned my parents over. "Mum, Dad, these are my friends from college, Hannah and Jack." They all introduced themselves in a friendly clump.

Hannah, it turned out, was one of those people instantly at one with speaking to grown-ups. This different voice came out as she shook their hands. "Lovely to meet you," she said. "Wasn't Amelie fab? Oh yes, we're in the same form group. Yes, I do Drama…"

The four of them starting talking, leaving Reese and me to fling ourselves together again. He pulled me in for a teddy-bear hug.

"So, you've met my parents," I said, stroking his cheek with my finger.

"They're lovely. Your dad has the most northern accent of all time though. I thought yours was strong… Man."

I giggled and faux-hit him, just as the loud strums of Mike's opening chord rippled backstage. Cheers from the arena thrummed through the air like a Mexican wave. The Contenders were starting.

Reese squeezed my hand. "Come on, let's go watch the show. Rob and the others have saved us a spot at the front."

Dad had already hilariously put his hands over his ears, complaining about "this racket", and Mum looked like she was sucking multiple lemons.

"I think it's time the old people left the building." She came over to kiss me on the cheek. "Congratulations again, honey. We're so proud. And it was nice to meet you, Reese."

He tipped his hat. "You too."

Her lips pursed, if only for a moment. Maybe I imagined it, or maybe it was because they were such Alfie fans and still struggling to digest this new plot line. I hugged them both goodbye, and after they left, the four of us were left standing in an awkward little circle.

"Right," Reese said. "Shall we go watch the show?"

He tugged me after him, and we all followed through the maze of corridors back to the gig. We squeezed past the barriers, and spotted Rob and the band, who high-fived us as we squidged in. The music cracked loud, my eardrums already buzzing. A few people recognized me from my show and came up and congratulated me.

"THAT WAS SO ROMANTIC," one girl from college yelled into my ear. "YOU ARE SO LUCKY."

I nodded because, right then, I was – the luckiest girl in the whole goddamned world. Reese passed me a hip flask of something strong and scorchy and I grinned and swigged more than I should have. He took a sip too, keeping eye contact with me as he did. Then he wiped his mouth and kissed me and kissed me and kissed me until at least two songs had passed and Rob threw an empty plastic cup at our heads. We broke apart and he stood behind me, his arms wrapped possessively around my waist. Occasionally he would just kiss the top of my head and it would melt all my insides into goo. I couldn't focus on the music, or the vibe, or the people telling me how well I'd done. I couldn't focus on anything other than I loved Reese and Reese loved me and, somehow, on this spinning orb crammed full of broken humans, we'd managed to find one another, and now the chaos of the universe made sense.

I kept sipping from the hip flask. Warm and fuzzy from alcohol and love, my face glowed red and I couldn't stop smiling. I remember thinking, *Nothing can ruin this*. Which is a silly thing to think really, because the moment you have such a thought, the world goes, *Oh, you think, do you?*

"I'm dying for a wee," Hannah yelled into my ear after the band had been on an hour or so.

Her saying it made me realize I was desperate too.

"So am I."

In true girl fashion, it didn't need discussing that we would go to the loo together. I unpeeled myself from Reese while Hannah waited impatiently, her arms crossed. Then we wove through the crowds, apologizing as we asked to be let through. The cooler air hit us as we pushed into the lobby and the band's music faded to thumps.

"I'm worried about leaving Jack with all that lot," Hannah said as we followed signs to the ladies. "But I'm actually busting."

"They're really okay."

"Hmm."

That was the first rupture. That "Hmm". Annoyance rippled across my skin. We pushed into the empty bathroom and I could still just hear the music as we both peed and flushed. When I came out of my cubicle, Hannah was reapplying her lipstick in the mirror.

"You seriously need to sort your face out," she said.

My hand went to my chin and my eyes went to my reflection. Red lipstick was smeared across the entire bottom half of my head. It looked like I had face scabies.

"Oh my god, I'm so glad it was dark in there," I said, before realizing something else and smacking my forehead. "Shit! Was my face like this when my parents were here?"

Hannah laughed and nodded. "Yes! I tried to make eye signals, but you were too busy making gooey eyes at Reese."

"Oh god. I'm going to die."

"It's fine. Just wipe it off, and I'll reapply for you."

I soaked some loo roll and got to work rubbing my face clean. The lipstick was surprisingly hard to remove, and Hannah giggled as I scoured myself like I was a grill pan with food stuck on it.

"I'm not sure I want to go through that again," I said, as she launched towards me with her lipstick bullet.

"Just stop making out so much, then it will be fine."

She instructed me to open my mouth again and leaned forward as she repainted my lips. With only my top lip done, she pulled away and tilted her head.

"Are you alright?" she asked quietly.

"Me? Yeah, why wouldn't I be?"

"It's just, what Reese did. You're handling it really well, but you can talk to me about it if you want. I mean, it was such a dick move."

I paused.

Time paused.

I mean, *What?*

Mistaking my silence for agreement, Hannah rattled on. "I know you're loved up, but did he have to gatecrash your big moment? And make it all about him? I'd be livid! I wanted to run onto the stage and yank him off. Bless you. You were so good at pretending you didn't care—"

"Because I didn't care," I interrupted. "I love him. It was a beautiful thing to do."

She raised both eyebrows. "*Really?*"

My pinpricks of annoyance morphed into giant oozing holes of anger. *How dare she?* I stuck out my bottom lip like a stubborn child. "Yes, really."

Jealous. She was just jealous – of Reese and me, of what we had. Yeah, she and Jack seemed into each other enough, but I'd been in one of those slow-burn, *we've-been-friends-first* relationships too, and, though things with Alfie felt safe and cute, they were nothing, *nothing*, like how I felt about

Reese. It was beginner's love. Slow-lane love. Love with training wheels on. It was dipping your toe into the shallow end of the pool, whereas Reese and I had jumped off a cliff into a giant sea of love.

And of course she didn't leave it, even though it was so obvious she should.

I stand here in the drizzle, looking up at the drab exterior of where a fairy tale came true but a new friendship floundered. I clench my fists, still angry at Hannah for not leaving it. Still angry at her for…being…

…right about you.

Hannah was so right about you.

Everyone was so right about you. Apart from me.

"Doesn't it bother you?" Hannah pressed. "That out of all the moments to tell you he loves you, he chose the one where he can promote his own music?"

I didn't reply. I was too scared of what would come out of my mouth. I spun and I left, with only one red lip on my face.

"Amelie? Amelie! Come on."

She followed me out into the lobby just as loud cheers erupted around us, signalling the song finishing.

"AMELIE?"

I stopped and prepared for an apology, not sure if I was ready to receive it. She ran up to me, her lipstick still in her hand.

"Look," she panted. "I know we don't know each other very well, and I really didn't mean to upset you. I'm happy you're happy, but...I need to warn you about Reese. I don't think I have properly. Things between you guys have gone so fast and I've just not had a chance to talk to you about it, and I'll kick myself if I hold my tongue. The thing is—"

I put my hand up. "Stop. I don't want to hear it!"

"You don't want to hear what I have to say?"

I shook my head. "No."

Why was she so determined to ruin things? Then it hit me... Hannah must fancy Reese! It all made sense. That's why she was so horrid about him, why she didn't approve of our relationship. Even why she was hesitant about getting together with Jack.

"I know you like him," I said.

It didn't sound crazy in my head at the time. Though now, in this car park, I almost can't bear to relive it.

Hannah's mouth dropped open into a giant "O". "Are you kidding?"

"Why else would you be trying to sabotage things?"

"*Sabotage?* What the fuck? I'm trying to be a good friend!"

"A good friend would be happy for me right now."

"MORE, MORE!" I heard the crowd shout through the arena doors.

Hannah laughed and started applauding. "Okay, okay. Well then, congratulations. Well done on being upstaged by your WONDERFUL boyfriend on the most important night of your music career. I'm so happy for you that you're in love with such a selfish twat."

"Hannah."

I just said her name. I didn't know what to add to it.

She looked at me with pity, and shook her head slightly. "Look. I can't pretend I like him. I actually can't stand to be around him. You're cool, Amelie. I don't know you very well, but you can do better."

"Please stop talking," I begged.

"Fine then. I'm going to go rescue Jack."

She pushed through the solid doors, just as more cheering announced the band had returned. I waited, stunned, for a second, my brain and body trying to catch up with everything that had just happened and all the emotions it triggered.

Anger – that she'd ruined my perfect night.

Confusion – it had all come out of nowhere.

Sadness – as I had no idea where our friendship could go from here.

And…insecurity – what if she was right?

She'd given me a niggle, an itchy piece of sand, and I didn't like how much it made me want to scratch.

I didn't scratch the itch though. For reasons I'm still trying to understand, here, in this car park, I closed my eyes and pushed the niggle down into my gut. Because the love of my life was on the other side of those doors, and he'd just made my life like the movies, and you don't want a piece of grit in a story like that.

I sighed – the sigh that ended a friendship. The only friendship I'd really managed to grow since I arrived. We wouldn't walk to English together after that day. Hannah was never cruel after that moment, just cold. No more invites to BoJangles or chats about coursework. Just tight smiles when we bumped into one another.

"She's just jealous," Reese said that night, as he tried to make me have sex in the dressing room.

"That's exactly what I thought! …No, Reese, come on. Anyone could walk in!"

But because I was so in love, and so convinced we were two pieces of a single soul that were meant to find each other, I leaned into his kisses.

"Ignore her," he whispered. "She's always been a spiteful bitch. I tried to warn you about her, but you wouldn't listen. You're better off without her, little one. Your friends should be happy you're so happy."

He wedged the door closed, and tried again.

"Let's make love. We can call it that, after tonight."

I found myself sinking into his touch and letting it happen, because he loved me.

You loved me.

You loved me, you loved me, you loved me.

The words I'd hang on to like an oxygen mask during everything that happened next.

Outside Your House

Whoop-de-doo for me. Mum and Dad want to have yet another conversation about how worried they are.

"College called." Mum's fingers clench the handle of her coffee cup. "They say your attendance has dipped below eighty per cent."

I just look at them, because I don't know what else to say.

But Dad's happy to fill the silence. "This isn't like you, Amelie. You've been going off for college every day. Except, you haven't. Where the hell have you been going?"

I shrug. "Around."

They share a look, and I reckon maybe I'm a little bit too old to be pulling the sullen adolescent act, but I'm not sure how to handle this. I've never been in trouble before. We've always sort of got on. I've not even really let them know how much it hurt to move down here.

Anyway, I don't have time for this because it's Sunday and I have plans. Plans to go stand outside your house and hang about like a stalker. You're away in London this weekend for a gig. I know this because Rob was chatting to Darla in music – one of the days I bothered coming into college this week – and I shamelessly eavesdropped. The gig's in Camden. You're all staying at your friend Harry's student house. She's coming too, of course.

But my plan looks like it's about to be delayed.

"They want us to come in for a meeting with the deputy head." Mum shakes her head. "Amelie, what exactly is going on?"

I look up at them over the steam from my coffee. "I don't know what's going on," I say, honestly. "I'm just…finding things hard at the moment."

"It's that boy, isn't it? It's that stupid boy."

"Don't call him stupid!"

"I didn't raise you like this, Amelie. I didn't raise you to screw up your life over some idiot who wears a stupid hat," Mum says.

"STOP CALLING HIM STUPID!"

I stand up, I spill the coffee, I almost knock the chair over.

I'm crying again already. I turn and flee to my room, slamming the door so hard that the framed photo of us falls over on my chest of drawers. More sobbing. More wailing. More words that describe crying, which I ran out of a really long time ago. But, for the first time in a while, it's not the sort of crying where I want to be left alone. I'm kind of doing that deliberate over-the-top wailing where you hope someone asks you if you're okay. I'm starting to want to talk about it. Because I've been trying to figure it out alone and it's getting me nowhere. There's a gentle knock on my door and a northern accent.

"Amelie? Can I come in?"

I wait for a second before I say yes, even though I'm glad he's there.

I turn over to face Dad, smiling wearily – my face no doubt red and blotchy and all the things it's been for ages now.

"I'm sorry," I say. "I don't want you guys to worry."

He closes the door behind him and perches on the end of my bed. "I know you don't, poppet."

I twist upwards, bringing the duvet with me, so I'm wrapped up like a glow-worm. Dad pats the space next to him and I shuffle down and lean my head on his shoulder. He sighs.

"I'll try and go to college more. I'm just finding it really hard, that's all."

Dad awkwardly rubs my back. "I know it's been difficult for you, coming down here," he starts.

I go to reassure him, but he doesn't let me.

"Let me finish. You've been great, Amelie. So mature, so selfless. It must've been so painful to leave your whole life behind. I hate that I wasn't able to get a job nearer home. I've let you all down."

"You hav—"

"Again, let me finish. What I'm trying to say is, that was already probably enough on your plate. Making a new life down here, making new friends, starting a new college. You were doing so well, I was so relieved. But, a broken heart. Having to deal with that on top of everything else..."

I'm not sure if he's talking about Alfie, or you, or both.

"I don't think heartbreak is given enough gravitas at your age," he continues. "Your mum and I are probably partly to blame. We just thought this Reese was a flash in the pan thing, that you'd be over it within a week or two. But then I remembered breaking up with my first girlfriend." He turns and smiles at me. "Jane. God, I was *obsessed* with that girl. I saved up all my money working at the chippy to afford this Elizabeth Duke ring she wanted from Argos."

I wrinkle my nose. "No wonder you guys broke up."

We manage to laugh. It's weird to think of my parents having relationships before each other, though I guess of course they did.

"Anyway, when she left me for Jamie Sanders, it really did feel like my world had ended."

He scratches his neck, smiling as he remembers the pain – which is reassuring, I guess. That maybe, with enough time passed, pain can be something you remember fondly because you're so certain that particular pain has healed.

"I was a mess, a complete mess. And I remember your grandma and pa kept telling me it was puppy love and I'd get over it, and I remember how frustrating it was, because it really was awful." He pats me again and won't make eye contact, like he can only be this open if he isn't looking directly at me, as if I'm the sun or something. "So, I don't want to be like them. I understand that you're very upset about this Reese boy, and I know the pain is very real. But you can't let it ruin your whole life, Amelie. College is important. Education lasts a lifetime. Whereas I promise you, *promise* you, that this pain isn't permanent."

I swallow and turn his words over in my mind. "The thing is, Dad," I say, needing to get it out, "I was really sad when things finished with Alfie. I know I got together with Recsc, so it may have seemed like I wasn't bothered, but I did feel like my heart was broken. I know what it feels like. Even if I couldn't show it." I pause and lean down to wipe a bit of snot onto my duvet. "But with Reese...I don't know." I'm unsure of my thoughts. So I close my eyes and let my gut speak to me. "I'm starting to think something wasn't normal, *isn't* normal about us. How I feel...I don't know...it feels like more than heartbreak, Dad. I feel like all of me is broken."

His hand clenches on my back. I feel his protective anger swell up like a bursting pipe.

After he's contained whatever emotions he needed to, Dad speaks again. "The college said your music teacher, Mrs Clarke, has spoken to you?"

I nod, surprised she blabbed. Though maybe she didn't have a choice.

"She thinks I should go to a counsellor."

I expect Dad to snort and say something like "Why would you need to go to a counsellor? You're not crazy, are you?" I mean, he's a YORKSHIREMAN. There isn't any problem that can't be solved by pretending it doesn't exist and having a cup of tea.

He doesn't though. There's just a long silence, and a sigh, and then, softly, him saying, "Maybe you should think about it. If you don't want to go to the one in school, we can look into booking you an appointment at one in town. We just about have the money."

"Really?"

"If that's what you need, we'll find a way."

A knock at the door, and Mum's standing on the threshold, looking nervous.

"All okay in here?"

Dad pats the other side of him. "Come on in. Amelie was just saying she might give the counsellor thing a whirl."

Mum puts her tongue behind her bottom lip, and I can tell she's not so keen on the idea. Although, I guess, if you want to have a repression-off, posh southerners are even more stiff-upper-lip than ruggedy northerners. She doesn't say she doesn't approve though. "The deputy head thinks it's a good idea. Maybe you can bring it up in the meeting?" she suggests. "At the very least, it may get college to see you're willing to take your A levels seriously from now on."

174

She perches on the end of the bed. "Because you are going to take them seriously from now on, aren't you, Amelie? Don't you still want to go to Manchester?"

I think about Manchester after they've left to do the big weekend food shop. I've not given it any thought since you. I'd been so desperate to go, but that whole plan was so entwined with Alfie and making it work with him. Do I really want to go still? Do I even want to go to university at all?

I'm left alone, to go as I please without them asking, and where I want to go is your house. To carry on this journey, to get over the finish line of it. But I don't rush there, like I thought I would the moment they close the door. Instead I find myself putting the kettle on, making a strong cup of tea, and sipping it while I stare at the kitchen tiles.

I feel a tiny bit lighter since I spoke to Dad, and I ponder on why. Is it because I listened to my gut? It told me to talk and I did. Do I need to ask my gut more questions? And actually follow through on the answers it gives me?

I put my tea down and hold my hand to my stomach.

"Is how I feel about Reese normal?" I ask out loud, like my tummy is a Magic 8 Ball.

I pause and see how it feels to let that question dissolve in.

No, my Magic 8 Ball tummy replies.

Tears jab at my eyes. I sniff and wipe them before they fall.

"Do I need to see a counsellor?" I ask out loud, cradling my stomach like I'm pregnant.

All there is is the tick of the kitchen clock, the steady hum of the fridge, and my gut – my gut that twists under my hands, sighs in relief, and says:

Yes, Amelie. Yes, you really do.

I'm standing outside your house, Reese, and I'm thinking about guts.

Not, like, the literal kind – not the ones that pour out of bodies in horror films. But the metaphorical kind. The feeling you get in your stomach that something is wrong or right. I guess another word for it is *instinct*. They always say we have more than five senses. We're not just smelling, seeing, tasting, hearing and touching things. Our bodies pick up on intricacies in other people's bodies, changes in the weather, tiny subtle hints from the universe, hardwired over thousands of years of evolution. Instinct is knowing someone's looking at you when your back is turned, or that icky blodge you get that something is wrong, even when everyone else is trying to convince you it's okay.

I'm standing a few metres down from your house, as I don't want your mum to see me. *Lurking* is the word for what I'm doing, and it's not attractive.

It was here that I started to be less attractive to you. It was here that it began. The unravelling – of how you saw me, and then of how I saw myself. I stood here, outside your house, on that night not so long ago, and I got that first tickle in my gut. The *something's-not-right* tickle. The lurch of an intestine taking a break from shoving food along to put up its hand and say, *Something's wiggy*.

Though, of course, you told me that my gut was wrong.

I wonder how many times in a given second girls are told that their guts are wrong? Told that our tummies are misfiring, like wayward fireworks. *No, no, no, dear, it's not like that at all. Where did you get that from? I promise you that's not the case. You are overreacting. You are crazy. You are insecure. You are being a silly little thing.* And, then, days or weeks or even years later, we look back on The Bad Thing that happened to us because we ignored all the signs, and we say to ourselves *I wish I had listened to my gut*.

It takes guts to listen to your gut, though.

It takes bravery to walk away from something because a part of your bowel tells you to. I mean, who does that? That *is* crazy.

Or is it? Or is it ignoring your gut that makes you crazy in the long run? Would I have so many dots on this map if I'd listened to my stomach? Would I have shed less tears?

Here is what I'm starting to think, Reese. I'm starting to think that some boys make girls cry, and then act like they're crazy for crying. I'm starting to think girls that cry don't cry for no reason. They're crying because their guts, or their instinct, or their psychic sense, or whatever the hell you want to call it, but the thing that's evolved to keep them safe is screaming *ABORT, ABORT* and yet they're too scared to listen to it. They're too scared that their gut is wrong and the boy is right. Because we trust boys. We trust them when they say they love us. We trust their instincts and their motives, and they're never as silly as us, are they? They are logical and reasonable and don't let feeble emotions get in the way of things. Who are you going to trust? The calm boy whose voice doesn't wobble, who can explain reasonably, and using examples, why everything is fine – or the crying girl saying she can *feel* something is wrong?

My gut told me something was off, right here, on this street. My gut told me to cry, and I did. My gut told me maybe this wasn't good news, but *you* told me it was okay and I believed you and then I cried some more. My gut told me at two a.m. the other week that I should get out of bed and go out in the cold and start retracing all the places you made me cry. I did as I was told.

My gut told me – in the kitchen, only an hour ago – that I should go and see a counsellor. I'm going to go. I feel better even at the thought of it.

I'm not going to ignore my gut any more, Reese.

But I did, back then. Here. Two weeks after your big declaration at the Cube.

Just two weeks is how long it took to unravel. I sat with you and the band every day at lunch, and I sat with you and the band in every spare moment in the music rooms, and I pretended I didn't mind that Hannah wrinkled her nose whenever she looked over. And with no Hannah and no Jack and no that lot, I had no other friends to hang out with. But I didn't mind, because I was with you, and any moment not with you was time wasted.

So, what happened here then?

Friday night always meant band practice in Reese's "garage", and Reese's garage was his ultimate pride and joy. In fact, if he'd had to choose between his penis and his garage, I think he'd have really struggled. It's nestled at the bottom of his garden, the inside covered in egg boxes and foam so you could make as much noise as you liked without annoying his posh neighbours. It was specially made for his music, like mine back home, but his was much bigger. This was all topped off with Reese's mum letting anyone hang out there for as long as they wanted. Because she would have done anything to make her Reese happy. Since we'd got together, I'd spent every Friday night sitting in the corner while That Band rehearsed. He'd stop for breaks, drag me over and kiss me, while the others didn't know where to look.

I arrived that night like I did any other…early, so we had time to do things before the others arrived.

"Hi, Ms Davies," I said as she opened the front door. "Where's Reese?"

She smiled her pinched smile that let me know for sure that she didn't like me, no matter how polite I was. "He's in the garage," she replied, while gently, but unmistakably, closing the door in my face.

My gut kicked my stomach. I stood on the doorstep, puzzled and embarrassed. This wasn't like usual. I mean, Ms Davies had never been an open fan of mine, but she'd never closed a door in my face before, no matter how much she resented me for taking away her quality time with her son, or whatever it was that made her hate me. She and Reese were very close. She came to a lot of his gigs, and pretty much seemed to let him do whatever he wanted, buy him whatever he liked, and let his friends around as late as he liked. She was always friendly to the band, but always a bit cold with me, which was jarring after being such a huge part of Alfie's family. This was a rudeness upscale though. And Reese wasn't usually in the garage when I arrived, either. He was usually in his room because his room had a bed in it, and we were very fond of Reese's bed.

Why had she shut the door in my face? I mean, it was *easiest* to walk around the house to get to the garage – better than coming through and taking off my shoes and all that. But surely a normal person would've said "It's probably easier for you to go round" to soften the blow of the door-closing-in-face situation. I shrugged it away though. There was no need to think the worst back then, so I made my way around his house in the dark, passing the little ornamental pond with bubbling water feature and the stone bird feeder next to the marble statue. I knocked on the garage door, smiling because I still felt loved and confident back then. "Honey?" I called loudly. "I'm home."

No reply.

Shrugging again, I pushed through to find Reese sat with his hat off, guitar in his lap, staring down at the floor.

"Reese?" I stepped over the empty beer cans and takeaway boxes cluttering the floor. "Did you not hear me knock?"

He looked up but he didn't really smile. Not with his whole face, like I was used to. "Oh, hi, Amelie." He said my name like he was bored of it. No beckoning at me to jump into his arms, no covering my face with kisses, no declarations of "I've missed you" even though it had only been hours since college.

Just: *Oh. Hi. Amelie.*

I tilted my head to one side, and made my first of two mistakes.

Mistake Number One:
I didn't ignore the fact things were obviously wiggy

You see, this was the first time I'd experienced one of Reese's moods, so I hadn't learned the rules yet. How was I supposed to know that, when he got like that, I needed to pretend everything was fine, or I'd only make it worse? I was a novice back then. I didn't know how scared I should be.

I walked over for a kiss and leaned in, but he just smushed his lips against mine. "Y'alright?" he asked half-heartedly, before looking back at his guitar.

"I'm fine. How are you? Is everything…okay?"

"Yeah, good." He plucked at his guitar then strummed a loud D major chord.

"Umm, okay."

The silence was beyond deathly. It was a new, alien silence that had never existed between us before. I couldn't handle it. The shock of it made my stomach hurt. Something was wrong, something *must* be wrong – things were suddenly so very different. In order to fill this silence of absolute doom, I made my second mistake.

Mistake Number Two: I mentioned his mother

"Your mum was a bit strange just now," I ventured, not realizing I'd just reached out a toe and dabbed it onto a landmine.

His head snapped up, his forehead furrowed, lip curled. "What do you mean?"

I knew right away that I'd fucked up. Big time.

"Oh, umm. Just now. I knocked at the door. I thought you'd be in your room because...you know. Anyway, she said you were in here. But she didn't let me into the house and made me walk around. It was a bit strange, that's all."

"Why would she let you into the house? It's easier to walk around."

"Yeah, I know," I quickly backtracked. "I guess it's just one of those weird things."

"I think you're the one being fucking weird."

My stomach fell out in horror as he squinted at me with total, defensive disgust. He didn't say anything else or comment any further. He just let me lie in the mess of my fuck-up, like a toddler stuck in their soiled nappy. He shook his head and went back to his guitar while I stood like a muppet, mouth open, tears stinging my eyes. He'd never sworn at me before. Ever. I watched him for a good minute – waiting for him to come back – as all these new emotions surged into my body. But he continued to completely blank me as a punishment. A ringmaster stepped into the hole that had opened up in my stomach and started introducing me to all the new, horrible feelings Reese's behaviour prompted. Emotions I'd soon be incredibly well-acquainted with.

Roll up, roll up. Ladies and gentlemen, I'm pleased to present to you – GUT-WRENCHING ANXIETY! Ever had that feeling in your stomach that you're in danger, even though technically you're perfectly safe? That's anxiety, folks. Your super-duper fight-or-flight system malfunctioning because it can't tell the difference between a giant boar or your boyfriend suddenly being cold and offish with you.

And, accompanying gut-wrenching anxiety, let's welcome another special guest. Will you please put your hands together for WTF? LEVELS OF CONFUSION. Ever had a conversation and then, suddenly, it's like a rug's been pulled out from under you? Everything tumbles out of control and your head's spinning and you have no idea how you got here? That feeling when your brain feels like a tipped-up beehive, and you can't understand what the hell's going on, or why, or what you can do about it to make it better again, or whether it's all your fault?

And, finally – last, but by no means least – please welcome in SHAME. Do you hate yourself? You should. Shame is here to tell you all the ways in which you should. It's going to trickle down into your soul and make you feel humiliated for everything that you are.

I didn't know what to do. This wasn't *Reese*. He was never snappy or cruel, and he never, ever ignored me. This wasn't the boy I knew and loved and adored. I felt myself well up, all the Gut-wrenching Anxiety, WTF Confusion and Shame zinging into my blood and making my limbs shake. His fingers scratched his guitar, his hair flopped out from under his hat, his eyes determinedly did not look up at me. After two deep breaths, I found it within myself to go and perch on one of his amps. I put my hands on my knees and wondered again what the hell was going on. Still he would not look at me. I reached into my satchel and dug out my writing book, flicking through it, reading back the lyrics we'd written that lunchtime, when everything was glowing and I didn't feel like he suddenly hated me.

There was you
There was me
It was inevitable
This start of we

I couldn't concentrate, but I made myself flick through the pages, refusing to apologize when I'd clearly done nothing wrong. Though I felt physically sick, something else rose in me too – my temper. Irritation laced my veins. I had thoughts I'd never had about him before. Thoughts like:

How dare you?

What the hell is going on?

What is wrong with you? This isn't okay.

So, even though I felt nauseous and disorientated, my anger allowed me to damn well flick through my writing book, ignoring his stupid and totally uncalled-for strop. Because I still had guts back then, you see. Guts and self-worth, and a trust in my own version of events.

Reese strummed a chord.

I turned a page.

He played a chorus.

I reread a line and scribbled it out. It was one he'd written, and it wasn't that good.

He sighed.

I pretended I hadn't heard.

And then, finally, he looked up.

"Alright?" he asked, like there was no atmosphere between us at all. Like he hadn't ignored me for fifteen minutes and sworn at me.

I plonked my book down onto my lap and crossed my arms. "Of course I'm not alright – you're being a total dick."

His face morphed from coldness into guilt, and, like a light switch, my boyfriend was back again. He strode over and dropped to his knees in front of me.

"Shit, Amelie. Sorry. Oh god, you're really upset, aren't you?"

I wiped under my eyes. "Of course I'm upset! You've ignored me since I got here, and you swore at me!"

"I know. I'm sorry. Seriously, I'm sorry."

He clasped his hands over my cheeks and brought me in for a kiss. I turned my head. "No! What's going on with you?"

"Nothing!"

I levelled him with a look. "Reese, come on."

He sighed. "Okay, okay. It's just...I had music this afternoon. And that fucking bitch Mrs Clarke has given me a D for my composition." He shook his head and clasped my hands tighter and, oh, the relief. I can't tell you what it felt like when that explanation tumbled out of his mouth. When he started being him again. My body gulped it in. It was over. Whatever that was, it was over. The universe made sense again.

"She what?"

"A D. I know! She said it was too simplistic. Can you believe that?"

A tiny part of me agreed with Mrs Clarke. Reese's chorus did come in too soon and too heavy, and you could tell where the song was going to go within the first sentence. I didn't tell him this, of course. Instead it was my turn to cradle his face.

"Aww, Reese, that sucks. I'm sorry. No wonder you're upset."

"I mean, what does that whore know? She's a music teacher. If she was actually any good at music, she'd be out playing it, wouldn't she? Not, like, fucking teaching it to loads of kids who are actually better than her."

I flinched at his language but let him whinge it out, instinctively knowing not to pick him up on it now. In time, he settled himself down and pulled me onto his lap. I wrapped my arms around his waist.

"Feeling any better?" I asked.

He stared straight into my eyes. "Much better. I wonder why."

We kissed like there was no tomorrow and certainly no band about to turn up at any moment.

"I didn't mean to get like that," he broke off to say, resting his forehead on my shoulder. "It's just, I was already down. Then I couldn't handle you being a bitch about my mum."

"What? I wasn't..."

"It's okay. I forgive you. Now... Let's make up." His hands snuck up the back of my cardigan. Reese pulled me in and kissed me aggressively, shoving all of his tongue into my mouth so I had no space to object to what he'd just said.

I was torn in two – between not wanting to let what he'd just said pass, but also feeling high on relief that everything seemed normal again. My stomach unfurled, my shallow breathing spacing out; his kisses got even heavier, my clothes got removed.

"Reese," I protested, giggling. "Your friends will be here any minute."

He smiled wickedly and leaned me back over the amp. "And?"

...And I wasn't actually feeling that comfortable. They really were about to arrive. And I was just about to start my period and didn't feel comfortable telling him about that either. I was also still thrown by everything that had gone down, and I really wasn't in the mood.

But for some reason I don't understand, saying no didn't feel like an option.

The guys turned up just as I was pulling on my tights again.

"WAHEY – LOOKS LIKE YOU GUYS HAVE CHRISTENED THE GARAGE," Johnnie yelled, bursting through the door and finding us dishevelled.

My entire body went red as Reese laughed and high-fived him. I pulled my cardigan further around myself, feeling weird. The sex we'd just had was different from the sex we usually had. It wasn't just that it was in the garage, but Reese had been different. All the other times before it had been amazing, like two people fusing – Making Love. But, this time, he hadn't really looked at me. And it was much rougher. Towards the end especially, it had felt like I might as well not have been there. But after we'd finished, Reese stared right into my eyes and said, "God, Amelie, you're gorgeous. I love you so much." It was so opposite to how he'd just behaved that I thought I must've imagined what went before.

He's just upset about his composition, I told myself. *That's what it is. You need to support him through this. That is what being a girlfriend is all about.*

"Are you ready to rock it?" Rob asked, picking up his drumsticks. "I've been thinking about this all day and I've decided we are actually Golden Gods."

They all laughed and I tried to join in, but it felt a bit too high-pitched and like I didn't fit.

"Not so sure about that, with Mr D in Composition here," Mark added, poking Reese in the side.

"Ooooh, harsh," the other two bellowed.

I thought he was going to react but he just laughed. "Umm, arseholes?" Reese said. "May I remind you who CARRIES this band?"

More ooohing and manly grunting and macho one-upmanship while they all traded insults about one another's mothers and musical abilities and penis sizes. I wondered quietly why it was okay for his friends to tease him about being a mummy's boy, whereas I had my head ripped off for the tiniest mention of her. Things felt weirdly dangerous, out of nowhere, like I'd woken up in a field of mines.

Until Reese held up his hand. "Can we stop being children already and just jam?" he said, boredom lacing his voice. Without argument, the band fell into line and started rehearsing.

I did what I always did – sat in the corner and quietly worked on my own songs. I checked my emails on my phone and smiled when I saw one had come in about a gig. Someone from a pub had heard me play at the Cube and wanted me to do a Sunday slot. I grinned and tapped out a yes, then felt sick the moment I sent the email. I channelled my nerves into working out my playlist. With the band's music throbbing in my eardrums, I nestled into a beanbag.

Planning set lists is one of my favourite things about a performance. There's a real knack to it, a science to building the right combination of songs to fit the gig and the audience. You need a big song early on to get their attention and for the crowd to relax that you're good. But you don't want to blow your best tunes too soon. You have to space the crowd-pleasers and know when to tone it down and how many quiet songs you can get away with in a row before ramping it up again. Reese's music faded to white noise as I guessed how a Sunday crowd would be feeling – hungover, tired, dreading work the next day? I'd need to keep the set low-key... Maybe open with "Come Away"?

I was so engrossed I didn't notice the music stopping after about four songs.

"Have we lost you, little one?" Reese was smiling above me. He patted my head and I looked up.

"Oh, you guys done?"

They all laughed. "No. Just taking a quick break. Look at her, lost in her own little universe," he said, adoration leaking from his every word. "Isn't she just the cutest?"

190

I beamed up at him and waved an apology at the band. "Sorry, I spaced out there. But before I did, you guys sounded *awesome*."

"What you lost in, little one? Writing a song about how good I am in bed?"

The others burst out laughing.

"Reese!"

He held out his hands. "Come on, Amelie, I was joking! That was clearly a joke."

The band's laughter confirmed they, at least, found it funny. With no choice but to shrug it off, I put my notepad back in my bag and stood up. He wrapped his arms around the small of my back, pulling me in for a kiss. "It really was just a joke," he whispered in a sort of apology.

"Okay, I know," I whispered back.

"Get a room, guys!" Rob shouted.

I pushed Reese off gently and he laughed into my shoulder, oozing affection. "I love having you at rehearsal. I sing just for you."

I rolled my eyes, even though I loved every syllable.

"Can you two stop being gross?" Rob called out again, holding up his drumsticks. "Some of us are alone in this world, and you two are doing nothing to make us feel better."

I giggled. "Aww, Rob, your time will come soon."

He didn't smile back, just stared at his shoes. Rob was the only virgin left in the band. I knew this because they brought it up at every single social interaction.

To prove my point, Reese broke away and jumped onto

his back. "Scared you're going to die a virgin, aren't you, mate?" he said, rubbing his clenched fist in his friend's hair while Rob yelped and tried to buck him off.

Rob made that wincing look all boys make when they're having an uncomfortable emotion but can't let it show because of male social conditioning.

"It's because I play the drums," he complained. "Drummers always have it hardest."

"It's because you have no game," Johnnie chimed in, unplugging his bass guitar from the amp. "I've seen you talk to girls. I have heard you actually ask a girl how her mother was."

They all descended into macho laughter as Rob glowed and protested. "That was Jessica. Her mum has CANCER! I was being NICE."

"Yeah, and how's being nice working out for your virginity status?" Reese asked.

I lost the boys to jokes otherwise known as "banter" and the second half of rehearsal. I was still getting used to how Reese talked about girls sometimes. There was more of a laddish edge to him than I was used to, and it left a sour taste. But I didn't like having negative thoughts about him, so I squashed them down. I got my notebook back and was finalizing my set list when Reese bounded over again, after only one song, like a puppy who'd been allowed to go play. "So, what you mysteriously doing over here?"

"Yeah, Amelie," Mark asked. "That better not be our psychology coursework you're doing. I've been pretending it doesn't exist."

I ran my hands through Reese's hair, my fingers curling up under the brim of his hat. "Actually," I told them. "I was planning a set list. The Red Deer just booked me for a Sunday gig."

There was a moment then, a very tiny one, where Reese's eyes flashed – or maybe I imagined it.

Rob spoke first. "That's so cool, Amelie. God, you are rocking it at the moment."

Johnnie gave me a low five. "Yeah, that's brilliant. Do you reckon you'll be able to sneak us in and get us served?"

I shrugged and waited for Reese's reaction. His face was emotionless for a second – his eyes blank, mouth set in a thin, straight line. Then it broke into a smile, making me doubt the five seconds where I'd felt certain that he hated me. "Amelie! You should've said! Wow. You're just racking them up, aren't you?"

"It's just a Sunday afternoon slot." For some reason it felt vital to play it down. "I mean, it will probably be soul-destroying. I'll just be sitting there, singing my heart out, while everyone ignores me and shoves their face into their roast dinners."

Reese scratched his neck. "Yeah, I guess it's shit if everyone is eating."

"Still though," Rob piped up, tapping his drumsticks together. "A gig's a gig. Is it paid?"

I nodded.

"Whoa. Cool. We actually had to PAY for our slot at the Turtle. You're running circles around us."

Reese took off his hat and squeezed the brim. "Yeah," he said. "But it's cheaper to book singer-songwriters than a whole band." Then he recovered and shrugged. "And, of course, Amelie is very, very talented."

I wrapped my arms around him. "You're talented too." This weird patronizing voice came out of my mouth that I didn't understand and instantly hated. He must've hated it too because he squeezed my hands and then dropped them like they were covered in fish juice.

"Right? Shall we go again?" he asked the band. "Rob, your drumming was shit in 'Nowheresville'. Let's do it one more time."

For the rest of rehearsal, it was like I didn't exist. He didn't look at me once. I mean, he was playing, I get it. But it was so different from normal. Usually he'd always glance over whenever he sang a particularly romantic lyric, winking to confirm it was about me, or say "Sorry, I need an Amelie top-up" and kiss me. But for the rest of that night, he was all music music music. I felt I was being punished for something, that I'd somehow upset him again on this evening of not-getting-anything-right. When Rob said, "Dude, can we take five?" he said "Not yet" in such a way that no one dared ask anything else.

I found myself perched on the amp, rigid with tension. Was I being dramatic? Probably. But I had no idea what had happened and where Reese had gone and why everything suddenly felt so wrong. I ran through everything I must've done to upset him, but I couldn't figure it out. It was so obvious I'd done something bad. Should I have kept the gig to myself? He'd always been so supportive of my music right up until that moment though. How was I supposed to know I shouldn't have told him?

Eventually, after way too long of me sitting on an amp and trying to contain the hurricane of stress raging inside of me, Reese stopped.

"Good work, guys, the Turtle won't know what's hit it," he said, shrugging off his strap.

I jumped off my perch and went in for a hug, desperate to make things normal. "Sounded great, as ever." I grinned at him, need pulsing through me.

He hugged me back loosely, then sort of shoved me off. "Thanks, Ammy. You didn't need to have stayed though."

Like a slap, it was.

When he said that.

"What?"

He looked past me at the egg boxes on the wall. "I mean, I'm just saying, if you've got other things you need to do, that's totally fine." Then, as if he wasn't quite finished *what-the-fuck*ing me, "We don't have to do *everything* together."

I tried to blink away the humiliation, as the band stood around awkwardly, pretending they hadn't overheard. It hurt for so many reasons. One, because he'd always wanted me there before. Two, because he knew full well that I didn't have other things I needed to be doing since falling out with Hannah. Three, because he'd waited until *after* I'd spent my whole evening sitting there like a melon before saying anything. Four, because he'd had sex with me before he told me he'd rather I hadn't come. Rather convenient...

Ouch. So much ouch. But "ouch" isn't an adequate word for the pain that rushed in.

"I know we don't need to do everything together," I got out, my voice wobbling. "You were the one who invited me round."

He smiled but not with his eyes and reached out, grabbing my cheeks and pushing them together. "Because I wanted to see this cute little face," he said in a squeaky baby voice.

"So..." I said, waiting for what normally happened. Which was that he would tell the band to clear off and we'd go to his room and act totally loved-up and gooey until it was way past either of our bedtimes. Johnnie, Mark and Rob also seemed to be awaiting the usual instructions. Yet Reese broke the pattern that night. He took off his hat, ruffled his hair, replaced it again, then spun away from me.

"Who's up for some tinnies?" He walked over to the mini fridge in the corner, collected some beer cans and flung them to each band member.

They caught them expertly, pulling back the tops and filling the room with hisses and fizzes while I stood there, watching, waiting, tears stinging in my eyes, wondering if...

"Oh dear, littlie, it's turned into a bit of boys' night tonight, hasn't it? It's okay if you want to take off. I'll understand."

"Oh, right."

There was no choice but to pretend I thought that was a totally cool idea. It practically killed me though, to say goodbye to everyone without bursting into tears. I hugged the boys goodbye. Rob even protested the plan. "Dude, stay and hang with us," he said. "You make the air in here smell nicer." But I had *some* pride, and, also, I could just sense Reese didn't want me there.

"I'm actually really tired," I said, wishing I had a better excuse. Wishing I had friends to hang out with so I didn't feel so needy and pathetic and useless and unlikeable – things I'd never really felt so painfully about myself until that evening.

"Bye then." I hovered at the door, waiting for him to stop me. Waiting for him to say, "Don't go, I love you." Waiting for him to be the boy he'd been very consistently right up till that night, until I'd somehow messed it all up.

Reese didn't stop me.

He waved, without even kissing me goodbye, and started laughing at Rob because he'd spilled beer down his shirt. I pushed through the door, and the noise of his laughter stopped abruptly as it swung shut behind me. I stood in his moonlit garden, still in shock, the night air not quite hitting my lungs properly. My head felt all buzzy – like it was fizzing from overuse, generating its own heat from the anxious thoughts spiralling inside of it.

What did I do?

What's going on?

Is it my fault?

Where did that come from?

I don't understand.

Does he not love me any more?

...How can I make it okay again?

The crying started in my throat this time, like a tickly cough, as I trudged my way across the grass back to where I came from. The itch spread to the inside corners of my eyes. My head felt too full. There were so many feelings and no space for them to go. I left his front garden and stepped onto the pavement and I got to this hedge outside his house, and found I couldn't take one more step. I dropped down so I was squatting, and weird hiccups of crying fell out of me.

They weren't really tears of sadness, more tears of confusion. I didn't know you could cry out of confusion before that night. Since I met you, I've learned of the giant cornucopia of different tears it's possible to make someone cry: tears of sadness, tears of emotional exhaustion, tears of anger that you're too scared to let out, tears of how unfair it seems, tears of *what-the-actual-hell-is-happening*, tears of shame for being yourself, tears of frustration because you know it can feel better than this, tears of hopelessness, tears because you're worried by how much you're crying... The list goes on.

Would I know about all those types of tears if I'd just listened to my gut that night?

Because my gut was screaming, *This isn't okay*. It was twisting and lurching around in my body, like an aeroplane dropping out of the sky. It was going off like a siren. It was jabbing all my emotional buttons – making me cry.

Crying is a very obvious sign that something isn't going right in your life. You should not ignore tears. I'm really starting to realize that. But, when I stood here – where I am now, holding my stomach and rubbing it to calm it down – I ignored my gut. I ignored my tears, and I would continue to do so for almost three more months.

Not any more.

I am standing here in the dark, and, before that, I was sitting in my kitchen, asking my gut if I needed to see a counsellor. My gut said yes.

I am going to speak to someone, Reese. I'm going to start talking about you, and you know what? I know that will make you panicky. There's a part of me that still doesn't want to upset you, despite everything you did. I don't want to betray you. I don't want to tell anyone how sometimes it was actually really, really awful between us, because admitting that is admitting to myself that you're not My One True Love after all. That hurts, because I really, honestly, thought you were.

Guts and hearts aren't always the most compatible – I'm starting to learn that. They pull in different directions, ignoring one another when they really shouldn't. I think I need help working out which one I'm supposed to listen to.

Because I don't want to cry any more. I really don't.

The Golden Jubilee Bridge, London

What are your plans this weekend, Reese?

Are you going to a party with her? Maybe you're rehearsing? With your friends and your self-esteem and your life without me in it – how I envy you. How I envy anyone who picks up their phone and has messages on it from people who like them enough to bother messaging them. What does that feel like? I've forgotten. My phone serves no purpose now, other than to taunt me with its complete uselessness.

Do you want to know my plans for the weekend? No, probably not. You don't give a shit. I'll tell you anyway.

I'm going up to London tomorrow. Which could sound exciting and impressive, if I wasn't going alone to try and exorcize the ghost of my ex-boyfriend. Yep, it's point number seven of the memory map and there's nothing else to do but relive that horrible memory.

Not just yet though.

It's Friday still and therefore not quite the weekend. Normally I have a free period on Fridays after lunch, and I sit in the refectory with my hoodie up, trying to drown out the sound of everyone discussing their weekend plans. Today, however, I'm in this beige waiting room, in a counselling place in town. I've been offered a cup of tea by a receptionist who takes cardigans to a whole new level, and it feels so bloody surreal to be here and going through with this. It's been a week since I promised my gut I'd come here, so here I am. I've refused to see the college counsellor, just in case they had to tell on you. I didn't want to take that risk. So I'm in Anonymousville Counselling, dragging my jumper sleeves over my hands, wishing I'd taken Mum up on her offer to come with me after all, hanging my head and pretending my life hasn't come to this.

Until, "Amelie?" A very thin woman with short hair is stood in front of me.

I nod.

"Nice to meet you, I'm Joan. Come right on in."

I scuttle after Joan, down a corridor, and into a room with two chairs facing one another. I hover and wait for her to gesture to one. "Please sit," she says, smiling.

So I do.

Then I wait.

She tilts her head, she gives me another smile. This is

so awkward. This is so awkward, so help me god. What am I doing here? I don't need counselling…do I?

"So," she starts, still smiling her smile. "Thank you for coming to see me."

"That's okay," I say to my shoes.

"I guess it's best to start with some housekeeping. As I said, my name's Joan. I want you to know this is a safe space. Anything you say in here is completely confidential. The only time I may have to break confidentiality is if I think you're at risk to yourself, or others. But, if that comes up, I'll talk you through it. For now, it's important you know that you can say whatever you want to say in here."

Part of my stomach uncurls, a part I didn't realize was tense.

"Now…" She crosses and uncrosses her legs. "What's brought you here? When I talked to your parents on the phone, they said you're struggling with your college work?"

I nod. There's no denying it.

"And can you think of any reason why this might be? Is anything going on for you right now?"

I pause before I nod again.

"Do you want to tell me about it?"

I open my mouth to speak, and yet nothing seems able to come out. I've not spoken about you to anyone, not once. But then look where that's got me. Joan waits patiently for me to fill the silence. The smile is back – kind, patient.

"This may sound stupid…"

"I promise you there's nothing you can say that's stupid in here."

I swallow. I twist my hands around one another. I stare the scribble of us right in the face and it hurts, still hurts so much.

"It's just…would you think I was really shallow and lame if I told you I'm upset because of a boy?"

Her smile is sad for a moment – knowing. "No, Amelie. I wouldn't," she said. "In fact, you'd be surprised by the number of people I see who say exactly this. Now" – she sits forward in her chair – "why don't you tell me about it?"

The train to London is crammed even for a Saturday. One of the lines has engineering works on, so when the doors open, the carriage already throbs with too many people with large suitcases and no seats left. I fold myself in next to the stinking toilets, my sleeve over my mouth. I stare out the window as the train pulls away and chugs towards the capital. I'm still feeling weird after yesterday's introductory counselling session. It's not raining, but the whole sky is just grey and eurgh, and no wonder everyone is out, just to try and cheer themselves up.

The weather was gorgeous the day we came up here…

❥ ❥

It was freezing though, and the train was mostly empty. We nestled up to one another, wrapping our coats together to make one giant coat. I laid my head on Reese's shoulder and he kissed it and I felt so, so warm and full. Things had been wobbly for a few weeks, but since I'd opened the first window on my Galaxy advent calendar two days ago, it had improved. My relief was so palpable I could practically taste it on my tongue.

Though my tongue was pretty busy with him.

"Reese," I laughed, pushing him off. "We're in public."

He put his hand up my skirt under the protection of our coats. "So? The carriage is half empty. No one will notice."

I pushed him away and worried he'd get pissed off, but luckily he laughed and the relief felt all the heavier for it. He'd been weird and distant after that night in the garage – not returning my calls very quickly, and, when he finally did, barely speaking down the phone.

"What's wrong?"

"Nothing."

"I feel like something is wrong."

"Well, there isn't."

"You're not talking very much."

"I'm talking to you right now, aren't I?"

The surging relief I'd felt whenever he finally called was quickly replaced with churning anxiety by the time I hung up. Reese had also started batting me off whenever I went in for a kiss at college, but then acting like he hadn't. This was combined with him occasionally going quiet and withdrawn, and acting a little bit like he hated me.

"Why would I hate you? You're my girlfriend," he said, the one time I'd felt brave enough to bring it up.

Quite frankly, it had been terrible – like standing on a rug that someone kept tugging and tugging so you never really had your balance. And yet, what made it worse was, Reese continued to pretend he wasn't tugging the rug.

But not any more. Well, not on that stunning morning whizzing up to London. He was back into us, and back into me. The rug had been put down. He made eye contact again, he looked at me like I was the best thing since all the things that were best since sliced bread. *It was just a weird patch*, I told myself. *Look how great things are now*.

Reese pulled back my hair, all the better to kiss my neck.

"You okay, my little thing?" he asked. "You're not still upset about that stupid pub gig, are you?"

I winced a little at the reminder. The previous day had been my pub slot at the Red Deer, and Reese and the band had come to support me. I certainly ended up needing support. The gig was *terrible*. I'd just sat on this stool in the corner, singing my heart out, while everyone ate their roast dinners and ignored me. Then some pissed-up football players turned up, and started shouting out demands for Bon Jovi and essentially booed me until I was almost crying.

"It was really awful, wasn't it?" I said.

More kisses of reassurance. "You did so well, considering it was so shit. I don't know why they bothered booking you if they knew the crowd would be like that."

"I still can't believe we're not going into college today. I never bunk off."

"Don't worry so much. It's my early Christmas present to you. Also, you need cheering up after yesterday."

I sighed. "Do you ever wonder if all this music stuff is worth it?"

"No." He stiffened up again. "I never doubt it for a moment."

I shook my head. "I was just asking."

"This industry will try and break you," he went on, like he'd been in it for a million years. "But you've got to be strong, Amelie. Only the really talented and the really strong make it."

"Of course." I nodded. "Of course."

He took a sip of his coffee and pulled the brim of his hat down. I searched his face for signs that he was going to go off me again. My tummy tightened, like someone had turned a screw on it, as I waited for his judgement. False alarm. He turned and gave me such a smile and leaned in to kiss me tenderly. I could taste his bitter coffee in my mouth when he pulled away. The sun hit his face through the window and he was gold. We were gold. The world was perfect again.

\\ \

Now, I'm squashed next to a toilet and thinking about a few things Joan said yesterday.

"So, your boyfriend?" she said.

"Ex-boyfriend, I guess."

"Yes, of course. I'm sorry. You say you still love him very much?"

I nodded, and gulped down the sob which had bubbled up by admitting that.

"Can you tell me a bit about why you love him?"

"What do you mean?"

"It's just, from some of the things you've said, it sounds like there were a lot of things going on between you. Even before you broke up, there was stuff that didn't make you very happy…"

I couldn't argue with that, even though I wanted to.

"…and so, it would be interesting to talk a bit about what you loved so much about him." She paused, waiting.

"Well," I started, grasping for something. "The thing about him is he's so charismatic. The whole room seems to beat around him. There's something special about that."

Joan didn't narrow her eyes, but she didn't look convinced. So I gabbled on.

"And, he's a really talented musician. He works so hard at it."

Another pause.

"He wears these hats all the time." I laughed fondly. "He just looks good, you know? He's so confident and good at talking to people."

Joan nodded. She remained unconvinced. Not that she admitted as much – you could just tell. "Thank you for telling me all that, Amelie. Can I ask what you loved about how he treated you? When you were together, what did he do that made you feel so in love?"

"Well," I started, sinking into the good memories like they were my cosiest pair of pyjamas. "At the beginning, he was the most amazing boyfriend ever…" And I told her about our fairy-tale first date, how you always walked me home, how I never doubted that you loved me because you told me all the goddamned time.

"What about after the beginning?" Joan pressed. "*Then* what did he do to make you love him?"

And that, Reese, that is when I ran dry.

"Is this really the sort of thing we're supposed to be talking about?" I asked, as a delay tactic.

"We're here to discuss whatever you want to talk about, and to examine the parts of your life you're struggling with at the moment. Amelie" – she leaned forward – "are you struggling right now?"

The familiar lump jumped into my throat, the familiar tears prickled my eyes. "I am."

"Because of this boy?"

I nodded. I sniffed and I snuffled. I pulled my sleeves down over my hands again.

"There's no appropriate or inappropriate reason to feel pain," Joan said. "You can't help feelings in life, even if you think the reasons for them are silly. Suffering is suffering. It really sounds like you're suffering right now. Would you agree, Amelie?"

I nodded and then started bawling. Surprise, bloody

surprise. She let me cry, this strange new woman. "It's okay to cry," she soothed and I cried harder.

"This is stupid," I kept saying. "Sorry for being so stupid."

"Why do you think crying is stupid?"

Because you told me it was, Reese.

"I dunno."

It felt like I cried for ever, but it can't have been that long because we still had time left afterwards for her to get to the crux of the matter.

"Now, Amelie, I'm going to ask you again. What did you love about this boy after the beginning?"

I opened my mouth but there were no words.

"Was this boy *kind* to you?"

I opened my mouth but there were no words.

"Did he make you feel good and safe?"

I opened my mouth but...you get the message.

"Sometimes," Joan said, "people we love can behave in very confusing ways. And if someone is treating us *inconsistently* it can have a confusing, almost drug-like effect on us."

My hands came out from my sleeves, like turtles who'd just finished hibernating. "What do you mean?"

"Did you ever feel...addicted to this boy?" Joan asked. "Did you ever feel like you were chasing something? Maybe you were chasing the feeling of how good it felt in the beginning?"

Do you hear that, Reese?

That is the sound of hammers hitting nails on heads. That is the sound of light bulbs lighting up, all ding-a-ling-a-ding-ding-ding. That is the sound of things falling into place. It is the sound of something making sense for the first time in what feels like for ever.

I looked up at Joan through my sodden eyelashes.

"Yes," I told her. "It did feel a bit like that."

She smiled again, but this time it was a little bit sad.

"Amelie," she said. "That doesn't sound like love to me."

We pull into London Bridge and I wait for everyone to filter out before I get off. People clutter the space where the doors open, stopping to sort out their bags and their buggies and their children, while new passengers try to board the train before the rest of us have got off. Joan's words echo around my ears as I step off and follow the ghosts of us through the ticket barriers. I can almost picture us ahead of me, like I'm watching the memory on a film. I see you reach your arm around and pull me into you. I stalk our ghosts out of the station, past the newsagent where you popped in to buy gum. The ghosts of not-many-months-ago head out towards the river, and I trudge unmerrily behind, inhaling the memory like it's the smell of my favourite dinner.

"Are we there yet?" I asked as we walked out onto London Bridge. "Are we there yet? Are we there yet?" I tugged on Reese's sleeve, play-acting like an impatient child. He kissed my forehead, like I really was a toddler being taken out for the day.

"Almost, almost, little one." He stopped and looked out over the water. "Wow, would you look at that view?"

I looked where he looked, and it really was something. All of London's top landmarks glowed in the winter sun, looking perfect and painted on and the sort of London you see in movies. I leaned over the bridge, taking it all in and grinning. This was only the second time I'd ever been to the capital, and it really was putting on a show.

"Let's take a photo." Reese pulled out his phone and yanked me towards him, angling it so Tower Bridge was in the background. "Smile!"

I leaned into his smell and posed. A clicking sound and we were suspended on-screen.

"Eurgh! Take it again! I look terrible!" I said, horrified. I'd blinked at just the wrong moment, and only had my eyes half-open, with no pupil showing. I looked like a zombie having a gurning fit.

"Yeah, but I look good." I thought Reese was joking until he put his phone back in his pocket and didn't take another shot.

I stand here on this same bridge and I dig around for my phone. I lean against the wall and scroll through my pictures until I get to that one. It doesn't take long to find because since you, I've had no need to take pictures. My folders used to be bursting with shots I'd taken out with friends – ugly-face selfies Alfie would send me to cheer me up, or memes building up from various group chats. It used to take me ages to scroll through all of those to find what I was looking for in my gallery. My phone regularly complained it was out of storage space, and I'd have to dedicate a good ten minutes to going through all the sludge, deleting things to make space for all the new photos arriving from people who loved me and sent me things.

Not any more.

It's been months, and yet, in just one scroll I can bring up that photo of us. That's how few new photos I have on my phone. I still wince at how ugly I look in it now. You sent it a couple of days after our London trip, with the caption, *What a sexy girlfriend I have.* You sent it three more times, zooming in on my face more each time. I had to pretend I found it funny otherwise you'd accuse me of not taking a joke.

"So, are we there yet?" I asked again, on this bridge.

He leaned in and kissed my hairline. "Almost. I told you: patience."

We walked hand in hand through the London streets and

it felt so good to have him back and his hand in mine. Despite the sunshine, the wind had a bitter aftertaste and we couldn't stay outside long without losing the feeling in our fingertips. Just when I thought I'd have to say something about the cold, we drew up to a pub tucked away down a little alleyway.

"We're here!" Reese announced, taking his hat off to mark our arrival.

"A pub?"

"Not just a pub. The start of something special."

I raised my eyebrows quizzically.

"But first, a drink! Wait out here, just in case they think you're underage."

I watched him disappear through the small entrance. It was one of those ye olde ramshackle places you could imagine Charles Dickens drinking in or something. I perched on an empty picnic bench outside, shivering but mostly just thinking how very exciting this was and how hugely in love I was. Reese returned, cradling two big glasses of red wine.

"Reese, it's only just gone midday."

"It will keep us warm and get us into the Christmas spirit. Come on, drink up."

He sipped his wine and looked at me like I completed his life.

"I love you so much." He reached over the table to clasp my hands. Our fingers were freezing but they felt warm the moment they entwined.

"I love you too." I remember he looked weirdly relieved that I'd said it back.

The wine did warm me up, in that squiffy, dreamlike, red-wine way. I sipped at it and contemplated the day together stretched out in front of us. "When are you going to reveal this surprise then?" I asked, draining my glass. "Why did you tell me to wear 'sensible shoes'?"

He flicked the brim of his hat. "Because, my wonderful girlfriend, this isn't just a pub. It is the starting point."

"Starting point?"

"Yes..." He paused for dramatic effect. "The starting point for a TREASURE HUNT!"

He made a drum roll using his hands on the picnic table and then he pulled out his phone and showed me the screen.

It said *Uncover The City: River Trail*.

"You're always saying how you don't know London at all," he explained. "So I thought this would be a fun way to see more of it. Get my girl acquainted with her southern side."

I took the phone from him and read through the instructions for how it worked. We'd get sent clues in messages that would lead us all around the banks of the Thames.

"Oh, Reese, this is such a lovely idea," I said.

His chest puffed up ever so slightly. "I know."

"So, how do we start?"

"We just send them the word *start* and then we get our first clue. I've added your phone to the team, so we'll both get the messages. Just in case one of us runs out of battery."

I looked up at him through my eyelashes. "So?" I said. "Shall we start?" The fact he'd planned this whole day had given me my confidence back. I'd been too nervous to flirt with him in ages, scared of how he'd react. But the thought that he'd put together something so special made me doubt I had reason to worry.

"Let's do it." He stared back, love in his eyes, enjoying my confidence.

We waited for our phones to buzz. After a thirty-second delay, they both went at the same time.

Ready for your adventure? Fly south down this regal street 19 23 1 14 12 1 14 5. What creature have you revealed?

We read it out loud. "Hang on," I said. "I think it's a code."

"Of *course* it's in code."

I winced at the dig and looked up to see him huddled over his screen. Instinct throbbed through me – a spidey-sense tingled and said, *Let Reese figure this clue out, it will make him happy.*

"Ooh, it's hard," I play-acted. I'd already figured out the numbers were related to the alphabet. "I'm crap at things like this."

He kissed the top of my head. "Don't worry, babe, I've got this."

I waited patiently while he muttered under his breath.

I'd never pretended to be lesser before that day. I'd never

pretended to be less talented, or less good at singing, or less anything than myself. Another red flag. Right there. As red as red can be. As red as the second day of your period.

Did I pay attention to it, though?

Umm, well…how has this story gone so far with me and stopping at red flags?

It was worth it though, because Reese looked so cute and proud of himself when he eventually figured it out. "I think the numbers relate to where the letters are in the alphabet," he said, eyes wide with childish excitement.

"Oh my god! Yes. You're right. Hang on… So, B is two? C is three etc?"

"Yes!"

"So if we put them together?… Hang on, let me use my phone to write it down."

He read out the numbers while I typed them out. Then we both peered at my screen.

"So we need to head down Swan Lane." He looked up and pointed at a road sign. "Oh my god, it's there! It's there!"

"It's there it's there!" I parroted with the childlike joy that surged through me at solving a clue.

He kissed me on the lips, both of our mouths fuzzy from wine.

"Let's go find the treasure," I said.

"I've already found the treasure."

He pulled me in for another one that tasted of blackcurrants and alcohol. Then, mid-kiss, he pulled away and hugged me so hard I could hardly breathe. We stood like that in the cold and I thought he was going to cry for a moment. We clutched at one another, and he smelled so good, and the hug was so strong and filled with urgency. It was exactly what I needed after the preceding weeks of weirdness.

Then he let go.

"Are you ready?" he asked me, the irises of his eyes dancing.

"Yes," I whispered. Though I'd never be ready for the ways he made me feel.

Typically, it's started to drizzle. I retrace the treasure hunt, following the scent of our ghosts. I wind down to the river. It takes a lot less time to walk it when you're not figuring out clues. But, even though it's raining, it's not so cold any more. You can feel a hint of upcoming warmth in the air, the edge of April rushing to greet us, and I'm taking my time. I try and soak up the memories of that day. Because, until it went sour, that day was another Good Time.

The treasure hunt led us up the river to St Paul's Cathedral and into this incredible rooftop bar where you can see the whole city. We took a break, and Reese managed to get served again and ordered us mulled wine. It was just about warm enough to sit outside by the patio heaters and sip it together, staring out at London and thinking how very lucky we were. I'd never felt more grown up in my life, or sophisticated, sitting sipping a weird-tasting drink, looking out at one of the most famous cities in the world, like it was a normal thing to do on a Monday.

"To us?" he said, clinking my glass.

"To us."

We crossed the Millennium Bridge and stumbled into the Tate Modern to collect two more clues. We giggled our way drunkenly around all the art we didn't understand.

"Why is there a poo on the floor made out of silver?" he asked. "Why has that won a prize?"

I giggled harder and kissed his wine-stained mouth. "Shall I just leave my pencil on the floor and see if people think it's art?"

The treasure trail led us back out onto the riverbank, past ye olde grandeur of the Globe Theatre, and into the pub next to it called The Swan. Evening was already beginning to fall and festive lights flickered on, punctuating the murk of the city, making everything magical. Miraculously, Reese was getting served everywhere we went. He held himself like the bartenders would be pathetic to even suggest he was underage. We took yet another break from the hunt, and drank yet another glass of red wine, and I started to feel very drunk. That euphoric drunk when you love everyone and everything and you feel woozy on just how good life can be.

I slumped into his shoulder as we watched London pass outside the window.

"I love you, Reese," I slurred. "I love you so much it hurts sometimes."

He smiled wonkily – tipsy, but not as annihilated as me. "If it doesn't hurt, it's not love," he said, kissing the top of my head again. "That's how you know it's real."

And I'd had so much wine, that had sounded romantic at the time.

"Let's give up on the treasure hunt and just stay here and snuggle," I whispered.

"What a perfect plan."

The sky got darker as the sun set over the water. He ordered more drinks. I can hardly remember the time or how it passed. I remember that walking to the bathroom took concentrated effort and my words came out heavy and slurred and made him laugh.

I'm standing outside The Swan now. The Globe is all lit up and fuzzy through the drizzle that has pinched the sun. The sky's dark from the rain, making it easy to peer through the windows of the pub. I can almost see us in there. That's where we sat, just there, by the window. The bar staff are probably still the same people. The world isn't so very changed, for everyone else. I see us finally looking at the time on his phone, laughing when we realized how late it had got, and stumbling out, arm in arm. I watch us pass through me, like I'm a ghost. I see the happiness bleeding off my face. I turn and follow us along the South Bank.

"Why is London so busy?" I complained, bumping into someone else.

"Because it's full of arse-weasels."

We laughed at the word *arse-weasel*. We started drunkenly yelling it out loud. We drew to a stop by some railings, where you could see St Paul's and the Walkie Talkie and the Oxo Tower and everything else that gets tourists excited.

"ARSE-WEASEL!" Reese yelled out over the river, and I bent over with laughter, thinking he was pretty much the best un-arse-weasel I'd ever met.

Now, I walk past the National Theatre. I watch the skateboarders rip their way around the skate ramp. I jolt to a halt outside the Southbank Centre.

This is the bridge. This is what I came for.

I sigh, and climb the steps, dodging people who aren't very good at holding umbrellas. Ready to immerse myself in the upcoming bad memory.

"Let's stand right in the middle," Reese said. "I want to see the whole city."

We wobbled out across the black water. The city sparkled around us, lit up to entertain and inspire. I remember feeling sorry for all the office workers storming past us with their heads bowed. Why were they missing so beautiful a view? An old busker was stood to one side, strumming his guitar, his case open in front of him with a splattering of coins inside. He was playing "The First Cut Is The Deepest" and his music sailed across the wind and into my heart.

Reese got out his phone again. "Let's take a photo."

I leaned into his face and tried my hardest to look pretty as he held it at arm's length for a selfie. We both looked so happy and carefree and loved-up on the screen, and I felt so high on *us* and how good the day was, and the relief that he'd come back to me again, that I…I…

…I made a mistake.

The busker finished his song and went straight into "Are You The One That I've Been Waiting For?" by Nick Cave, one of my absolute favourites. I knew that song. I LOVED that song, and I loved Reese, and I was blind drunk, so I thought of the most perfect thing to do about all these combined circumstances. Bolstered with yikes-knows-how-much red wine, I let go of his hand, I crossed the bridge, I smiled at the busker, stood to one side of him, and I started harmonizing with him. It was seamless. The old man grinned over, like he'd suspected this would happen all along. Our voices matched perfectly. I had literally no stage fright. I sang out to Reese and into the city night. I thought he'd *love* it – his own dedication, just like he'd given me at the Cube. We were so in love only a moment ago. He'd been looking at me like I couldn't do anything wrong, ever. It didn't occur to me this would be anything other than gratefully received.

But Reese didn't look delighted like I'd expected. In fact, he *winced*. I struck a bum note instantly, as Gut-wrenching Anxiety and WTF Confusion swooped in like a seagull dive-bombing me for some chips.

I've got it wrong, I've got it wrong, I've got it wrong. I've ruined it, I've ruined it, I've ruined it.

And even though my brain was shouting *DISASTER, DISASTER,* I couldn't stop singing as that would've made it even stranger and too awkward. So I had to continue dueting with the busker, despite it being a huge mistake. A few people noticed us and smiled as they walked past, dropping a coin in. I pushed down the sick feeling in my throat and finished what I'd started. I could no longer sing to Reese though. Not now his arms were crossed, his head tipped at an angle, a look of repulsion on his face. So I turned back to the busker and sang to him, like we were a duo who'd been doing this for years. He was in his late sixties and wearing this rainbow jacket. By the end of the song there was even a little crowd around us, and we got a scattering of appreciative applause and more coins were lobbed into the busker's case. He nodded his head at me, sensing it was a one-song thing.

"You can really sing, little lady."

I smiled, even though I felt sick and like I was going to cry and that my universe had imploded.

"Thank you."

I turned back to my boyfriend. He had his phone out and was immersed in his screen, ignoring me and my song. I felt the busker watch me watching him.

"Be careful of Mr Grumpypants over there," he warned, before strumming the opening chord of "Wonderwall".

⸱ ⸱

Oh, what your life has come to when you wish you'd taken the advice of an elderly busker wearing tie-dye.

⸱ ⸱

I shuffled towards Reese, my face sheepish, my throat tight. I felt so, so embarrassed. *What was I thinking? Why had I done that? Why did I need to show off?* It had just felt so right in the moment, when I should've known it was stupid and wrong. He reluctantly looked up.

"Y'alright?" he asked.

"Yes." I didn't know what else to say.

"What was all that about?" He nodded his head towards the hippie singing Oasis.

I shook my head. "I don't know. I thought..." I could hardly form words. My throat felt like it had been snatched out. I literally couldn't talk. My brain was foggy from wine, yes, but it was more than that. It was like he'd trodden on my vocal cords, like they were an escaping mouse he needed to trap by stamping on its tail. "Are you angry?" I managed.

He screwed up his face. "Why would I be angry?"

"I don't know. You seem…off. You're being weird."

He shook his head. "*I'm* being weird? You're the one who just randomly started busking with an old mental."

"I just thought you'd like it…" My voice sounded so pathetic. *I* was so pathetic.

Even now, standing on this bridge all these months afterwards, I cringe at myself.

No wonder he left you. You are so stupid and weird and embarrassing. No wonder you are on your own now. You will always be on your own because you're so needy and desperate and odd.

He started walking towards the north side of the river. He didn't take my hand or put his arm around me. All I could do was scuttle after him. I knew I shouldn't push it. I knew I'd messed up somehow but also sensed that talking about it would make it worse and would annoy him more. Disgust him more. Put him off me more.

Don't say anything, don't say anything, I chanted to myself.

224

Leave it be, leave it be. You'll be rewarded if you just leave it be.

And yet I couldn't. My brain was going so nuts, the *need* for relief from him was so strong, that I poked it, despite myself.

Also, I was quite drunk, which didn't help.

I stopped on the bridge and burst into tears, just like that. It took him a moment to sense me not following. He turned around, and I swear I saw him roll his eyes at my tears.

"What is it?" he asked.

"I know you're mad at me," I sobbed.

"I'm not mad at you."

"I'm sorry I sang with that man. I don't know what I was thinking."

"'It's nothing. I don't care. Come on, let's get some ramen or something."

I tried to push the tears back in, but they wouldn't stop falling. Tears because I was so mad at myself for ruining the day. Tears of shock that it had all fallen apart again so quickly. Tears because he was looking at my tears like they were made of shit.

"Just tell me if you're upset. Please. It will make it easier."

"For fuck's sake, I'm not upset! Why are you being so crazy?"

That was the first time.

The moment we lost our *calling-me-crazy* virginity.

And, a bit like after having sex for the first time, once you've lost it, you just keep doing it.

I sniffed and I paused. *Was* I being crazy?

"So you're *not* angry at me?"

He sighed. "No! I'm just cold and drunk and hungry for noodles." He held out his hand. "Can we go?"

I sniffed again and I nodded, feeling so silly, feeling so *crazy*.

I took his hand and we walked over the bridge, dodging passers-by. I should've felt better. He had told me that he wasn't angry, he had told me that I was imagining it. I should've believed him. I should've trusted him. And yet... I could sense that he *was* still angry. That, for some reason or other, I'd pissed him off. Because he was gripping my hand a bit too tightly, and he wasn't looking at me. His mouth was set in this thin, firm line. We merged into the crowds around Embankment and found somewhere to eat noodles. We sat on high stools at a table adorned with tinsel, sobering up and slurping our soup. He got out his phone again.

"Is your ramen good?" I asked.

"What? Yeah. It's fine."

More silence.

"I had a really nice day today."

He half glanced up. "Huh? Yeah. It was alright, wasn't it?"

More silence.

"Thank you so much for taking me out. It really cheered me up."

"Don't mention it."

More silence.

"Reese?"

No reply.

"Reese?"

A look. One of mild irritation.

"Yes?" A question of mild resentment.

"I love you."

A full ten seconds before he replied. Even when it came back my way, I knew he didn't mean it. Not in that moment. Not a jot.

"Yeah, Amelie. I love you too," he told his phone.

I'm here again and eating ramen again. The soup's warming me up slowly. They've sat me at the counter because I'm alone. I look over at our former table where we sat mostly in silence – me unravelling, you not seeming to mind, or even notice.

I slurp at some noodles and think about what it means to be crazy.

How do you know if your reactions are crazy or not? Who's in charge of deciding that? In our relationship, it was you, Reese. And, after that day in London, you started calling me crazy a *lot*. And the not-hilarious consequence of that was that I *did* start to go a little crazy. It became self-fulfilling.

> Amelie: Where are you? I've been waiting at the
> corner for half an hour now.
> Reese: Didn't I tell you? I've got band practice
> tonight.
> Amelie: No, you didn't tell me...thus why I've
> been waiting.
> Reese: I did tell you! God, you're not going to get
> all crazy now, are you?

Or...

"I feel like we never see each other any more."

"We see each other loads. We're seeing each other right now."

"This is the first time we've been alone together all week. And you're about to head off to rehearsal."

"So you want my band to fail, is that it?"

"That's not what I said."

"I never thought you'd be like this."

"Like what?"

"Like this! All crazy and needy and insecure..."

...

"Why are you crying? Oh my god. I can't handle this, Amelie. What's going on with you? I swear you're mental sometimes."

Or...

"What's going on with us?"

Sigh "What do you mean?"

"I feel like something's off."

"You always feel like something's off."

"You're not how you used to be."

"I could say the same about you."

"What does that even mean?"

"When we first got together you were so chill, and now you're all needy. I can't always be here for you, okay? That's not fair. Why don't you go see your friends or something? You're putting so much pressure on seeing me."

Crying "I'm not! You've not been free all week and I've not said anything."

"Until now. Great, you're crying again. Here we go…"

"I don't know why I keep crying."

"It's not attractive, you know that, right? I mean, how am I supposed to get in the mood when someone is crying all the time?"

Cries harder

"Was this boy ever kind to you?" Joan had asked, towards the end of the session.

I think about this question as I pay for my ramen and wait for it to stop raining so I can go home.

"Of course he was kind to me," I'd said, still always defending you.

"Okay," she said. "But was he consistently kind? Kindness

isn't a reward for good behaviour, Amelie. It should be a given."

Here's the thing. I'm sure you'd tell Joan that you *were* kind. I'm sure you'd baulk at the suggestion that you were anything other than an amazing boyfriend, trying your best considering how freaking crazy and hard work I was.

Joan had asked me another question.

"Have you been in any other relationships where someone *was* consistently kind to you?"

I'd nodded because I have. With Alfie.

The rain still hasn't stopped, but a group have come into the noodle place, shaking off their umbrellas and eyeing my space, all like, *Move please, it's our turn.* I touch my heart, rubbing it like it will stop the burning. It still twangs whenever I think of Alfie. I'm mourning you, Reese, but I'm also mourning Alfie. I never got time to mourn him before. I was so swept up in you that there wasn't a huge amount of time for the guilt and the regret of how much it hurts to break another human's heart. I guess we're about to get to me and Alfie. That's the next stop on this magical mystery tour of my crying. Each one is getting more and more painful, but I feel it working; I feel the pieces start to make sense, though I'm still miles away from seeing the finished puzzle as a whole.

I'm instantly drenched again as I walk towards Charing Cross to go home and stare at the walls and not write any music. As I squelch in my Converse, I think about the word *consistent*. It's not the sexiest of words, or the most romantic.

When you close your eyes and imagine your ideal person, it's not the word that arrives right away. You tend to go for words that, you, Reese, comfortably inhabit. Words like *charming* and *exciting*. I cannot think of anything Alfie ever did that was exciting. That's not what our love was. I never felt like I was on the top of a roller coaster about to drop. I never felt anxious butterflies in my stomach while I waited for his messages, because I never had to wait for his messages. I didn't get that sick feeling before seeing him, wondering what kind of Alfie I'd get that day – a loved-up Alfie, or a sulky, *I'm-going-to-act-like-I-hate-you-but-deny-it* Alfie. He was just always…Alfie.

"Were the highs with this boy worth the lows?" Joan had asked, going right in there.

I push my ticket through the barrier at the station, plucking it out as the flaps swing open to let me through. Alfie never gave me the highs you did. I never felt like I was in a movie with him, or that the world had stopped rotating. I felt good and nice and *safe*, but never giddy.

But I never felt crazy either.

In fact, Alfie spent his whole time making me feel anything other than crazy.

"Of course you're crying," he'd said, clutching my hand in the Botanical Gardens. "Don't beat yourself up about it, Ammy. Your parents are moving you away to the other side of the country. It's categorically shit. Crying is a totally normal thing to do."

Then he'd cried too, because of how much he'd miss me.

Alfie was consistent, and, because of that, I wasn't crazy. I was calm, I was chill – I was all the things you wanted me to be, Reese. But I was incapable of being those things with you. The more you wanted me to be that "chill" girl – the more you made it clear that your love for me depended on it – the less chill and more crazy I got. Because you *weren't* consistent. One day you'd be all over me, making my anxiety disappear, being kind and considerate and amazing and everything I'd always wanted. "God, I love you, I love you so much," you'd tell the whole lunch table, and the rest of the band would groan while I glowed. But then, later that afternoon, we'd walk past a girl and you'd say, "Wow, she's so pretty," then get in a mood with me if I dared to be upset.

I'm starting to realize something. I'm starting to realize that craziness may not always come from within. I'm starting to think lows aren't worth highs – not in love. Not in something where the most important thing is to feel safe.

Consistency is underrated.

The train pulls out of the station, and the rain starts to fleck the windows. As ever, I start to cry again. A little snuffle, turned towards the window so the other passengers won't see. This cry isn't for you, though. This cry is for Alfie. Because I had a consistent boy, and do you know what I did with him?

I ripped his heart out of his lovely, safe chest.

That's what I've got to face next. That's where I have to go back to next.

Alfie.

The Leadmill,
Sheffield

"What can I do for you, duck?"

I want to cry with joy, just because someone's called me *duck*. I feel ten times better already.

I hold my phone into my hair. "Hey, is that the Steel hotel?"

"Yes it is."

"I'm just checking my booking has gone through. I did it online, but I never had a confirmation email, and I'm supposed to be staying there tonight."

"Hang on, what's your name?" I give it to her, feeling sick with nerves as I hate speaking to people on the phone, and she hums under her breath as she clacks her keyboard. "Where are you, where are you...? Hang on, here! Here you are, duck. Oh yes, I see. It got stuck in our system. Good thing you called."

"You still have a room available, right?" My voice wavers.

"Oh yes. I'll book you in. Don't you worry about a thing. All sorted! Have a lovely journey here."

I hang up my phone and stare at the wall for a really long time. I've been staring at the wall a lot since seeing Joan. Staring…thinking…remembering… I shake myself out of it, look at the time and swear.

Both my parents are in the kitchen as I wheel my little overnight suitcase in, both trying to hold back their smiles.

"You all packed?" Mum asks.

I nod.

"And Jessa is looking forward to seeing you?"

I nod. Does a nod count as a lie? They'd be devastated if they knew I was going up on my own, staying in a hotel by myself, and planning on not seeing anyone. I used all my gig money to book the train and the hotel.

"Can you give me a lift to the station?"

Dad couldn't be gladder to provide transportation. He chats happily as he swings my luggage into the boot, swings his body into the front seat and pulls out of the car park.

"You going to visit all your old haunts? he asks, without waiting for my reply. "The Leadmill and the Botanical Gardens, I bet? That's where I always knew you were. Jessa and you have so much to catch up on. Has she got a new girlfriend yet? Ended it with that Pippa or someone, didn't she? Don't worry about seeing your auntie. I've not told her you're coming. I thought you'd just want to focus on your friends, you know? Anyway, we'll all go back up as a family for Easter. Oh, I'm jealous! Are you going to get a Broomhill Friery? Send me a photo if you do. Let me live vicariously through you."

I keep up the facade that I'm travelling up to have a jolly good time. They've both been happier since I started seeing Joan. And, for the last month, I've been making myself go to all my lessons, making myself face you in the college canteen, and trying to make myself write songs again. My composition is almost on track for its mid-May deadline.

In fact, a lyric about this weekend and everything I need to confront keeps cartwheeling into my brain.

If you can't really remember it
Does that make it less real?

But I'm not sure how it fits into the song I've been writing.

I hug Dad goodbye at the station. He hugs a bit too hard, and tells me he loves me, which makes us both awkward. I wave behind my back as I push through the barriers and up to the platform, before slumping onto the predictably-a-bit-delayed train.

I try not to think about it all the way into London and I just about manage.

I try not to think about it all the way through London on the Tube and I just about manage.

I try not to think about it while I wait for my train at St Pancras and I just about manage.

I try not to think about it as I find my seat, and find someone else sitting there, and have that awkward *You're sitting in my seat* conversation which makes my shyness rash bloom. I sit with my head leaned against the window and watch us roll out of London and into commuter belts, and gardens backing onto the railway tracks, and into meadows and the British countryside. I don't read a book, I don't listen to music, I don't write lyrics in my journal. I just try not to think about it. After an hour or so, we chug past the big bubbling chimneys of the Midlands. I watch them stretch into the spring sky, pouring steam from their tops. These chimneys always signal the beginning of the North, to me. We'd look out for them from the car, when we used to drive back from visiting Nanny, before she died. "Can you see the chimneys, Amelie?" Dad would ask. "It means we're coming home." Any person who regularly travels from north to south knows these chimneys, has some kind of connection to these chimneys. They whizz past as I look out the window...or have I told you that already...and it signals the North and where it happened and...oh god, oh god, I'm biting down on my clenched fist.

I curl my legs up on the seat, hugging myself.

I had a tough session with Joan yesterday, you see.

"You seem to keep going over the good times with this boy," Joan said. That's what she calls you. *This boy.* Because I've not told her your name. "But it may be worth remembering the not-so-good times, too. So you're not romanticizing the relationship too much. Does that make sense?"

It does, and it makes me feel proud. Proud that I thought to make this memory map, even before I met Joan. Proud that my instincts this could help heal me were right.

She asked about some bad times, steering the questions in a way so I felt relaxed enough to reveal things.

Two weeks ago, we talked a lot about your attitude towards girls. Did you respect them? And I thought of quite a few bad things to say.

"Well, he sometimes said off things about girls," I found myself telling her. "Like, whenever we watched a TV show, he'd always comment on girls' appearances. Like 'Oooh, she's not very pretty' or 'Oooh, nice arse', and if I called him out on it, he'd say something like 'Come on, I'm a guy'."

"And do you believe that all guys talk about women that way?"

I shook my head, because no, no I didn't. Because Alfie never spoke about girls that way. My father never did.

Then, last week, we talked about how often we'd seen each other.

"I don't want to hear about the first couple of weeks," Joan warned. "What about after that? You say he started being unkind about spending time together?"

And, once again, I found I had plenty to say about you,

Reese, and plenty of it wasn't particularly good.

"Well, he acted like I was weird for wanting to spend time with him. Whenever I asked if he was free, he'd get all off-ish. He'd make plans with everyone other than me."

"So that wasn't very kind," Joan stated.

"No," I replied. "I suppose it wasn't."

"And do you believe that it's weird for a girlfriend to want to spend time with their boyfriend?"

"No. I mean, not all the time. But, some of the time. My ex, Alfie – he never made it feel strange that I wanted to spend time with him."

"Well, probably because he wanted to spend time with you."

"And Reese didn't…"

She paused. "I think it's a positive thing you had this relationship with Alfie before this boy," she said eventually. "It's good to have something healthy to compare your experiences to."

That was the first time she implied you and I weren't healthy, Reese.

And, at our session yesterday…

"This may be difficult to talk about, Amelie. And I want you to know this is a safe space, and we don't have to talk about anything you're not comfortable with."

"Uh-oh," I joked, to cover the twist in my guts.

"But I wanted to talk today about your physical relationship with this boy."

That's when I got the first weird thing. The first

supersonic pulsing of *WRONG WRONG WRONG, NO NO NO* going *ZOOM ZOOM ZOOM* through my body.

"Do you mean sex?" My throat shut down, my fingers trembed under my pulled-down sleeves. My breathing sped up, hurting my lungs with each inhalation.

"Yes," Joan replied. "If it's not too painful, I think it would be useful if we talked about what went on in your sexual relationship."

I'm going up to Sheffield. I'm going up to Sheffield, where it happened. We've just gone past the chimneys and we're getting closer and it's all coming up and it's all coming back and I don't know if I can stand to think about it.

"Come on," you always used to whisper when my clothes were already off and therefore I already felt vulnerable. "Let's try it. Just once. Aren't you curious?"

"No."

I would always say no.

"Everyone does it now. It's not a big deal."

"No, Reese."

Then you'd sulk and you'd cross your arms and you'd get into a huff, and sometimes, you'd refuse to have sex the usual way, even though I was totally up for that.

"Are you okay?" Joan had asked yesterday in her office. "Amelie? Are you alright?"

It was only then I realized I'd started crying and shaking uncontrollably.

Not now.

No.

I don't want to think about it now. This part of the trip isn't about me, it's about Alfie. The tears that he must've cried because of me. The tears he never should've had to cry.

The train announcement system dings and reminds me where the buffet car is, and I manage to pull it together. I've unfurled my body by the time it chugs into Sheffield.

Not just Sheffield.

Home.

The sense of belonging smacks me warmly in the face. My stomach settles, and I feel an easiness unleash itself inside me. I know this city. I know its roads and neighbourhoods. I know its shortcuts and secrets. There are memories of my life everywhere. I step out of the station into the square, where the giant steel fountains gurgle out welcoming water. For once, it's not raining. The sun is out, hitting everything and tingeing it gold. I don't have enough money to spend on a cab, so I wheel my way towards the hotel. Memories ignite and dance all around me – practically all of them happy ones.

I grew up in this city. I became me in this city. I learned to walk and talk and grow and make friends and go to school and fall in love. Here, by the gargling fountains outside the town hall, I spent so many summers after school – sucking on ice lollies, daring Jessa and Kimmy to run through the water jets. Over there, in that shop, is where I bought my dress for the Year Eleven leaving ball. I used to sing in that little pub on the corner, on Tuesdays, when they had an open-mike night, Alfie urging me on most weeks.

"If you keep doing it, it will get less scary," he insisted.

"I know that makes sense in theory," I'd always reply. "But, for some reason, the nerves don't care that I've done this a million times before."

"They will. They'll get the message some day."

Alfie…

I find the hotel. The lady at reception recognizes me from the phone. "Oh, you made it then," she says, sounding genuinely delighted that I'm here. I'm on the top floor. I'm given a key card that works on the lift.

"Have a good day," she calls after me as I pull my stuff into the lift.

"Thank you."

I fumble my way into my room – dropping my key card twice before I manage to get me and my stuff into it. The fire door swings shut behind me, leaving me in this little box of my own loneliness. I've never stayed in a hotel by myself before. It strikes me that no one in the universe right now knows where I am. I hoist my suitcase onto the little sofa, I draw the curtains so I'm sat in the dark, and I perch on the end of the bed.

I'm not in the same hotel as where it happened.

I couldn't afford it, for one.

Also, I couldn't. Just couldn't…

I have a sudden need to take a shower. A really long shower, scraping my skin clean until it is red raw. I peel off my clothes, ignoring my reflection in the mirror. It's a budget hotel, so the water pressure isn't great, and there's black mould in the tile grouting. But the water's so hot it scalds my skin and I stand under it and shiver, even though it's so damn hot and I find I am sobbing.

Sobbing and screaming and smacking my fist against the mouldy tiles…

…

…

…

…This is what happened in Sheffield.

I looked up from the book I was reading and saw the chimneys hurtling past outside the train window. I smiled, snapped a pic, and sent it off to Jessa.

Amelie: THE CHIMNEYS! HONEY, I'M COMING HOME!

She replied instantly.

Jessa: Welcome back to the North! I cannot WAIT to see you, GC. See you at the station. You better not have some goofy accent. xxx

My smile was the sort of smile that unravels your guts. I couldn't concentrate on my book, I was smiling so hard. I'd forgotten how good it felt to have friends. To feel loved and connected and have my phone going off with messages from people who cared enough about my existence to send them. I'd vaguely kept up with Jessa, but not properly. I'd started to worry I was so annoying that no one would want to hear from me. That I'd only irritate them if I got in touch. So I'd stopped replying to messages, believing they were only sent out of politeness anyway. But I'd felt so lonely the past couple of weeks that I'd broken and fired one off to her.

Amelie: What if I were to come back one weekend?

She'd replied instantly.

Jessa: OH MY GOD, YES. MAKE THIS HAPPEN NOW xx

I was so high from the love that I'd booked it right away, even though the train costed a fortune because it was right before Christmas. And with that smile in my stomach on the train, I knew I was right to come back. This was just what I needed.

"So, what you doing up there?" Reese had asked, the night before when I was packing.

"There's a gig at the Leadmill. An early one, and I'm friends with the band. It's just a trip home, really."

He took off his hat, put it on my bed, and gave me a huge hug out of nowhere. Then he drew back, holding me at arm's length. "Is *he* going to be there?"

"Yeah, maybe." Although I knew for sure I'd see Alfie. "We're just friends though."

Reese rolled his eyes. "Whatever."

"It's true! We broke up before I even knew you. And I've not spoken to him in months."

"Well, I'll meet up with one of my exes this weekend, shall I? One I've written a song about? See how you like it?"

My tummy instantly went into spasm. I wouldn't like that – not one bit. I often tortured myself with thoughts of Reese's exes. I'd never been a jealous person until we got together. But there were at least two girls in college I knew he'd slept with, and the merest whiff of thinking about it made me want to vomit. In my head, his exes were so much better for him than me. They were less needy, and so chill and cool and everything a girl is supposed to be.

"Reese, I'll probably hardly speak to him. I just really need to see my friends. You're always telling me you wish I had more of a life. Well, this is me having more of a life."

"With your ex."

"You know I only love you."

"Well, make sure you send me lots of messages."

We kissed and it was okay and I was so happy he wanted me to send him messages. He cared, he really cared. What a relief!

My mood was beyond giddy as the train pulled into Sheffield. I spotted Jessa as I pushed through the barriers and my heart full-on cartwheeled when I saw who she'd brought with her.

Standing there, hair a mess as always, sheepishly holding a sign that read *Amelie*, like he was a driver picking me up from the airport.

Alfie.

Something strange happened.

I love him, my head told me.
I love him, my heart told me.
I love him, my soul told me.
I love him, my everything told me.

For a second, we locked eyes, and for a second, I have never felt clearer about anything in my life. I loved Alfie. Alfie and I were supposed to be together. I was an idiot. Reese was an idiot. What the holy fuck was I doing with him? Why did I let him treat me the way he did? Oh god, what had I done? *I love him I love him I LOVE HIM.*

I could hardly walk, but I somehow managed to wobble over.

And then, like most people who have moments of pure clarity but are stuck in situations where it's not appropriate to act on them...I pushed it down and told myself it hadn't happened.

"Oh my god," I said, instead of hello and *I love you I love you I love you.* I dropped my bag and we all smashed together into a hug. I could smell Alfie through the mesh of our bodies. He smelled of safe and comfort and good and nice. We all started laughing, giggling in a huddle, until we broke free.

"And she's crying," Jessa said, tilting her head with affection. "I told you she would, Alfie."

He smiled at me too. In a nice way, though one with a guard up because neither of us knew who we were to each other any more.

I laughed and pushed the tears back into my eyes. "You just surprised me, that's all." I looked at Alfie again. "A good surprise," I added.

We stared at each other a second and I felt it, I just felt it. *I love you I love you I love you,* he was saying right back. *I love you, Amelie. I love you.*

Jessa ignored us or didn't see it. "Right. Here's the plan," she announced. "Back to mine. Get a proper brew on. Mum's desperate to see you, so you may have to endure her endless questions about down south for a while – sorry about that. Then my world-famous mac-and-cheese, you and Alfie feel weird and awkward around each other, then we meet everyone else at the tram stop for the gig."

"Jessa!" Alfie and I both said, exasperated, at the same time. She cackled again.

"Oh come on, let's just embrace the awkward! When was the last time you two actually spoke to one another anyway?"

We both walked with our heads bowed, towards the bus stop. "A couple of months," I eventually said.

"Lemme guess?" Jessa shook her head, still laughing. "You were both too proud and thought the other one was off not missing you, so you pretended you weren't missing them and now you're in a communication cold war?"

"Jessa!" Alfie warned sharply, which wasn't like him at all.

She put both hands up in surrender. "Calm down. I'm just trying to help."

I managed to catch Alfie's eye and give him my best *This is awkward* smile. He received it and nodded, the ease of our communication slipping back seamlessly – never a misread message, never a misunderstanding. I felt too many emotions all at once. They all knock-knocked on the door to my stomach, demanding to be let into the adrenaline-party, arguing over who had the most important reason to be there.

Knock-knock-knock went Guilt, saying, *Well, hang on, why the hell hasn't Amelie even TOLD Alfie about Reese? That's a terrible thing to do! I just really want to be allowed inside to truly make Amelie fixate on how she's a deceitful liar. Can I get a plus-one too?*

Confusion then joined the argument. *Umm, sweetie, what about Reese? Aren't you supposed to be in love with him?*

What's going on here? Can you even love two people at the same time? Hmm, shall we spend some time being confused about being confused?

Joy, however, was determined to override everything. *THIS FEELS SO GOOD!* she shouted into my insides. *Amelie, doesn't this feel NICE? It's like you're YOU again. Ignore Confusion and Guilt and just ENJOY feeling good about yourself for the first time in months.*

But Jealousy pushed her to one side. *What's Alfie been doing these last months without you? Why hasn't he called? Has he been with other girls? Is he in love with these girls? Even though you promised you wouldn't fall in love with anyone else? I mean, you didn't exactly hold up your end of that bargain, did you? How can you expect him to? Oh, I hope you don't mind, but I've just squeezed some high-concentrate droplets of nausea into your stomach. That's okay, right?*

And finally, Pain hit, just as we hopped on a bus that would take us back to Jessa's house. It grasped my wrist and said, *This hurts, Amelie. All of this is really terrible and painful – ouch ouch ouch!*

The bus rumbled past all my old haunts, past the university buildings, up past the Crookesmoor parks. It even went past the end of my old road, and Pain really took a hold then, prodding me like a child exploring a puddle with a stick. I went quiet and bit my lip.

"You okay?" Alfie asked. "This must be weird for you."

I smiled sadly. "You too."

His hand tightened on the bus rail. "You have no idea."

Many things passed between us as the bus flung itself up another giant Sheffield hill. I got a flash of what my life would've been if my parents hadn't moved. Alfie and I would still be together; I wouldn't even know Reese existed. I couldn't begin to imagine that. I knew, then, I was being unfair. I needed to tell Alfie. Much as it was going to break both our hearts, I had to be honest. I owed it to Alfie, and I owed it to Reese. I'm not sure what I owed myself, but I was in such a confused state I couldn't even begin to figure out what I wanted or deserved. I still can't.

"Alf?" I said.

"Yeah?"

"I'm glad you came to meet me at the station."

A smile broke over his face. "You are?"

I nodded. "We probably need to talk at some point today."

His smile got even bigger, misreading it entirely. "Great. Yeah, you're right. Let's talk."

We never got time to talk. We got off the bus and went into Jessa's house, which felt so comforting and festive with the Christmas tree up and cards hanging all down the stairs. She was right, her mum bombarded me with questions as I drank countless cups of sugary tea.

"Yes, they're settling in well. Yes, it is much warmer down there. Yes, fish and chips is much more expensive, everything is. Yes, it's been hard but we're doing okay. Yes, I guess it is exciting to be so close to London. No, I've not seen any shows yet. No, we're staying down there for Christmas. I know, I know. Our auntie's coming down to us, as Dad can't get time off work. Yes, it's a shame. Yes, my music's going okay." I told them about the Cube and Alfie actually stood up and hugged me in congratulations.

"Amelie, that's insane. I can't imagine how hard you must've found that. I'm so, so proud."

I didn't want to let go of the hug. Every word he said was like medicine to me. He got it, he just got it.

Then the mac-and-cheese was ready, and we all sat with Jessa's parents to eat it – laughing and reminiscing about the good old times, my smile hurting because it was so out of use. Jessa and I retired to her room to get ready. I dumped my bag on the camp bed she'd set up and dug around for a change of clothes.

"Vintage dress and a granny cardigan?" she asked, as I pulled just that out of the rucksack. "Man, you've changed."

"Shut it, you." I chucked my cardigan at her.

I took time with my appearance because I wanted to look nice for Alfie, because I was a horribly confused person. I couldn't help it. I fought Jessa for mirror space and actually bothered to put on a bit of mascara. Jessa asked some questions about down south but I deflected them. I couldn't tell her about Reese. Not before Alfie. It wasn't fair. Anyways, she was more than happy just to fill me in on all the gossip I'd missed. She was definitely over Pippa, for certain this time. Harry and Charlotte at school had split up, and I gasped because they'd been together for ever. Ralph from the band we were watching that night was a mess because he'd found out his girlfriend had cheated. "We're hoping he can hold it together." Sixth form was going well but they missed me of course. "None of us as much as Alfie though," she added, quietly.

"He's...he's been missing me?"

She turned away from applying eyeliner in the mirror. "Amelie, he's been a bit of a mess, to be honest."

"He has?"

"Yeah. He's been weird and miserable since you left. Spends all his time in the Science labs. I hope you didn't mind me bringing him along. I told him you wouldn't."

"I don't. I'm glad." I felt the familiar sting of lurking tears. "Oh, Jessa, I've been so stu—"

My phone buzzed.

Reese: So, what's your plan for tonight, Little Miss Up North? I miss you xxxx

It was the first time he'd messaged me first in ages! And he said he missed me! And he'd put kisses on the end!

"Everything okay?" Jessa asked, as I sighed into my phone.

I smiled up at her. "Yeah, fine. Just a message from someone down there. Hang on." I twisted, to block her from seeing my screen. I wondered if I should wait a while before replying. I mean, it was rare for Reese to message me first.

251

I should try and hold on to the power a bit more. Make him wait for it. I couldn't do it though. I tapped out a reply straight away.

> **Amelie: I miss you too. Going to Leadmill tonight for a friend's gig, remember? It's so nice to be back. What you up to tonight? Xxx**

A knock on the door. Alfie's voice. "Are you done yet? Your mum's talking about the horrors of your childbirth again."

Jessa groaned, leaning over to open the door. "She will NEVER forgive me for that forceps delivery."

I clutched my phone to my chest, just in case he could read my screen from two metres away. He'd changed into his usual gig attire: black jeans with a black T-shirt. It struck me how very different he was from Reese – with his hat, and carefully curated outfits, the way he held himself like he believed he should be allowed even more space, whereas Alfie always folded himself away.

"You look nice, Amelie." I blushed, and Guilt jumped back out from her hiding place.

"Thank you."

Jessa, sensing the tension, stood up and chucked a collection of make-up into her bag. "Come on, lads. We need to meet the others."

I checked my phone as we were leaving, and I checked it on

the bus. Everyone was so excited and happy to see me when we stepped off.

"GRANNY CARDIGAN IS BACK WHERE SHE BELONGS!" Kimmy yelled. I was enveloped in a group hug, which felt just wonderful, but also went on a bit long considering how much I wanted to check my phone.

WTF Confusion was back. I could see that Reese had read the message but there was no reply. The euphoria I had initially felt at receiving it was draining away fast, replaced with anxiety about why he hadn't replied. Maybe I'd been too keen? Why didn't I wait longer before I replied? I'd been needy again. He wasn't going to miss me, now that I'd reminded him of how desperate I was. Why couldn't I be *cooler*? Also, what about Alfie?

"Earth to Granny Cardigan!" Kimmy yelled. "We need to get in before seven if we don't want to pay entrance. Ralph said they've put our names on the door."

I shook my head to jog myself out of my spiral, and tried to focus on enjoying the present moment. I was back with my friends, people who truly loved me for who I was. We walked in a line past the Hallam campus, taking the piss out of each other, mainly Alfie, as was our custom. I kept my distance from him, feeling weird and scared about our upcoming conversation, trying to figure out how to tell him. I was running through possible lines that might lessen the emotional blow.

"I wasn't expecting it, it just happened."
"I do still love you, I always will..." No, that one wasn't fair.

"Please forgive me."

"I'm so, so sorry."

"I think, if you'd met him, you'd like him." And that one was a lie.

There was a small queue outside the Leadmill when we arrived, but we knew the guy on the door – Jonesy.

"Amelie!" he exclaimed, spotting me. "I've not seen you around here for ages."

My tummy bubbled at being recognized and missed. "I've moved down south," I explained. "I'm only back for one night, to watch the guys."

"No way! That sucks. We have a folk night next month, and I was totally going to book you."

I held out my hand for him to stamp. "Maybe I can come back up for it?" I suggested.

"Yeah, great idea!"

I turned to Jessa. "I could stay at yours again, right?"

She pulled a *Well, duh* face. "Of course you can. You need to visit MORE, I reckon. You've left it too long, it's made things weird."

I thought about how right she was, as we stepped into the club. I was up here and I felt better and more me and I should come back more. It was good for me. I started to imagine my life. How it would feel if I came up at least once a month. A happier existence began to stretch out in front of me – filled with good memories, waiting to be made.

But, of course, after that night, I wasn't welcome at Jessa's any more.

Nightclubs in daylight are a funny thing. It's almost like they shouldn't exist. They should appear only when night falls, like some kind of magical circus. In this spring sunshine, it's hard to picture what the Leadmill's like after the daytime dims. It's hard to really imagine the shivering clusters of people queuing to get in, the music throbbing through the soles of your shoes, the giddy, fiesta feel of the smoking area. Today there are remnants of the night before everywhere – a puddle of sick dried on the pavement, smatterings of cigarette butts that haven't been swept up yet, the odd, discarded half-drunk bottle of beer that someone didn't quite finish before they got in. But even with all that, standing here, looking up at it right now, I can't match this quiet building with the humming club it becomes each evening.

There's nowhere to sit, so I stand – my arms wrapped around me to keep in my emotions. I managed to scrape myself off the shower floor and wrap myself in enough cardigan to stand the Sheffield wind, and then I walked straight here.

I'm not sure I can do this.

I'm not sure I can remember this particular night.

But something is telling me I need to.

The Leadmill was exactly how I remembered it, as I checked in my coat and scarf and stepped out onto the sticky dance floor. Even with it decked out for Christmas, fake trees hanging upside-down from the ceiling, it felt familiar. It even smelled the same. That stale, almost-sicky smell when a club hasn't warmed itself up yet with the heat and stench of dancing bodies.

Jessa clapped me on the back.

"Still the same?" she asked, reading my mind.

I twisted around to smile at her. "Yes, thank god."

She, Alfie and I went to the bar to order some lemonades, while Kimmy and the others went to chat to some sixth-formers. The bad thing about being known on the circuit was that everyone knew we were underage. So we never got served, and we always got chucked out at ten thirty. Every two minutes I was encased in a hug by an old acquaintance, shouting "HOW IS IT DOWN SOUTH?" and saying they'd missed me. It was lovely to see everyone but it was distracting me from the very pressing matter of summoning the courage to talk properly to Alfie. The dance floor slowly clogged up as people took up their spots to get a good view. Ralph's band were pretty popular in Sheffield, though they hadn't been able to break out to other cities yet.

I felt Alfie's hand on my shoulder.

"Shall we go to our regular spot?" he asked me.

"Why break with tradition?"

He steered us to the right-hand side of the stage, halfway back. Alfie had used actual physics one day to explain to me how sound travelled, and that therefore this was the best place to stand. Since then, every gig we'd been to, we'd manoeuvre ourselves there and feel smug about our superior knowledge of acoustics. People started jamming in behind us, trying to push us forward with the weight of their bodies, but we stood firm, occasionally letting some people in front. Someone bumped me, shoving me back into Alfie, and he grabbed hold of my shoulder to steady me.

"Watch it!" he yelled at the pusher-inner, who ignored him. Alfie turned to me, his hand still on my shoulder. He blushed. "Sorry," he added.

"It's fine. Thank you."

We stared at one another, his hand not leaving my shoulder, my shoulder not wanting his hand to leave.

"We need to talk," I spluttered out. "At some point tonight, it would be good to talk."

Alfie smiled. "Yeah, of course. I was going to say the same thing." His smile grew, his eyes glowed with happiness, confirming my suspicion that he thought this would be a happy conversation. Once again, my body had no idea how to react. Just the thought that it wasn't over for him wobbled my love for Reese. Or maybe it just reignited my love for Alfie. I guess one of the biggest misconceptions about love is that you can only love one person at one time. Whereas I'm starting to think hearts can compartmentalize. That a heart can grow walls in itself, with chambers specially reserved for each person we fall in love with – making it possible to have feelings for one person without that impacting the feelings you have for another.

I didn't know what to do. I felt like time had slowed, giving me extra time to figure out how I felt. I was going to break Alfie's heart that night when I told him about Reese and how I'd broken our deal, and yet I really, really didn't want to. I didn't want to shatter the wall he'd built for me in his heart. The thought of Alfie knowing…of me taking out scissors and severing us from each other… Every instinct in my body told me it was the wrong thing to do.

We were plunged into darkness and the crowd started clapping before I had a chance to figure it out. Jessa, to my side, turned around and said, "They're on." I clapped and put my hands around my mouth to whoop.

Ralph, the apparently heartbroken lead singer, said, "A-one, a-two, a-one, two, three, GO!" and the stage was blasted with light as they opened on their most famous song "On A Lazy Afternoon". Everyone went nuts. Well, as nuts as a crowd full of folk fans can go. I found my head nodding to the music, enjoying how tight they were, the depth of their sound, the gravelly quality of Ralph's voice. They bled smoothly into the next song. Their set list was on point, they'd really honed it since I'd last seen them. I knew a few of the lyrics and I sang along, my face stretched into a smile, the music momentarily distracting me from the drama of my own life. If Ralph was upset, he wasn't letting it ruin his performance. I felt Alfie reposition himself behind me, then I felt his hands tentatively weave themselves either side of my waist. I closed my eyes, savouring how it felt. Not stopping it, though I knew it was wrong. He rested his chin on my shoulder – how we always used to stand at gigs. It dug into my skin as he sang along too and I stood there and let it happen because I'm a bad person who truly deserves everything that happened next.

After six straight songs, Ralph took the mike off the stand, and signalled for the lights to go up.

"Now, we're about to do one of our favourites," he said. "'Hounds of Love'."

We all cheered, because their cover of that was truly perfect. I'd sung it with them so many times, walking home after a night out.

"Now, we actually want to do something a bit different tonight. A very dear friend is back with us this evening…" I realized at once they must mean me. And, yep, Ralph scanned the crowd with both hands above his eyes, found me, and winked. "Can we please bring the brilliant Amelie onto the stage."

I started shaking my head.

"She's shy, but she's brilliant. Come on, everyone, clap her into it."

Applause started. Jessa turned around again, grinning manically. "HA HA – SURPRISE!" she said.

"You cow!"

"If I'd told you, you'd just have got stage fright and ruined your trip. Go on, up you go."

The clapping got louder. I started to feel a little bit ill, but, I'll tell you what, my nerves weren't as shot as usual. I think they were used to being wrung by then, by the complicated and uncertain business of being in love with Reese.

I twisted in Alfie's arms. "Did you know about this?" I asked him.

He shook his head. "No. You know I would've told you." He raised both eyebrows. "Up you go."

My feet moved for me. I mouthed "You're dead" at Ralph as he helped me onstage and hugged me hello. "Come on, it will be a laugh," he said into my ear. "Anyway, you sing it better than me. You always have."

Everyone cheered louder as I was handed the mike and given a stool to perch on. And, you know what? In that moment, I wasn't nervous at all. I was staring out at a home crowd. I saw so many faces of people I knew, who cared about me, who understood me. Memories of all the gigs I'd done here before, in all the different growing-up incarnations of myself. My Sheffield friends knew me only as Amelie, the girl they'd watched grow as they grew too. Everything I said or did was filtered through thousands of shared past experiences, instead of down south, where nobody knew me, and my life felt like an audition I was failing.

I smiled, I heard the intro, I opened my mouth and I began to sing.

How I loved that song, especially the way Ralph had arranged it. It's all about being scared to love someone, the fear that it will rip you apart like a pack of dogs. I felt so free and full as I sang to my old friends, in my old haunt – like the last four months hadn't happened and I was still just simple Amelie, living her quiet little life in Sheffield, dreaming of one day being able to sing every day. On the last verse, Ralph joined in, harmonizing, and then, without needing to discuss it, we made eye contact, nodded, and both held out our mikes to let the crowd finish the last bit. Everyone joined in seamlessly, shouting along, making my tummy feel wonder at the existence of other good humans. I scanned the crowd and I found Jessa giving me a thumbs up. I found Alfie. His eyes were moist as we acknowledged each other and my smile grew wider. I put the mike back to my mouth to finish the final two lines in falsetto, still looking out at everyone and...

And...

And...

...

There.

There you were, Reese.

Standing at the back of the crowd, the sorest of sore thumbs. Not where you were supposed to be – back in my new life, not replying to my message – but here, in the Leadmill, your hat jaunted at an angle, a smug grin on your face as you saw me notice you and I jolted with shock.

You were here.

Here.

You had come.

The song finished. The applause was bountiful. Ralph held up my arm and made me fist-pump the air, while I stared out in stunned wonder.

Reese.

Reese was here.

In *Sheffield*?

My brain just kept hitting the *reject* button, unable to comprehend this complete unlikelihood. Ralph sped into their last song as I was lowered back onto the dance floor. I walked towards Reese and it felt like the sea was parting. I passed Jessa and Alfie, who had no idea that he'd arrived, or even that he existed. They both beamed at me. Alfie's hand was held up, ready for a high five. I put my finger up, signalling *One moment* – though, honestly, I did not have any plan in my head about how to handle this situation in a way that didn't scatter mess over everyone, and everything, but mostly myself. Alfie tilted his head in confusion and I gently pushed past him.

Reese just stood there – waiting, smiling, not coming towards me – letting me chase him for the final section of the journey. I shook my head in disbelief when I reached him.

"What are you doing here...?"

He broke me off by pulling me in for a kiss – the sort of kiss there's no getting out of. There was no time left to work out the best way to tell Alfie, or the others, or to try and make this not the mess it was about to become. All I could do was surrender to his mouth, and try and make myself feel happy that he'd come all this way, despite the fact Alfie must be watching. He cupped my face in his hand and broke off to grin at me with all his teeth.

"God, I love you," he said, before returning his lips to mine. And I was sucked back into our vortex. *He came all the way here to see me! He MUST love me. How could I ever doubt him?*

"Amelie? What the hell is going on?"

Alfie was at our side, the very picture of pain. Without missing a trick, Reese held out his hand, like we were all grown-ups at a business meeting. "Hi," he shouted over the music, "you must be Alfie. I'm Reese, Amelie's boyfriend from back home."

If I close my eyes now, on this pavement decorated with last night's vomit, I can still see the precise moment I watched Alfie's heart break.

His eyebrows drew up for a second before the reality hit. Then his face spasmed into grief.

I squeezed Reese's arm, trying to stop him, though it was too late and I had no idea what to say.

"Amelie?" Alfie's voice could hardly be heard over the band. "What's going on?"

My mouth dropped open. Words completely and utterly fled from me.

Finally I managed, "I was going to tell you."

I felt Reese's grip tighten on my waist.

"Hang on," he said. "You've been up here all day and you've not told your ex that you're with someone else?"

Now two boys were hurt. Now two boys were mad at me. My stomach sloshed into a pool of nerves. I wanted to cry – even though I was the baddie here, I was the one causing all the pain with my cowardice and confusion.

"I was waiting for a good time," I tried to explain to both of them. Then I turned to him. "Reese, I didn't know you were coming."

He actually snarled in response. I never thought people snarled in real life, but he did. "Just as well I did." His voice was colder than liquid nitrogen. "God knows what sort of 'good time' you'd be having if I hadn't surprised my supposed girlfriend."

The word *supposed* hit me like a bullet. It was a warning. He knew as much, and I received it as much. I felt so sick. I felt the need – the desperate need – to make it all okay again. But how?

How?

And Alfie Alfie Alfie, who seemed stuck to the floor.

"I didn't…" I started to say. Not sure which boy I was talking to. "I wasn't…"

"I'm going," Alfie said. He was there one moment, and then he was gone, his mad hair bouncing through the crowd. I watched him leave and couldn't even function because I felt so guilty. It took a lot of strength to turn back to Reese, and his face was quite the picture too.

"What the actual fuck, Amelie. I can't believe you've not told him."

I shook my head slowly. "I was going to. We're broken up anyway."

"It didn't look that way."

His eyes had gone cold. God, I hated it when his eyes went cold – how they'd glaze over like rice pudding that gets a skin if you leave it too long.

"I was *about* to tell him." I tugged at Reese's shirt, trying to get close to him, but he pushed me off sharply. "I was! I was about to, then I got called up onstage."

"Well you're never one to let the opportunity to show off pass, are you?"

My mouth fell open again. "What?"

"I'm just saying, for someone who supposedly has stage fright, you spend a lot of your time ensuring you're the one onstage, getting all the attention."

"Is that what you really think of me?"

He stuck out his bottom lip, refusing to retract the insult.

"I'm sorry," I started begging. "Reese. I'm so, so sorry.

265

I'm so happy you're here. I can't even tell you how it felt when I saw you in the crowd."

He blinked, not dislodging the rice pudding skin. Panic crawled in. The band finished. Everyone started clapping and calling for more.

"Reese!" I flung myself at his chest and he smelled slightly, of travelling and being on the train too long. I sensed that he wanted me to praise him, so I obliged, muttering sweet compliments into his neck. "No one's ever surprised me like this. It's so romantic. Alfie is nothing, nothing. I promise. I was just worried about his feelings. I mean, I have a heart. You wouldn't love me if I didn't have a heart. But he's the past. You're my future. You're my forever. And you're here and it's amazing and I can't stand you being mad at me. Please, Reese. Please."

The encore finished by the time he managed to stiffly pat my back.

"You're really glad I came?" he asked. "Your face when you saw me – it looked more like shock."

"I was shocked," I admitted, relief soaking through me that I'd got through to him. "It was the last thing I was expecting. But it was a good shock."

He held me at arm's length, and the coldness of his eyes melted away. The sides of them crinkled in a smile. He was back. Thank god, he was back. I still had Alfie to sort out, and a huge amount of mess to clear up, and I knew that I'd played it all so very wrong, but at least Reese was back.

Or, well, I thought he was, until Jessa turned up.

"Amelie, what the actual hell is going on?" She appeared at my side, clutching a plastic cup of water. "Alfie's outside in a right state." Then she clocked Reese and how I clutched at his arm. "Who the shit are you?"

"This is my boyfriend, Reese," I said. "He's come up to surprise me."

"Your boyfriend?" Jessa muttered almost to herself as she digested it. Then she shook her head and her face hardened. "Well, congratulations, Ammy, on breaking Alfie's heart. Again," she added.

"I can explain—"

"Explain to him, not me. He's the one crying outside on the pavement."

Alfie was *crying*? That knowledge hit me like multiple tons of bricks. My already liquid stomach churned into a whirlpool.

Maybe, in time, I'll be able to think about how my decision in this next moment made what happened next happen next. Maybe if I'd been colder – more like you – and just shrugged and thought, *Well, Alfie needs to get over it*, then I could've stopped it. I wouldn't have ended up sobbing uncontrollably on a shower floor. I would've been able to sit down the next few days without wincing. I wouldn't have bled into my knickers for days, having to wear a sanitary pad, but not in its usual position.

But I'm not cold, I'm not like you. I couldn't handle that

I'd made Alfie cry. So I turned to you and I set the wheels in motion.

"I need to go after him," I said.

"Are you joking?"

"Five minutes."

And, before I could let Reese scare me out of it, I pushed through the applauding crowd and ran out into the cold night air.

Alfie was sat maybe ten metres away from the club, against the wall, in this very spot. His long legs were sprawled outwards, his head falling down towards them. His body shook with tears. I'd made him cry in public. A boy. How much do you have to really hurt a boy for him to shed all societal expectations and cry in front of people? That's how much I hurt Alfie. Seeing him like that made me start crying too – the sort of tears that stream silently from your eyes like a river.

"Alfie?"

He flinched, but didn't look up. He sniffed hard and rubbed his face with his arm.

"Alfie, I'm so, so sorry."

I couldn't have meant it more – never have I spoken a truer sentence. I started crying harder than him, which was inappropriate and wrong, considering it was all my damned fault. I sat down next to him, and he still didn't look up. We both cried for a minute or two together in an almost companionable, snuffly silence.

I wonder if the salt from our tears is still in the concrete, crystallized beneath my feet? If there are traces of it remaining underneath my shoes?

I found my crying hit a new peak, as crying can do sometimes. When the grief hits so hard that sobbing takes on a realm of its own. The pain in my stomach was so raw, the reality of everything so heartbreaking, that I let out this weird howl and demolished myself there on the pavement. And Alfie, always with a heart so big, always thinking about others before himself, saw me combust, and put his own pain aside to comfort me.

"There there," he whispered, putting his arm around me as I juddered and screeched and howled and generally cried in the ugliest possible way. "It's going to be okay."

"I'm sorry," I whimpered, over and over, meaning each and every single apology. "I'm so sorry. Honestly, sorry. I'm sorry. I'm so, so sorry. Alfie, I hate this. I'm sorry. I have to tell you how sorry I am. Sorry, sorry, sorry." Another wave of pain hit and he hugged me so tight and so hard and I thought,

This is the last time you'll ever hold Alfie this close, and that's all your fault, and that led me to cry further.

His chest shook and my head shook on it. I felt my hair dampen with the tracks of his tears. Then he gently pushed me away.

"Who's that guy, Ammy?" he asked, wiping his nose. "What's going on?"

"He's…he's…I didn't mean for it to happen."

"Do you…do you love him?"

I wish he'd asked a different question – one which was less "yes" or "no". One that would paint a fuller, kinder picture of all my conflicting emotions. But Alfie had just flat-out asked, trapping me into a simpler, more painful truth.

More tears shot out of my eyes, as I nodded, ruining us for ever.

"For fuck's sake, Ammy. You've only been gone a few months."

"I know, I… It's all been so confusing—"

Alfie cut me off, interrupting me for the first time. "Did I mean nothing to you? That you're able to get over me that quickly?"

"I…I…"

"What about our pact? What about Manchester?" His anger stopped his tears, while mine only increased. He shook his head. "I'm so stupid. Shall I tell you how I thought tonight would go? I was going to tell you that I've not been able to stop thinking about you since you left, that I've been too scared to message you, but that, actually, if we could

270

be alone, we could talk about what a stupid idea this whole break was." He shoved his hands into his hair, pulling it up on end. "I was going to see if you wanted to get back together. I thought we could travel to each other at weekends... God, and this whole time...you're with someone else? Some guy who wears a FUCKING TRILBY?"

I shook my head, I cried harder. "I'm so confused, I don't know what I feel, I just... I'm sorry, Alfie. Really."

He put up his hand, stopping me from detailing my feelings. "No, *I'm* sorry. You're not who I thought you were at all. We don't have what I thought we had. How could we? When you've just...just..."

He stumbled to his feet and I stumbled up with him, desperate to reach out and grab his arm, desperate to make the pain stop. I watched him come to terms with *What Actually Happened*, replacing his story of *How He Wanted It To Go*. I sometimes think maybe all the tears we cry are due to this huge gap between the how-we-think-things-should-go and what-life-actually-gives-you. Alfie wiped his nose on his T-shirt.

"I hope you're very happy together," he said, hollowly. "Sorry if I caused a scene."

He turned and walked away into the night, and my arm reached out, wanting so much to call him back. But for what? I was with Reese. I had chosen him. I'd chosen being whisked off my feet rather than the steady ground beneath them. I didn't want to mess with Alfie's head with all my selfish declarations of compartmentalized hearts. He deserved someone whose heart was fully his.

"I'm sorry," I whispered out into the night, where it crystallized on my breath and vanished among the Christmas lights. I guess there was no way I wasn't going to break Alfie's heart that night. There was no way I could've spared him the hurt of me choosing Reese, of me breaking our pact, erasing the future we'd planned together. I really did feel like my heart was breaking, though, which didn't make sense because the boy I supposedly loved was waiting for me inside the nightclub. I wiped under my eyes, took a few calming breaths, and turned to make my way back inside.

I showed my stamped hand to Jonesy, who nodded me through, smiling. The darkness hid most of my crying face. It was calmer now the band had finished. I stood on my tiptoes, but couldn't see Reese anywhere.

The panic re-sprouted and my priorities shifted back to him. Where had he gone? Why had he gone? Surely he must understand that I had to follow Alfie?

I spotted the top of Jessa's head at the bar and I tapped her on the shoulder. Her face soured when she saw it was me.

"How's Alfie?" She didn't ask after me, though it was clear I was upset too.

"Not good," I admitted. "I tried. But there's not much I could say."

She shook her head. "You've hurt him bad."

"I know."

"What's happened to you, Ams? Who's that guy?"

"Have you seen him?" I asked desperately. "Where has he gone?"

She wrinkled her nose. "Yeah, I've seen him. He was a complete dick to me and then he left."

Reese had left? The panic spread through me like a superbug.

"Where did he go?" I found myself grabbing her arm, and she looked down at it like I'd gone mad.

"He said he couldn't be arsed with this and that he was going home."

"He's going HOME?!" Oh god, this was bad. This was going to be so bad. I'd ruined it all. I was so stupid and ungrateful and he'd come all this way and I'd just run after some other boy.

I now felt sick at the thought of losing him, especially when I'd just full-on sacrificed my love for Alfie for him. That couldn't be for nothing. It couldn't, it couldn't.

Jessa lowered her voice. "Ams, he called you a bitch."

"What?"

"A bitch. He called you one."

"He wouldn't." My brain rejected it the moment she said it. No. No, no, no. He wouldn't do that. That made no sense. Reese loved me. He'd come all this way.

Jessa leaned back. "You saying I'm lying?"

"I don't have time for this. I have to go!"

"What the hell, Amelie? What's going on? He called you a bitch, to my face. And what? You're going to chase after him? I know I've only just met the guy, but why would I lie to you?"

"He won't have called me that."

"AMELIE, HE CALLED YOU A FUCKING BITCH!"

I kept shaking my head. "Well, I am one, aren't I?"

"Are you crazy?! You're not a *bitch*. You're being right weird today, but you can't let him speak about you like that. Amelie? Amelie! Where are you going?"

"I've got to find him."

"No!" Jessa said.

I fled through the crowd, pushing my way out. I felt so sick, and the only way to feel better was to get to Reese, to make it right, to apologize, to smooth things over. I can't explain why this seemed so very important, but it did. It felt like life or death. It felt like my only purpose for existing. Reese *was* my only purpose for existing. I was obsessed with him, addicted to him, addicted to how it felt when he loved me, even if it wasn't all the time.

I burst out into the cold air again, stomping through the puddles of Alfie's tears.

"AMS," Jessa called after me, running after me. I stormed ahead, making her run to catch up. I had to get to the station. I had to stop him. I'm not sure why, but I had to. "Come back to mine," she pleaded. "We'll talk about everything. Alfie, this Reese guy, moving down south. Please. Come on."

"I don't want to talk, I just need to find him."

"BUT HE'S CLEARLY A DICK!" she shouted, grabbing me to try and grind me to a halt.

This, I couldn't handle. For some reason I still don't understand, disliking Reese was a deal-breaker. I'd lost Hannah over it, I'd lost Jack, and now I was about to lose Jessa because – I don't know why, please explain to me why – I could not be around anyone who didn't like the boy I loved.

"Fuck off," I shouted, although I had never, ever, told anyone to fuck off in my whole life. I shook her off and broke into a run towards Reese, wherever he'd gone.

I didn't have time to worry about Jessa hating me, I didn't have space to feel guilty about Alfie any more. All I cared about was finding Reese, and making it okay. I hurtled towards Sheffield train station, looking out for his hat. Self-hatred pulsed through me with every step I took.

I'm a terrible person. I ruined everything. No wonder he acts as if he doesn't like me sometimes, I don't like me either. I hurt people. I'm selfish and terrible and crazy, and I can't believe he came all this way and I treated him like that.

I spotted him by the water fountain just outside the train station, and almost collided with a lamp post.

"Reese!" I called.

He was sat on a bench, looking at his phone, acting like he didn't have a care in the universe. He didn't reply or even look up.

"REESE!"

Still no reaction. I walked over, out of breath, my stomach hurting from stress, my heart banging too hard from the hurt and unknowing.

"Reese."

I stood over him, but he still refused to look up as he scrolled through some music blog. I sat next to him on the bench and he didn't even flinch. I could've been a ghost.

"Reese." I started crying again, shuffling closer, wanting

so much for him to notice me. But he refused. He scrolled and scrolled, he shrugged off my advances, he went back to his phone.

It's such a simple torture – the silent treatment. As basic as tripping someone over or pulling their chair out before they sit down. And yet it's so very effective. When someone has the willpower to pretend you're not there, it nullifies you. How do you fight against that humiliation?

"REESE!" I screamed, and a cluster of pigeons flapped away in anguish. My voice echoed around the steel of the water fountain, my tears became sobs once more.

Finally, he looked up.

"What?" The disgust on his face could sour milk.

"Reese, I'm sorry. Where did you go? What's going on?" He shrugged and returned to his phone.

No.

I couldn't bear it. I'd only just got him away from his phone. I reached out, grabbing it from his hands like an actual crazy person.

"What the fuck, Amelie?"

"TALK TO ME!" I screamed. "WHY WON'T YOU TALK TO ME?"

"Are you done?" he asked, totally unmoved. If anything, he sounded…*bored.*

I felt like all my sanity had drained out of me. All my ability to see straight or act and behave like a "normal" human was supposed to, gone. All I knew was that I had to get through to him. I could handle him hating me, I probably deserved it.

I could handle him screaming at me. I could probably even handle him breaking up with me – just as long as I felt he was there. That he cared about me at all. His total lack of emotion only made me more emotional. I knew the harder I cried and the crazier I got, the more repulsive I was becoming, but I couldn't help myself. I had to break through. I had to, I had to.

"REESE. PLEASE, REESE. YOU'RE KILLING ME! TALK TO ME."

He stood up and walked away towards the station. I chased after him, wailing like a cat who'd been trodden on.

"I ONLY WENT AFTER ALFIE BECAUSE HE WAS CRYING. IT'S YOU I LOVE. YOU KNOW IT'S YOU I LOVE."

He entered the harsh strip lights of the station, where announcements told us about the very few trains leaving Sheffield that late at night. A few drunken people clutching baguettes looked up blearily as I stormed in after him.

"So you're just going to leave?" I yelled at his back. "Go home in the middle of the night? And what? Not talk to me ever again?"

He carried on walking and I carried on scuttling after him. I glanced up at the board, and *aha!* There were no trains going to London. It was too late. He had to stay. He had to stay with me. Reese looked up at the board and I felt him notice it and figure out the same thing. I stopped behind him because I suddenly felt slightly afraid. His back radiated a blast of danger.

I sniffed and tried to wipe away my tears with my hands. I stared at his back, desperation oozing out of me. Waiting… waiting…

He turned and made himself look at me.

"There are no trains," I said.

"So it appears."

"Reese, I love you."

He tilted his head to one side. "Do you really though, Amelie?"

"Yes! Of course I do! I'm here, aren't I?"

The relief that he was speaking to me. The relief that he was looking at me. I saw his walls begin to crumble and I dared to hope that we could get over this, that we could mend this unbearable anxiety in my stomach.

"You just ran after him," he whispered. "I came all this way, and then you run after another guy."

My heart flooded itself with love. He sounded genuinely sad. I couldn't bear the thought that I'd hurt him. I would've done anything to make it better.

"I love you," I repeated, wanting to soothe him so much, to reassure him of how much I cared. "Seeing you in the crowd was one of the best moments of my life." And my memory was already rearranging itself, telling myself that was the truth.

The tiniest hint of a smile. "Really?" he asked, thawing.

I wanted to throw myself at him, but I held myself back, sensing I needed to convince him a bit more yet. "It was like a fairy tale."

"It was a last-minute thing. I only booked the hotel this morning."

I smiled shyly. "You've booked a hotel?"

He nodded. "Yes. A really posh one. Well, as posh as you can get in Sheffield."

The joke told me we were getting there. And he'd spent all this money and come all this way. *He* must *love me.*

I held out my shaking hand. "Can we go to this hotel then? Talk things through?"

He let me squirm on the hook a moment or so longer.

Then he smiled.

Then he said, "Or maybe, instead of talking, you can make it up to me?"

He wrapped his fingers in mine and pulled me into him. The drunk people cheered for us as we kissed under the announcement board. Then he tugged on my arm, and he started walking me to the hotel he'd booked. The hotel where it happened.

"You'd do it if you loved me."

"But, Reese..."

"Everyone does it."

"But..."

"Is it because of him? Because you still love him?"

"What? That's nothing to do with it. I'm here because I love you!"

"I came all this way. Doesn't that mean anything?"

...

"It's not even a thing. Other girls do it all the time. Why are you being so frigid?"

"But…"

"I'll go slow. We'll take it really slow. Please."

…

"Please, Amelie."

I didn't want to. I really didn't want to. I'd said "no" so many times. "Never" even more times. There was not one part of me that wanted to do it.

…

"I love you, Amelie."

"I'm not sure."

"Just try. For me, try. I thought you loved me."

…

"Look, I'll take it slow. Really slow. I promise I'll stop the second it hurts, but it won't."

"I really don't want to, Reese. Can't we just…?"

…

The way he looked at me. I would lose him if I said no. I really wanted to say no. My arms were crossed over myself, my head down. He kissed my neck. Started to take off my top while I clung back to it, not even wanting to be naked.

"We love each other. It's not a big deal. Stop making it a big deal. Don't you love me?"

"Of course I love you."

"Then show me. Try."

…

No…

No no no no no…

"I guess I can try."

I'm back at my hotel and I'm screaming. I'm under the showerhead again and I'm still screaming. I feel like I've been screaming since it happened but no one can hear me. They must be silent screams. Or it's just I have nobody left in my life to listen to them, to care about them.

You lied, Reese.

You said you would take it slowly, but you didn't.

You said you would stop if it hurt, but you didn't.

In fact, when I said it was hurting, you only got rougher.

I've not let myself think about it until now. Now I'm scared I'll never be able to stop thinking about it again. Whenever I close my eyes, the memory regurgitates on me.

And it wasn't just how you were during it that messes with my head, Reese, but also…

Also…what you were like afterwards.

How you kissed away my tears, rubbing my nose with your nose like we were cute Eskimos.

How you said, "That was amazing," like it was.

How you fell asleep, without asking me if I was okay, even though I was so clearly not okay. You rolled over, ignoring the mess we'd made on the sheets, ignoring your girlfriend staring hollowly at the ceiling and in pain because of the way you'd been. You started to snore and I listened to the noise of it, and to the sounds of the city outside, and I focused on getting through each five-second interval for quite some time before I was able to take myself to the shower and collapse onto the tiled floor in shock. It doesn't make sense. None of it makes sense. Yet it happened, it happened, it happened and it can never be taken away.

The next morning, Reese woke me up with room service. He'd even got them to put a carnation on the tray. Between mouthfuls of croissants, he leaned over to kiss me, tucking my hair behind my ear and looking at me with such tender love that I started to think maybe I'd imagined the Reese he was the night before.

"I love you so much." He squeezed my hand as we checked out.

"I love you too," I found myself replying.

The receptionist overheard, sighed and said, "You guys are so cute."

I found myself thinking, *Maybe we are.*

I'd left my bag at Jessa's, but I couldn't face seeing her and explaining everything. Not when my whole body hurt. So I just left with what I was standing up in. The train journey was agony, sitting for that long. Reese winked at me and then took my fingers to his mouth and kissed them. He rested his head on my shoulder, and he whispered how much he loved me and how great last night was and how special it was that we'd found one another. And it started to melt in. Because what else could I do? Focus on the previous night and what had happened? It seemed so strange, so surreal, that he could be like that – just take what he wanted when it was clear I hadn't wanted to give it – and then be like this. The two didn't fit. So maybe I'd exaggerated his brutality, him ignoring the fact I clearly didn't want to? Or maybe he'd just got carried away and didn't mean it, or didn't realize I was hurting? Which doesn't make sense, because I'd started crying. I'm not sure how he missed that.

He was perfect the whole way home, as I left the North and the scattered carcass of my old life behind me. We whizzed past the chimneys and he fell asleep on my shoulder, and I felt so safe and so full and so glad he was back. That I'd managed to save it. Save us. I could just push last night aside. It was a puzzle piece that didn't fit. It was the Bounties left in an empty tub of Celebrations – just leave them behind and pretend they're not there.

He was wonderful as he walked me home, kissing me and saying he couldn't wait to see me at college the next day. He was wonderful that night, sending me funny messages full of kisses.

"How was your trip?" Mum asked when I got in, not noticing I didn't have my bag with me.

"Great. It was great."

I got into my room, and I crawled onto my stomach, lying face down in bed. Memories started resurfacing and I felt the desperate need to shower again.

My phone went.

Him!

It shook in my hands as I read it.

Reese: We are perfect together and I love you so much xxx

It was just what I needed. It just about made it all alright again.

***

I've been naked on the floor of this hotel room for most of the night. I got up once, to wrap myself in a towel. I've not slept. I've just sort of cried and huddled and shivered and wailed. The hotel is silent at this early o'clock in the morning. I peel myself off the ground, turn on the shitty complementary hairdryer and point it at parts of my body to warm up. I manage to pull some clothes on, then see in the new day by staring at the wall and shaking violently.

Alfie's mum can hardly contain her surprise when she finds me at her door – at eight o'clock on a Sunday morning.

"Amelie! Oh my god. Hello."

"Is Alfie up?" I don't have the energy for basic pleasantries.

"I don't think so. But I can wake him, if you don't mind waiting in the kitchen."

She invites me in, without asking me why the hell I'm there, and why so early in the morning, and why I'm not down south, or why I deem it appropriate to just turn up when I'm so very responsible for breaking her son's heart.

"Wait here. Feel free to make a cuppa."

I've always loved Jan. I've known her since I was five – she picked me up from music lessons, shared the school run with my mum. She'd always let me choose what to sing along to on the car stereo.

I take a seat in this kitchen I know so damn well. I let warmer memories crowd into my annihilated brain. Memories of Alfie and me attempting to bake beetroot brownies and how they turned to mush. The endless cups of tea, sat chatting to his family about science or Sheffield Wednesday football club, or how well my last gig went. The covert kisses we snuck in, between family members coming in or out – me giggling into Alfie's chest the one time his brother walked in on us mid-kiss and yelled, "EWW." I bathe in the warmth of these memories and they light the tiniest of flames in me. Until I realize that is all in the past and I'll never be able to undo what's happened, and Alfie hates me, and I have no idea what I'm doing here, only that I couldn't not come.

I hear his mum's muffled voice through the floorboards. The creak of Alfie stirring awake.

"*Amelie's* here?" He says it so loud I can taste his confusion on my tongue.

My heart thrums as I wait to hear him swear, or refuse to come down. He has every reason to. He owes me nothing. But I must've known for certain he would come down, that's why I came. Because I can rely on him.

And here, here he is, thumping down the stairs, appearing in the door frame.

His mouth collapses open when he sees the state of me.

"Hi," I manage, drinking him all in, wanting to cry just at seeing him. He's pulled on some baggy jeans and that T-shirt he loves so much with the periodic table on it. His hair is messed up. Jan's not come down with him.

"Amelie, what the hell's happened?"

I can't cry. Not yet. It wouldn't be fair to him, and I've already been so unfair to him. Me being here right now is unfair too. So I hold it together. Just. Though I'm ripping at the seams. It feels like I'm held together with Pritt Stick that's melting in the sun.

"Can we go for a coffee?" I ask.

We don't talk as we get coffee from the place we always got it from. Every big talk we've ever had we've had in the Botanical Gardens. We instinctively know we need to save it all for there.

We clutch our cups and sip at them, even though they're still a bit too hot. The gardens are beautiful and bursting with blossom. Magnolia punctuates the blue of the sky, and carefully-tended beds host cute crops of flowers. It's cold though, and I'm declimatized to the northern chill. We wipe dew off our bench, then we tuck our coats under our bums and sit down anyway.

Just Alfie's presence brings me temporary calm. I forgot what it feels like to be near him. Even before we were together, he was like slipping your feet into your favourite pair of slippers. We stare out at the red and yellow of the manicured flower beds.

"I know I've said it before, but I'm sorry."

Alfie sighs and won't look at me. Not in the way that Reese would refuse to look at me – like it was a punishment – more in a *please-give-me-a-minute-and-then-I-promise-I'll-be-with-you* way. I leave the silence to settle, I leave him the time he needs to break it.

"Why are you here, Ammy?"

"I don't know," I reply, honestly.

At that, he turns to me. Alfie doesn't just look at me, he really takes me in. I see his eyes search mine, I see them scan my red-raw face, my shaking, skinny body.

"What's happened to you?" He asks with such genuine care that I almost combust.

"I don't know." Then I do start crying a little. Not to make him feel sorry for me, or to trick him, but only because I can't not. I start talking, words pouring out of me. "I came up here because things aren't good, and I'm trying to figure out what happened... Alfie, I'm so sorry about what I did to you... I can't even... I'll never forgive myself. I don't want to take the blame off me – but I think maybe it hasn't all been my fault. I think... I think... He...he..."

Alfie shakes his head. "Ammy, if you want to cry on someone because it didn't work out with your new boyfriend,

I'm really not the person to have picked."

"I know. I get that. But that's not what's happened. Sorry, I know I'm being so unfair, but I don't know who else to tell…" His anger, though totally justified, adds to the pain and guilt surging through me, yet I desperately gallop on – the words are desperate to come out. "Alfie, it's not about breaking up with him, it's about everything that happened before that. Some…really dark stuff happened, and I'm only just letting myself remember it…"

I start shaking in my coat, the memory crashing over me again and again, like I'm trapped in a rip tide.

"He did something bad…he did lots of bad things…"

At that, he softens. He reaches out and puts a hand on my shoulder. The undeserved kindness almost ruins me.

"Amelie. Let's take this slowly. What happened?"

I start sobbing rawly. I drop my coffee cup. The lid comes off and it spills all over the concrete, spraying my shoes. "I feel like I'm going mad," I tell him, ignoring the mess.

"Talk to me, Amelie."

"I don't deserve you. I don't deserve your kindness. I don't deserve anything good."

"What? Ammy. What are you even saying? You're scaring me a little."

I feel so guilty for confiding in him – this boy whose heart I broke – and yet, I came here, I clearly need to be around him. Alfie gives me some time, acting like he's fine. Though, when he bends down to pick up my cup, I see his hands wobbling.

Eventually I manage to say, "Sorry. It's so inappropriate for me to be telling you this. After how I treated—"

Alfie interrupts me. "Let's worry about you and me and what happened another time. Look, before all this, we were best friends. You're still my best friend... Oh god, I didn't mean to make you cry harder."

I snuffle, but it doesn't stop snot dripping into my mouth. *You're still my best friend.* Those words. How generous they are...the safety I feel. Though I'm crying, it feels good. I want to tell my best friend about what happened.

"The boy who came up to Sheffield a few months ago... Reese. His name's Reese. Well, we're not together any more. But that's not why I'm so upset. Well, that's not only why. Alfie? I've been remembering things. I came up here because something happened that night we went to the Leadmill. And I've been trying not to think about it, but now I can't think of anything else, and I'm not sure I understand what happened."

Alfie's hand on my shoulder tightens ever so slightly, and I sense him forcing himself to loosen it again. "Did he hurt you, Ammy?"

I pause. Then I say, "Yes."

Alfie lets out a big breath.

Then I add, "He did something really bad."

Alfie throws his head back to the sky. He takes his hand off my shoulder and I'm already panicking that he's the wrong person to tell, that this is all about to get worse, that this is the stupidest idea ever. "Ammy?" he asks the sky quietly. "Did he make you do anything that you didn't want to do?"

I pause. Then I say, "Yes."

Saying it out loud releases something. A part of my stomach that's been constrained since the last time I was here. The unravelling feels amazing for the tiniest of moments, but agonizing, rip-roaring pain fills the gap. I start crying again.

Alfie stands up and walks away for a moment. Hands in his hair, face tilted towards the sky. Then he's back by my side, and he's crying too.

"Oh, Ammy," is all he manages, before he pulls me to him, and lets me bury my face into his coat. We sit there, both sobbing, as the magnitude of what I've just admitted drowns us both from the inside out. A few dog walkers notice us, then pretend not to notice us crying silently on the bench.

I close my eyes and feel Alfie's grief and his kindness. I feel, for the first time in so long, that I am in the right place at exactly the right moment. What a person he is, to be able to push aside all the pain I've caused him and still be here, cradling me in his skinny arms, stroking my tear-damp hair.

"Do you want to talk about it?" he asks. "I'm here, if you want to tell me what happened. I'm not sure if I'll say the right thing, but I can try."

I sniff. "I'm not sure I can. I just... Alfie? I know I hurt you, I know I hurt you so much. I know I went back on our plan, and it was wrong, and..."

"Please. We don't need to talk about that right now. It's not important."

I shake my head. "No, but you see, it *is* important! Because I'm trying to figure out why I got together with him, why I hurt you, why I got so lost, and how that's led to everything. I thought, at the time, it was just that I'd fallen in love, but...but...I've been seeing this counsellor." I swallow. "And I've started telling her about what happened. She says that love isn't supposed to go how it went with him. She's making me start to think that it wasn't actually a relationship at all. That maybe it was something darker."

Alfie's still struggling to control his emotions. I see his fists clench and unclench, his knees bobbing up and down madly as his foot bounces. "I'm glad you've got someone to talk to about it, Ammy. Honestly, I can't tell you how relieved I am to hear that."

I take a breath. "I think it's helping. I mean, everything feels worse rather than better. But worse in a better way, if that makes sense? Like, I'm finally starting to understand what happened. And, Alfie..." I reach out and I take his cold hand in mine. I squeeze his fingers. "...I don't want to dodge all responsibility for how much I hurt you, but I'm starting to think that Reese is partly to blame; that he was controlling me, almost. It wasn't a kind relationship. It felt like I got caught in a tidal wave...that nothing I could've done could've stopped what happened from happening... I'm probably not making sense."

A late-arriving tear runs down Alfie's cheek.

"I just found myself outside your house, because I realized it's not just me who's been messed up by all this – it's you too. And I thought it might help you understand it."

Alfie's able to look at me for the first time since I told him. He stares right into my eyes. "Tell me everything, Ammy," he whispers. "I want to understand it."

We sit until our arses are numb, and our tears just keep on coming. I start at the beginning. I start with the day I didn't send that message telling him I loved him. I skip over the bits that I know he will find painful, and I stop when I get to that night. Because I'm not ready to give words to that night yet, and Alfie's assumptions are near enough the mark. I can feel his body soften as I fill in blanks or replace his own dark fantasies about what happened with the truth.

"I just assumed you never thought about me," he says through tears. "That the break-up didn't mean anything to you."

"Alfie, I thought about you every damn day." And he lets out a guttural sob.

Sometimes we tell ourselves stories of *How Things Should Go*, and we get angry and upset when life doesn't go to plan. And, sometimes, I've realized, we tell ourselves stories of *Let's Imagine The Worst And Pretend It's The Truth*, without actually checking in with real life to see if our dark make-believe is grounded in any reality. And it causes such pain, us being lost in daydreams of *if-onlys* and *I'm-sure-it-won'ts*.

All of us. And so, I begin the process of dismantling Alfie's *Imagining The Worst*.

For the first time since I met Reese, I really start telling someone about him. Someone I know. And, together, Alfie and I begin to understand. Sometimes that's all you can do in life, when it comes to pain – try and understand it. We all carry scars and scorch marks around with us. We cuddle up each night with ghosts of damaging memories – we let them swirl around our heads, never able to settle or heal because we can't make sense of this terrible thing that happened to us, and why we're finding it so impossible to get over. You can't force pain to leave until it's ready to. Like the most annoying party guest, it only leaves in its own sweet goddamned time. Meanwhile there's nothing you can do but carry it until it's ready to be released. But understanding the pain – why it's there, why it's not leaving – it makes that burden much easier to bear.

In time, we silently stand together and walk back to Alfie's house, picking up another coffee on the way. We sit on his wall and slurp at it, going over it all some more, until the coffee's gone and all the words I can manage have come out and it's almost time for me to get the train home.

"I guess I should go." Alfie looks at the time on his phone. "I've got loads of chemistry write-up to do before tomorrow."

"Yeah, my train's in an hour. I should go get the bus."

Alfie looks at me – really, truly, looks at me, with nothing but love and kindness. He smiles sadly. Part of me thinks I don't deserve it. But being with him, if only for two hours, has reignited the part of me that believes I do. That we all deserve to be treated kindly, no matter how inclined we are to fuck up.

"I'm so sorry, Alfie," I say. I will never have said it enough times.

"I'm so sorry too, for what you went through. Are still going through." My throat closes again but I manage to stem the tears. "Stay in touch, yeah? Let me know how you're getting on?" I nod and nod. "And keep talking to that counsellor lady." I nod again. Alfie's head twitches towards the house. I sense this is goodbye now. "I'm always here for you, Ammy," he adds, finally. "You can call any time."

Tears twitch at the edges of my eyes. My voice comes out like a tortured mouse. "I'm always here for you too."

We hug goodbye. So hard. Neither of us quite wanting to let go, and yet knowing this is the only way. I want to cry, yet again, because I know this is the end of us. I will never know if we'd have made it if you hadn't come into the picture, Reese. If we'd have gone to Manchester and made it work and done everything we'd promised. Part of what I need to get over is the *what-ifing* over Alfie and me.

"Apologize to Jessa for me, won't you?"

"Tell her yourself. We all miss you, Ams. Come back and visit soon, yeah?"

I trundle my way to the bus stop. The last time I was here, the last time I walked along this road, I didn't carry the scars I carry now. The ghosts of past-Amelie brush past me – oh, how carefree she was. I will never get her back.

I will never be the girl I was before you and what you did to me.

But I can understand it.

That is what I tell myself as the train pulls out of the station, as I leave my home behind and travel back to the strange town filled with bad memories, which I'm now supposed to call home. As I lay my head against the window, I whisper it to myself over and over.

I see the chimneys, spurting steam out into the air.

"I want to understand it," I say out loud.

I want to understand it.

Music Classroom

Something strange has happened.

You sent me a message at two a.m. last night, two weeks after I returned from Sheffield.

I read it as I'm brushing my teeth and mentally gearing up for yet another lonely day at college, and yet another strenuous hour of counselling.

Reese: I think I'm still in love with you. x

"You okay?" Mum asks over breakfast, as I stare at the message and then stare at it some more. And then, after I've finished doing that, I follow all the staring with staring at the message some more. "You've been rather absorbed in your phone this morning."

I manage to look up and smile at her and not look at my

phone for thirty whole seconds. "I'm alright. Sorry. I, umm, just…got a weird message from someone."

Mum wrinkles her nose. "Someone hasn't sent you a dick pic, have they?"

I drop my phone in a clatter. "Mum!" I laugh in shock. "How do you know about them?"

"I read about them in the newspaper. I can't see the point in it myself. Maybe if they were more attractive to look at I'd get it, but…"

"Mum!"

She starts chuckling and I find myself laughing too, right down into my stomach.

"So it's not a penis photo then?"

"MUM!"

"You can tell me if it is. I'm cool. I can handle it."

"It's not. Oh my god." I pick up my phone from where it fell to the carpet and reread it. My laughter stops. "It's a message from Reese, actually."

Mum's laughter stops instantly. She closes her eyes and pinches the top of her nose, before arranging her face into a neutral nothing. "Oh…"

"Yeah."

"I didn't know you were still in contact with him."

"I didn't either."

I've been trying to talk to my parents more about everything. Joan suggested it. "You shouldn't have to go through this all alone," she said at last week's session. "Maybe open up a little?"

298

"But what if they don't understand?" I'd replied. "What if they think it's all my fault?" And I'd taken a tissue from the familiar box.

I read the message again, and again. I'm reading it so much that I miss my mouth and drip porridge onto my floral dress.

"Bollocks." I get up to dab it off. Mum wets a paper towel and hands it over.

"You weren't very happy when you were with him," she mutters, as I attack the stain. "And you've not been very happy since it ended." She pauses, and I see her weigh up every word carefully, reaching for the ones that will cause less damage. "We were worried about you, Amelie."

"I know."

"You know we'll never tell you what to do, Amelie, but… but…maybe really think things through before responding."

"I wasn't going—"

She held up her hands. "I'm just saying."

I've decided to shelve how I feel about this message until I speak to Joan later. I'm finding it very hard to trust my own instincts about anything, you see. Joan's been making me revisit our memories, Reese, and she's been taking out this supersonic magnifying glass and holding it up to each one, forcing me to see it in a different way. She says things like:

"Do you really think your first date was romantic? Have you considered that maybe it was quite manipulative? I mean, he said he wanted to get to you before anyone else did? That doesn't seem very healthy to me."

And...

"None of the things you mentioned wanting in this relationship seem that 'crazy' to me. In fact, they seem quite normal. Have you thought about whether this boy was the one with the problem, not you?"

After every session I feel a bit lighter and a bit cleaner, and a bit like I may actually like myself and not think I'm a crazy fucked-up mess. It's a physical effort waiting for each counselling session. Every hour I see Joan I feel like I'm given a huge gasp of oxygen, before I have to plunge back into the depths of college and having no friends to talk to, and having to see you with her. My lungs hurt, and every week I worry I may not be able to make it until Friday. I absorb and absorb and hurt and hurt and then run to Joan's and vomit it all up, and get her to make sense of it. And then grab another breath.

I'm so glad I only have this morning to get through before my next session – especially after your message.

I call goodbye to Mum, turning down her offer of a lift. It would get me in too early, and it's gorgeous out. I also need time to reread your message and figure out what the hell's going on.

It's like you know, I realize, as I'm staring blankly at my reflection, combing my hair. You can sense the bond between us loosening. You always had that psychic sense, you could always tell when you'd pushed me too far, been too distant for too long, made me start getting angry and fed up and thinking I deserved better. Then *BAM* – back came

Reese, the boy I thought I loved, rather than the cold, unfeeling silence I'd been dealing with for weeks. Now I'm finally starting to see you for who you are, rather than the you we both told ourselves you are, and you can obviously sense it, so *BAM* – here comes the message I've been longing for. The reason I've checked my phone every minute of every day since we broke up.

I collect my bag, stuffing in my notepad filled with new song lyrics and my completed English essay. Joan said that "this boy" had taken up too much of my life already, and I shouldn't let him take up any more. "You're letting him win, Amelie," she said recently. "Don't you see? If you let all this affect your music and your exams, you're still letting him in, you're still letting him have control over you."

So I've been turning up to lessons, and trying to write songs again, and just about coping with seeing you about the place. There are exams to revise for and coursework to get handed in this week. Generally I've been doing okay… a little better… Apart from those times when you pass me, and I'm back in that hotel room, and I start shaking uncontrollably and have to go lock myself in a toilet cubicle and shove my head between my legs and relive the whole damn thing like it's happening right that moment, and start crying and shaking harder, and it takes me at least ten minutes to get a grip on myself…

…Other than that, I'm doing okay.

I look at my phone again. It will have told you I've read the message. I wonder how often you're checking to see if

I've read it yet, to see if I've replied. As I lock the front door, I almost feel sparks in my fingers.

Power.

Right now, with this message on my phone, and you knowing I've read it and it's my turn to reply, I have the power. I am in control. I have the ball in my court. Is this how it always felt for you? Were you fizzing, and smug about yourself, being able to relax because you weren't the one waiting for a reply? I smile, enjoying the feeling, thinking how very rare it is. Or was...

Then.

"Amelie?"

I launch out of my skin.

"What the fuck, Reese?"

You're here outside my flat, with my favourite hat on – the one with the yellow trim.

"Can I walk you to college?" you ask casually, like the past few months didn't happen.

I can't... I don't know... What's happening? Why are you here? You're never here! I only speak to you in my head now.

"What are you doing here?" I ask.

"You've not replied to my message."

I start walking, not waiting for you to follow. My legs want to march away, they're aching to run, though my heart is telling me to slow down and let you catch up. Or is that only habit?

You fall into step, your longer legs making it easy to keep pace. "So?" you ask.

I try not to look at you, but I sneak a glance and it's a mistake. You look tortured. You look like you mean it. Your eyes are bloodshot from lack of sleep and wide with desperation. I feel my fingers twitch with the power again, though the electricity splutters as I'm still so thrown that you're even here.

"I didn't know what to reply," I say. Even though I owe you nothing, let alone a reply.

"So you don't know if you love me?"

I throw my head back to the sunny sky. "Reese! What the hell are you even saying?"

We're at the corner by the zebra crossing. I step out but you reach and grab my hand, pulling me back onto the pavement. "I miss you," you say. "I think I've made a mistake."

Here's what I know I should do:
- Feel nothing
- Tell you to fuck off
- Proceed to fuck off

Here's what I actually feel:
- SO, so relieved
- Happy
- Hopeful, thinking, *I knew it! I knew it. I knew if I was patient, you would come back to me. I knew you could never really love her, when you loved me so hard! Maybe it could work this time? Even after everything.*

Here's what I actually do:

- Say nothing
- Let you hold my hand

"You're not saying anything." You fill in my gaps for me. "Look, Amelie, I'm sorry. I'm so sorry for going off with her. I wasn't thinking." I start counting the clichés, to give myself a distraction from all the happiness I feel but also know is wrong. So wrong. "It didn't mean anything. I was just confused. She doesn't compare to you." I drop your hand and cross the road and pretend this is me being strong, but it's not like I've told you to piss off. I know I'm entertaining you, and the horrendously dangerous possibility of Us. You know it too. We walk our usual way to college, like back in the good days, and the bad days, when your silence along this path was akin to torture.

You promise me the world. You apologize for everything you think you've ever done. You miss out real apologies though – like for what happened in Sheffield, and all the other times after that, and all the ways you dissolved everything I was, until I was only salt water. Instead, you apologize for what you *think* I'm mad at. "I was scared by my feelings. The first time we got together, I was drunk. It was all her. I was too drunk. I mean, if it was the other way around, you could say she took advantage."

I've waited so long to hear all this. Every word melts into my heart. Relief pulses through me, releasing each muscle. It always used to be like this between us – me holding my breath and holding my breath and holding my breath and then, just when I thought I would pass out, you'd come back to me. Your love would come back to me.

This is the longest you've ever made me wait though.

I've passed out and regained consciousness so many times. It's been months, Reese. *Months*. But you've come back, you've still come back, and that makes me fizz with joy. But…but…

It's also been long enough for me to get help, to know that maybe this isn't healthy. I keep walking. I keep putting one foot in front of another. I hold on. I don't say anything back. I'm seeing Joan – she will help me make sense of this. I don't trust myself to make sense of anything any more.

Ironically, you can't handle my silence. "Amelie, please talk to me. This is torture. Are you even listening? I love you. Did you not hear me? I love you."

I snap for a second, and let my guard down. I spin to look at your beautiful, desperate face. "You have a really weird way of showing it," I say.

Your eyes widen, I see you gear up for an argument, one you will win, no doubt. Yet, you throw me off again.

"I know," you admit. "I'm sorry, Amelie. I'm so sorry. I'm such a fuck-up, I'm such a fucked-up mess." You stop and lean against someone's garden wall. I cannot help but stop with you. I've never seen you like this, not ever. You take off your hat, and look so vulnerable without it. You squeeze it in your hands, ruining the brim. "I don't know what's wrong with me, Amelie," you choke out. "I feel like I'm broken.

I know I always made it your fault, and I know I hurt you, and I'm sorry. Because it's me. I'm the problem. What's wrong with me, Amelie?" Your whole body's shaking. "WHAT THE FUCK IS WRONG WITH ME?" Then you cry. You collapse and dissolve in on yourself while I stand here hopelessly, in total shock. "Amelie, I need you." You look up at me through your tears. "You were so good for me. So good."

My heart starts to lurch towards you, like a dog dragging its owner on a lead. Because I love you, Reese, and I can't bear to see you like this. My head starts joining forces. It starts having dangerous thoughts like, *Maybe this is the breakthrough we needed* and *He must love you, look how much he is hurting. This must be the truth.*

You are crying. You, not me. Here, in a public place. Where anyone could walk past. We're even. You've finally made yourself cry, rather than me – and maybe, just maybe, everything between us will be okay.

I reach out to comfort you, knowing physical contact will be the undoing of me.

"I'm such a mess. Amelie, help me. I love you. You're the only one who can…"

And, just before I make contact with your shoulder, there's a voice.

Run.

Run, it whispers. *Now! Go! Flee! It is not safe to stay here.*

My hand pauses in mid-air. Where's this voice coming from?

I'll tell you where.

It's my gut.

And I promised myself I'd listen to it. I clutched it and I solemnly swore and I must I must I must listen to it. Because listening to my heart got me nowhere, and neither did listening to my head. It's my gut's turn to have the steering wheel. I promised.

I don't touch your shoulder. I don't say "There, there". I don't let the fairy tale come true – not yet. The only way I can walk away now is by telling myself that, if you *really* love me like you're claiming to, then you can wait.

I take a step back and you look up, tears still on your cheeks. "Amelie, please? At least sit down next to me. I need you. Please."

I shake my head. "I've got to go to my music lesson." I take another step back.

"Music can wait! Amelie." You tap the space next to you on the wall so desperately it's almost a command.

You're saying my name so much. You never used to call me by my name. It takes every ounce of bravery I have to refuse. "I'm sorry you're upset," I say. When I speak, my voice sounds different. Calmer, deeper, quietly powerful. "But I really am going to be late. Let's talk later." Then I turn and I walk away from you as fast as I can.

"Amelie? Can you stay behind a moment?" Mrs Clarke asks. "I just want to go through your composition coursework."

I sway from foot to foot anxiously as her finger traces over my musical score and she mutters the lyrics under her breath. I stare at her wedding band and wonder if she's happy with the person she's married to. If they make her feel safe and sure, rather than tense and like something is wrong with her. I hope it's the first option. I know she's just a teacher and is only doing her job and all, but I do feel like she really cares. That she actually, properly, wishes me to feel safe and secure too. She runs over the lyrics one more time before looking up with a smile.

"This is great, Amelie. Just great."

I let out a long sigh of breath. "Really?"

"Yes. I mean, the second verse needs work, but all second verses need work. You've got a day or two to get it just right." She hands my open notepad back to me. "It's nice to have you back."

Even with everything going on, my face cracks into a smile to match hers. "What do you mean?"

"You know. You doing music again. Turning up to lessons, even. It's a bit of a relief to be honest, though I'm probably not allowed to say that."

"Thank you. Though you're right about the second verse. I'll tweak it."

Mrs Clarke pulls back my pad to look at it again and she reads the song title out loud: "'The Places I've Cried'. It's such a good idea for a song."

I laugh. "How would you feel if I told you that it was actually Mr Jenkins who gave me the idea?"

"Oh god – for that V&A project he had the assembly about?"

"Yeah. I've been making a memory map to donate, and that's what gave me the idea for the song."

"Yikes." She smiles. "Never tell him. He'll be insufferable in staff meetings. Whoops. I'm probably not allowed to say that either." She stands up, picking up her coffee mug. "Right, I've got a free now. Lots of exciting marking awaits. What are you up to?"

I shift from foot to foot again. "I was actually going to ask if I could sit here for a while? I have a free, and I find the library hard to work in…" And I'm hiding from you. "Would that be okay?"

She holds out her arm. "Of course. My classroom is your classroom. Good work, Amelie. I can't wait to hear you record the finished song."

"Me neither."

I watch my teacher leave. The noise of corridor activity is slightly louder as she swings the door open and then muffles when it swings shut again. If I sit in that corner, then you won't be able to see me through the glass. No one will be able to see me. And that's just what I need for the next forty minutes, before my appointment with Joan.

I allow myself five minutes to fantasize about everything that happened this morning. I doodle biro hearts as I play all the Disney outcomes in my head. Here's a lovely fantasy about you begging for forgiveness for weeks. You'll happily do everything I've ever desired to prove your love for me, and then we'll reunite stronger than ever. Here's just a really good kiss I'm imagining, clutching each other on the garden wall I didn't sit on.

"Stop it," I say out loud.

I'm here to remember. I'm here because this music room is one of the places I cried. It's nondescript. It looks pretty much like every classroom in any educational establishment. There's a faded wall display as it's not near open evening yet so it hasn't been replaced in ages. The tables are arranged in a horseshoe shape and they all have wads of chewing gum stuck underneath them. It's a room that's always too cold in winter and too hot in summer. Just your everyday, typical classroom, and you made me cry in it.

I close my eyes.

"Crazy," I mutter under my breath, repeating your words. "You've gone completely crazy."

I open my eyes again and find I'm smiling. How strange it is, that today of all days – the day I decided to remember this particular cry, this particular cry started by her – you have told me you still love me. That she meant nothing to you.

Life really does go full circle, doesn't it? You may have to wait a hell of a lot longer for it than you'd like to, but, in the end, you really do get back to your starting point.

Her…

I'm being a bad feminist really. Calling her that.

Her name is Eden.

"I can't come to yours tonight," Reese said, without looking at me, in the refectory. "I'm songwriting with Eden."

That was his first mention of her and it didn't go unnoticed. Show me any girl whose little ears do not prick up with female intuition when their boyfriend randomly drops a new girl's name into conversation.

I worked really hard to not show any emotion on my face. I was getting good at it. I'd found that, if you can keep your eyebrows still, it sort of stops the emotional responses in the rest of your face – like your eyebrows are the things that unleash tricksy, telltale signs of your inner distress.

"Who's Eden?" I asked as neutrally as I possibly could.

"You know Eden! Everyone knows Eden."

"I don't know Eden." I was trying to come to terms with multiple instant anguishes. Firstly, he'd just cancelled plans to see me. Again. Even though we hadn't spent any proper time together in weeks. Even over the Christmas holidays, I'd hardly seen him. "It's not my fault I have to go see my stupid dad," he'd said, making me feel guilty, though he'd only gone to see his dad for two days, which didn't explain the rest of the lonely holidays. Secondly, because of the cancelling, I was now facing yet another night in on my own, trying to work out how to explain to my parents why I have literally no life. I could hardly stand the thought of it. Alone, just staring at my phone and wondering when he was going to message me. Feeling euphoria whenever it flashed a different colour, and then despair when I realized it wasn't a message from Reese – it wasn't a message from anyone – just my phone telling me my battery needed charging. Thirdly, I was certain that Reese cancelling again meant that *He Didn't Love Me Any More*, and that caused such heart-wrenching anxiety I knew I wouldn't be able to eat for the rest of the day. He hadn't even got me a Christmas present, claiming the treasure hunt and trip to Sheffield was one: "Anyway, why do you need presents to feel like I love you? That's a bit insecure, isn't it?"

And now, *now*, on top of everything, I had to deal with some random girl called fucking *Eden*?

"Oh god, you're going to kick off, aren't you?" he said, already pissed off.

"What? Why?"

"Look, Amelie. I can't spend every waking moment of my fucking time with you – that would be weird."

The band, as always, were sharing a plate of chips between them and pretending very hard not to listen in on our domestic.

"I'm happy that you're songwriting," I protested, feeling my face go red. "I didn't say I wasn't."

"I can see it on your face though. You're so pathetic sometimes."

Ouch.

Ouch ouch ouch ouch ouch.

The band put chips in their mouths and wouldn't look at me. They all got out their phones and pretended to be immersed in their screens.

Reese carried on. "Sorry, I didn't mean it like that. Come on! That was a joke. Can't you take a joke? Look, I only said it because it's just, it's a bit weird that you don't have any friends, don't you think? It puts so much pressure on me to see you all the time."

But you don't see me all the time, I thought. *In fact, you've not spent any time outside college with me for over a week.*

I kept my face neutral, because I didn't want to cry. Not here, in front of everyone. Not again. He found me so disgusting when I cried.

"I told you, it's fine." I leaned over and tried to kiss him in a sexy, breezy manner.

"Eww, Ams, your breath stinks!" He pulled away and laughed, reaching out to grab a chip while I stayed there, still mid-pucker, and let the humiliation soak through me.

I have no friends and no life and my breath stinks and even my boyfriend doesn't want to see me because I'm so pathetic.

Self-hatred is like a snake that eats its own tail. It feeds off itself – the bacteria of it spawning more bacteria until the infection is out of control. I'd really started to hate myself in those weeks after Sheffield. I'd lost all my friends. I lost all my confidence. Why wouldn't I? Reese was telling me I was pathetic. He made me feel like it was only out of charity that he hung out with me at all. He'd started saying mean things, on the rare occasions I spent any time alone with him. He'd tap my stomach and say, "How many pasties did you have in Sheffield then?" then call me "oversensitive" when I got upset. He increasingly got rough when we had sex – he'd even called me a slut.

"Reese," I'd said, covering my apparently disgusting body

with his duvet. "I don't like it when you call me a slut during sex. Not ever, really."

"I didn't call you a slut!"

"You did. Just now."

"No, I didn't."

He stood up and wriggled into his jeans. "You hearing things again?" When he turned, a smile was on his face. He leaned over and kissed me gently on the lips. "Hearing voices is the first sign of madness, my little crazy cuckoo." Another kiss, a really sweet one. Then he got out his phone. "Shit, the band are about to arrive for rehearsal. You better go."

So I collected my things and pretended I didn't mind that I wasn't welcome at rehearsal any more. I pretended we'd had a most marvellous time.

"I love you," I said, as he piled me out of the door.

"Yeah, whatever, slut." I gasped, and he laughed and wagged his finger. "Now that time I really *did* say it."

He was joking with such conviction that I started to wonder if I had actually imagined him saying it the first time. Oh god. Maybe I really was going mad? Poor Reese, for having such a pathetic crazy girlfriend, I must be such a burden.

I really did feel like a burden. I stopped trying to talk to anyone, because I just assumed they wouldn't want to talk to me. I stopped even being that nice to my parents, who kept asking me what had happened and why I was being like this and where their nice daughter had gone. Reese was the only one who wanted me, and even he didn't want me around very often. Crazy, pathetic me.

So the snake of my self-hatred continued to eat itself. I was so twitchy and nervous and filled with self-loathing that I almost didn't blame him for wanting to spend so much time with Eden.

Here, in the classroom, I shake my head, because – for the first time today – I think about Eden. Does she know about your message? Or that you followed me to school? Have you even broken up with her yet?

I bet if she does have any suspicions, you call her crazy. Like you did to me.

"This is Eden," he said the next day, bringing her to the table and introducing her to the band. She went around hug-patting everyone hello, like self-confidence wasn't a big deal.

"Greetings, earthlings," Eden said, laughing at her own joke.

Immediately I hated her. She was everything I was not – cool, edgy. She had a nose piercing and wore ripped jeans and this red crop-top thing with bat-wing sleeves. Who can wear red without feeling like it's wearing them? I'll tell you who. *Eden.*

I, of course, was introduced last.

"This is my girlfriend, Amelie," Reese practically mumbled,

gesturing to me before slumping on a chair the other side of the table. She waved hello unenthusiastically.

"Hi," I said, trying my best to come across well. "Nice to meet you."

"Same. I saw you win the talent show. You're really good." It didn't feel like it was a compliment. Reese sniggered as she said it, for one.

I pressed on, determined to be a good example of a girlfriend. "So you write songs too? I've not seen you around the music rooms."

She rolled her eyes. "God, no. I think studying music ruins music. You know? I do philosophy, economics and photography." She sat down easily, the boys moving their chairs to make room. "No one can analyse music. I mean, it's art. Whoever became a proper artist by writing an essay about art?"

"This is what I've been trying to say." Reese leaned over, his eyes wide with agreement. Meanwhile, my jealousy was so putrid I could've spat and it would've burned a hole through the table.

"I mean, I know I'm a good songwriter," Reese continued, "but that slag Mrs Clarke keeps giving me Cs because she says I can't keep within the marking criteria. I mean, did John Lennon write songs that followed a list of freakin' criteria?"

Rob took the last chip. "You're comparing yourself to John Lennon now, Reese?" he interrupted. "That's healthy. Totally healthy."

"Oh fuck off."

316

"Calm down, mate," Rob said. "I was only joking."

My stomach started sloshing from side to side again. Somehow this was my fault. Even though Rob had said it, I knew Reese was somehow going to make it my fault.

As I predicted, he nodded his head towards me. "Of course, *Amelie* here is the perfect A-grade music student. Aren't you, bubs? Your songs match all the *criteria*."

I flinched and smiled through it. This was one of his special attacks. One that – when I go over it afterwards, trying to prove that Reese WAS angry and he WAS attacking me and I WASN'T imagining it – makes me feel like I'm trying to pin down a butterfly. Because he didn't technically actually say anything *bad*.

"Criteria songs? Great!" Eden chirped, making it clear she thought it was anything but. She twisted her of-course-perfect body towards the band. "So, your name, dudes! It's such a good name for a band. Who came up with it?"

"Reese will claim it's Reese," Johnnie said.

"It was me! How many times do I need to say it?"

"Totally me," Rob argued. "I remember it perfectly. We were in Chicken House, and I had an epiphany. It was the most amazing moment of my entire life – even though I got food poisoning afterwards."

"Dude, you keep telling this story like it's true or something," Reese said, laughing.

Eden giggled and Eden fitted right in and Eden was one of the gang already. Good for fucking Eden! "So, it was you who came up with it?" she asked him, and I swear to god and baby Jesus and everything in between that she was most certainly flirting with him, right in front of me. She was leaning forward and making full-on eye contact.

"Yes, it was me. We did come up with it in Chicken House, but it was all me."

She asked question after question about the band, and Reese answered most of them, though the whole band seemed equally pleased to be the centre of this attractive girl's attention. I kept opening my mouth to try and join in but found I didn't have one useful thing to say. I had no personality to contribute. Because everything I thought about saying, I weighed up in my head beforehand and then decided it would probably piss Reese off, and I didn't want to piss him off when he was sitting next to a pretty girl. So I just sat like a goldfish, gawping, as she laughed at his jokes and he turned on his charm, and it was like watching the start of a romance film – one where a couple instantly clicks – and that would've been great, except *I* was his girlfriend and I was sitting right there. Trying not to cry.

Always, *always*, trying not to cry.

The bell rang, signalling the start of the afternoon and my formulaic music lesson. But Reese had one parting shot for me as we all gathered up our bags.

"Eden, you should totally come to rehearsal tonight," he told her. "I have a soundproof garage at the back of my garden. We can show the guys the songs we worked on?"

She shrugged. "Sounds great."

SHE SHRUGGED? I wanted to shake her. Did she not

318

realize how hard it was to get into rehearsal? It was easier to get into that London nightclub all the royals go to. Did she have any idea, ANY IDEA, what a big deal this was? And she just shrugged? I wanted to go to the garage! I SHOULD have been going to the garage. I was the one who was his GIRLFRIEND.

"Great. It starts at eight. I'll message you my address."

"Cool. I'll see you later. It was great to meet you guys." Eden didn't even have a bag. She just carried some leather-bound notepad with her, and slipped her phone into the bony arse of her jeans. "You too, Amelie," she added as an afterthought.

I didn't cry that day. I held it in. I know, who would've thought I was capable? I swear to god, Reese, if you knew how many times I'd *wanted* to cry and managed to stop myself… Well, if I'd cried all the tears I'd wanted to, some bloke called Noah would've turned up in a large boat in preparation.

I don't really want to bore you again with the conversations we had about Eden, as you found them so boring to begin with.

But they all went a bit like this….

"Eden is so chill. I've never met a girl so chill."

"Are you saying I'm not chill?"

"Whoa. And, listen to what you just said. That's pretty unchill."

And…

"Eden's completely opening my mind up to how to write a song."

"Really? How?"

"It's kind of hard to explain. But we had such a good session last night. I learned so much."

"Oh…"

…

"And Eden also said…"

And…

"Eden's got so many friends, you know? I've met so many people since I met her."

…

"It's nice, isn't it? When you've got other things going on in your life?"

"What's that supposed to mean?"

"Oh god. Calm down."

"I have friends…"

"I wasn't saying you didn't. I was just saying, Eden… Anyway, no offence, but you don't have any friends really, do you, littlie? Don't get upset! I'm not being mean. It's true! It is though, isn't it? Oh god, I can't believe you're crying again. You're always fucking crying. What is it now? What have I done now? I can't be around you when you're like this. It's not healthy. I'm worried about you. You need to be more chill."

"Oh, like Eden?"

"You're mental. You're actually fucking mental."

And…

"So what are you doing tonight?"

Sigh "You know what I'm doing. Band rehearsal."

…

…

"Is…*she* coming?"

"I knew it! I knew you were about to ask that."

"Well, is she?"

"Yes, she's coming. I've told you. She's helping us write some really great stuff."

…

"You're going to let your jealousy get in the way of my band succeeding? Is that what you want? For me to stay with you always and not do anything or have any life or write any songs because you're too jealous and needy?"

"I'm not jealous. It's just…you see her a lot, Reese."

"So?"

"So, I don't know."

"I'm not allowed to have friends now? Is that it? Just because you don't have any fucking friends doesn't mean… Oh, what a surprise. You're crying again. Have you thought that maybe you don't have any friends because you literally just whinge all the damn time?"

"I'm sorry! I don't know why you put up with me."

"Sometimes I don't either."

One day, not long after I met Eden, a miracle occurred. Reese agreed to spend time with me. Actual time with me. He was even the one who suggested it.

All the terribleness of the previous weeks vanished the moment he said, "How about we sack off lessons and I treat you to a trip to BoJangles?"

"Really?" My voice squeaked with hope. God, I was pathetic. I was so, so pathetic.

He laughed and ruffled my hair. "Yes, really, you wotsit! You're my girlfriend! Why wouldn't I want to hang out with you?" He wrapped his arm around me, pulling me into his coat as he steered me away from my English lesson. Reese was being so nice again, just like at the beginning.

I'd made myself not message him first or call him first or bring up Eden in any way, for an entire week. It had been a huge challenge, and my heart hurt every morning as I woke up, checked my phone, and saw he hadn't messaged. But it had finally paid off! Maybe I *was* too needy. He clearly just needed more space, like he said. And love is about giving people what they need. I'd cracked the code, the code of how to get him to love me again, and it felt fantastic.

"I've missed you." He kissed the top of my head, making

love ooze out of every fibre of my body. "We need to spend more time together."

I nodded – the epitome of cool and chill. "Shall we get the truffle crumpets?" I suggested.

"I mean, that is just one of the best ideas in the whole goddamned world."

We wandered into town, arm in arm, bodies entwined. If you'd have walked past us and you were in a lonely place in your life, we would've made you feel lonelier. We were *that* couple. We walked through icy patches and Reese got obsessed with sliding on them like he was a kid. "It's the most satisfying feeling ever," he cried, while I laughed and hugged him so hard.

We arrived at the cafe and he picked the table with a squishy sofa, pulling me into him after we ordered melted truffle chocolates on crumpets. He talked a lot about his band, but I didn't mind because he was stroking my hair and in love with me again. He could've been talking about paint drying and trainspotting and *Antiques Roadshow* and it would've still felt like gold was tumbling out of his mouth.

"I'm really into this new direction we're taking..." he said. "The others are reluctant, but they just can't see what I see. It's not a risk..."

I nodded and agreed, because he loved it when I nodded and agreed.

The crumpets arrived with a big teapot, and he took them without thanking the waiter.

We stuffed our faces and moaned about how good it all

tasted, swapping crumpets halfway through because we'd picked different flavoured truffles.

"I definitely picked the best flavour," he confirmed, after taking a bite of mine. I nodded in agreement. I would order his flavour next time.

It was all going so well, and I was so, so happy, and I really thought it would last for ever. And if not for ever, then maybe for more than an hour, at the very least. But then I messed it up again, as I always did.

"So, yeah." Reese pushed away his unfinished crumpet. "We have a gig on Saturday. At the Jeeves and Wooster. It's going to be the perfect opportunity to try out this new sound."

I clapped my hands together in pure happiness for him. "Reese, that's great news!" The Jeeves and Wooster was a cute little venue I'd played a month or so before. The room only fitted around fifty people, but the crowd was amazing – really engaged. It had been full of slightly older music obsessives who couldn't always get the train into London on week nights. I'd felt horrible all the way through my set there though, unable to focus on the applause, because Reese had sent a message right beforehand, saying he couldn't make it. Not even giving me a reason why.

"I know, right? It's about time they bloody had us, to be fair. But I went around with Eden, who knows the manager, and we sang them two of our new songs and he really liked them."

Hang on.

A new Eden bomb had just exploded.

He'd been out with her? Again? He'd been pitching himself as a musical act with just *her*? Green, sharp jealousy zipped through my bloodstream, alongside white-hot rage. I knew I shouldn't say anything. I knew that would make things worse.

"You didn't tell me you and Eden were gigging together now," I said quietly into my mug of cold tea, and Reese's whole body stiffened with annoyance.

"Don't do this." His voice was firm. "Not when we're having such a nice time."

I couldn't accept it. My insecurity writhed inside my body, like a squirming toddler on the cusp of a tantrum. I sipped more cold tea to try and quell it, but my instincts were yelling, *WHAT'S GOING ON? SOMETHING IS GOING ON WITH HER. YOU ARE RIGHT ABOUT THIS. I PROMISE YOU, YOU'RE NOT BEING CRAZY, YOU ARE RIGHT ABOUT THIS.*

"Do you fancy her, Reese?" I asked, even quieter. But the way he erupted suggested I'd thrown a pint over his face and demanded a paternity test.

"Are you actually kidding me?" He shook his head. "Are we really going here? Again? When we're having such a nice time?"

I knew I should apologize. I knew I should say I didn't mean it. But the itch was so itchy and the need to scratch so desperate. I'd rather be splattered with blood than swallow down all these feelings.

"I don't think I'm being unreasonable," I started.

"You never think you're being unreasonable. However, here we go again."

I sighed and put my palms over my eyes. "Reese, are you honestly saying you wouldn't be upset if I suddenly started spending all my time with another guy and started a band with them without telling you? And never called you? Or messaged you back? And when I did speak to you, all I could speak about was how amazing this other guy was?"

"No, I wouldn't mind at all," he said. His face was getting redder but his voice was cold and controlled. "Because I'm not fucking mental!" He crossed his arms and stared at me like I'd shat myself. "You're the one who went up to see your ex and didn't even fucking tell him about me. And I'M the one who is in the wrong?"

This argument again. He always brought that up when I got sad, which always threw me because that was the night it happened. The tears. They were coming. *Here we go again...* But I blinked them away because they only ever made things worse.

"Have you thought about *why* I spend so much time with Eden?" he asked.

I shook my head, waiting for the insult, my hands trembling around my cup.

"Because she doesn't put all this pressure on me like you do! Because I can RELAX around her. Do you have any idea how much hard work you are?"

Don't cry, don't cry, don't cry.

"When we first got together, you were so relaxed and

happy and...attractive. Now you're just..." He let me fill in the blanks.

I focused so hard on not crying that I almost forgot how to breathe.

A tiny part of me had a thought. And that thought was: *I was relaxed and happy and attractive because you were treating me well. I was chilled out because I trusted you to do and say the things you said you were going to do. I was happy because I felt like you loved me for exactly who I was and didn't need to hide any parts of myself in order to win affection. I was attractive because I felt attractive, because I wasn't being ignored or undermined or put down or made to feel that, whatever I did, it was never enough. If only YOU would go back to the way YOU were, then I could easily go back to the way I was. I swear it's not all on me. I swear, I swear.*

But I blinked back tears and allowed his character assassination to continue, because I believed I was the mess he saw in me.

"You're so paranoid. I swear I worry about your mental health. Nothing is going on. Nothing!" He took off his hat in exasperation. "Though if there was – I mean, the way you are right now – could you blame me?"

I shook my head. No, I couldn't blame him.

"I tried to take us out and have a nice time, and now you've just ruined it."

"I'm sorry. I'm so, so sorry, Reese." My voice was more squeak than voice.

He rolled his eyes. He actually rolled his eyes.

"Maybe it's better if you don't come to the gig." He looked out the window as he said it, so he didn't have to watch the heart he was smashing.

My mouth fell open. *"What?"*

"I won't be able to concentrate on my music if I'm worrying about you being all psycho."

"But…" *Don't cry, don't cry, don't cry.* "But we always go to each other's gigs."

"Yes, well, maybe we shouldn't," he told the window.

I felt I'd reached a whole new realm of nauseous. I was so angry at myself, hating myself so much. Why didn't I just keep my mouth shut? Why didn't I just eat the freaking crumpets and enjoy us being back to how we were? I *must* be crazy, and I *must* be jealous, and I *didn't* know why he put up with me. Why would *anyone* put up with me?

His face was totally blank while I fell apart, lacking any expression at all. "I do need a bit of space from you, Amelie. You're too much, you know? It's not fair on me."

"You want to break up?"

No.

No no no no no.

"I'm not saying that – god! Stop being so dramatic. I just need space…"

Space? More space?! I hardly ever saw him. I considered how truly terrible I must be, that he needed space from me after only one crumpet together. I must be the most annoying human in the universe.

"If that's what you need," I said, my voice cracking.

"Don't start crying again, will you? It's so manipulative of you."

I gulped. I pressed my lips together. I blinked upwards. I did exactly what was asked of me.

"Okay."

"Stop crying!"

"I'm not crying."

"Look, it's fine. I'll call you, alright?"

"Okay."

"Are you being snippy now?"

I pressed my lips together harder. I shook my head. "No," I said robotically. "You need space. It makes sense."

He reached over and patted the top of my hair like I was a dog. "I do. Cheers, littlie. I do love you, you know. You're so cute."

He said it as he was already getting up and leaving, already on his phone, checking his messages from Eden. "Gotta dash – bye."

I watched him leave and kept breathing deeply before I checked the time with shaking hands. Ten minutes until my music lesson.

Get off the sofa, I told myself. And I managed it. *Leave the shop,* I told myself. And I managed it. I didn't cry. I just broke the journey from BoJangles to college into teeny tiny segments of steps to get through. *Can you get to that streetlight without crying? Yes, yes you can, well done. Can you get to the post office without screaming at the top of your lungs? Yes, just about – congratulations. Look, there are the college gates. I dare you to make it all the way to them without your knees buckling and you crumbling to the floor. Dare accepted, you say? Well done. You did it. High fives. Now, here's another dare: sit through your music lesson without falling apart.*

I collapsed into this very corner, except the classroom wasn't empty then. Mrs Clarke streamed in and started explaining our coursework to us, and I tried to lose myself in the lesson. I'd always been able to escape into music, but you eclipsed my brain, you eclipsed that capacity. In fact, I've started to realize that you eclipsed every single part of me that made me *me*. There is nothing in this story that isn't about you. I have been eroded away – my friends, my hobbies, my quirks – anything that made me interesting or happy or someone you would want to know, it's all gone. I've been smoothed down to a flat stone that just has your name carved onto it.

I sniffed. I snuffled. I blinked at the ceiling. I muttered under my breath to get a grip on myself. I held my breath. I did every possible thing you can think of to not cry but the floodgates were determined to open, the dam was determined to burst.

"Now, the hardest part of the composition will be…"

Mrs Clarke said, just as a lone tear plopped down my cheek. I rubbed it away, hoping no one would notice. But another one plopped out the other eye. I couldn't stop sniffing. People started to look. I rubbed my nose on my cardigan and kept swiping the tears as they arrived.

Please stop crying, I begged myself. Not here, not in front of everyone. Not again.

But *plop, plop, plop*. Soon I couldn't stem them. They splashed onto my exercise book, making the ink swirl and smudge and the paper bubble.

"You'll be marked not only on the quality of your composition but..."

The conversation kept replaying in my head.

"You're a bit too much, you know?"

"I just need space."

"You're so manipulative."

I cried a tear for every name Reese called me. Everything that he believed about me that I believed too. In that moment, I felt nothing but sadness for him, for having to put up with me. Poor, poor Reese for having to deal with crazy, nutso, insecure, boring me – when he could be with girls like Eden. Girls who made him shine.

Plop, plop, plop, plop. My exercise book was a swimming pool. You could teach children to swim on it, and they'd definitely need armbands. A boy next to me, Michael, kept glancing over whenever I sniffed. He saw the tears landing onto our desk. I couldn't take it any more. I collected up my things and stuffed them into my bag.

"Mrs Clarke? I have to go. I don't feel well."

"Are you okay, Amelie?" she asked, noticing my rivers of crying, but unable to do much about it as she was mid-lesson.

I was out of the room before I could even reply. I flung myself into the girls' toilets and – oh, yes, you've guessed it – I cried.

I pull up your message again. And, for the first time ever, the unimaginable happens. I feel a bit sorry for Eden.

Sympathy, rather than jealousy.

For so long she's been my nemesis. She's been my albatross. She's been the focus of my insecurity and self-hatred. I've obsessed over her almost as much as I've obsessed over you. Why couldn't I be more like her? Why was I so, terribly, like myself? Why couldn't I be cool and calm and chill and funky and all the things she could give you but I clearly could not? I hated her for being so much better than me in every conceivable way.

I was so crazy. Or so you said…

"*There's nothing in it,*" you said. "*Stop being so paranoid,*" you said. "*Why are you so insecure?*" you said. "*I can be just friends with a girl,*" you said.

And I wonder, Reese. I wonder.

Is she worrying about me now? Is she asking you the same questions? Have I become her albatross?

My gut says: *Perhaps.*

Perhaps, now you have her, you miss parts of me. Perhaps you're asking her why she can't be quieter, or more this, or more that, or more anything that isn't like her, so she – *abracadabra* – suddenly feels insecure and like she's going mad. Because I bet you're telling her there's nothing to worry about when it comes to your crazy ex-girlfriend. Whereas, from this message on my phone, there is a lot for her to worry about after all.

I know all this. I know you're bad news. I know my gut is right. I know that Joan is probably going to have pretty severe opinions about this message. And I hate myself for thinking this, and I hate myself for being so weak but, Reese, oh my god… How much I want to meet you after school and dissolve back into what we were.

I don't know how to stop me.

Please, someone, stop me.

"He said he loves me," I tell Joan. "He says that it was all a mistake with her. He says he wants me back."

I'm smiling because saying it out loud does make me very happy indeed. I'm expecting her to go nuts. To tell me it's a terrible idea. To ban me from seeing him again. To grab my hands and scream, "Noooo!" I prepare to get defensive. Joan's face remains totally neutral however.

"I see," she replies. "And how does that make you feel?"

I tilt my head, slightly annoyed by her lack of response.

"Confused," I answer honestly. "I know he did some bad

things…" I've told her about Sheffield. I've told her and I've screamed and I've cried. She's been giving me techniques on what to do when the memory surfaces, like a train hitting me out of nowhere. "I know he's not perfect," I stammer on. "But maybe he just needed this time, this space, to realize what we had? And now it will be amazing? Like it was in the beginning?"

She's quiet again, and yet I can fill the silence with what I know she's saying in her head. Because there's a little voice in my head too that's yelling, *This is ridiculous! Love doesn't work like that! You were miserable with him! You've been broken since you met him! That's not love, that's not love, that's not love!* But I don't want to listen to this voice, because this voice means I won't get to kiss you again. I won't get the thrill of you looking into my eyes like I'm the only one who will ever matter. I'll miss out on the potent surge of love I get whenever you finally come back to me, and how it tastes so much sweeter when I've had to work for it so very hard.

"Do you really think things will be different?" she asks. "If you're really honest with yourself, Amelie, do you think this boy won't hurt you again?"

I can feel how carefully she's picked every word, like she's chosen each one from a line-up and then assembled them into that question, using a pair of tweezers.

I'm about to open my mouth to defy her, to defend you – then my stomach twists.

It has something to say.

My gut.

334

My gut says… *No.*

I close my mouth, not wanting to admit it. Because admitting it means this is the end of us. The end of the good and the thrill and the mess but, oh, how amazing it could be. I'm not sure I'm ready to let go of that. I'm not sure I'll ever be ready to let go of that.

Joan talks again. She uncrosses and recrosses her ankles. She doesn't look directly at me, rather to the side of my face, her eyes skimming over the box of tissues that sit on a table between us.

"Sometimes," she says, "when someone doesn't treat us well and attacks the essence of who we are, that causes a trauma. It's natural to want to be loved – it's the most natural thing in the world. So, when we love someone and they hurt us, our brain doesn't like it. Our brain doesn't like trauma, it doesn't like feeling unsafe, and sometimes it comes up with unhealthy shortcuts in order to trick us into feeling safe."

She's speaking so matter-of-factly, so calmly, that I can't help but listen.

"One of the things the brain does to feel safe, is it creates an intense bond with the person who hurts us. It's the ego's way of protecting itself. You may have heard of Stockholm syndrome?"

I nod. I remember it from some old James Bond film where the girl falls in love with her kidnapper.

"Well that's an example of a trauma bond – falling in love with your captor makes it a hell of a lot easier to handle the fact you've been kidnapped." She pauses, still not looking at me or forcing the issue, just quietly urging me to listen. "Another thing to consider, Amelie, is that if someone is inconsistent with how they treat us…our body can get addicted to being in a nervous state. Waiting for it to get better, feeling sick and depressed and terrible when it doesn't – but then we get a flood of happy hormones when this person is finally nice to us again. It's a bit like being on drugs. You're never sure when you'll get your next 'hit' of niceness.

"Now if you combine a trauma bond with this constant state of emotional and anxious arousal, well…it's very powerful. Your pull to this person is incredibly strong. Your feelings for them are incredibly strong…"

Here. Here is when she looks at me. Joan sits up and stares me right in the eye.

"But it isn't love, Amelie," she says. "Those feelings are not love."

She doesn't tell me to never see you again. She doesn't tell me what to do next. She quietly presses about whether, one day, I want to tell my parents everything. As always, I shake my head.

It isn't love, Amelie.

When I come out of counselling there's another message.

Reese: I need to see you. Please. BoJangles. I love you xxxxxxx

It isn't love, Amelie.

What is love? I wonder, as I step out into the warm day and look at the leaves fanning out from the tree branches. I'm alone, as usual. Is love never having to say you're sorry? Is it grand, romantic gestures? Is it fireworks and *can't-get-you-out-of-my-head* and *I've-never-felt-this-way-before*? Is it constantly checking your phone and feeling sick when you've not heard from them but then pure euphoria when you have? Is it hiding the bits of yourself they don't like, but it's okay as long as they're really good looking? Is it butterflies? But not, like, always nice ones, but nervous ones every time you see them – not just because you're excited, but also because you're scared you'll get it wrong? Is it knowing you can't live without them? That you need them so much and so utterly that you're willing to give up everything else just in exchange for how it feels on those rare good days? Love hurts. That's what they always say, isn't it? Is it real if it's not hurting? Can you trust it's love if it doesn't punch you in the face?

I start walking towards town, reading and rereading your message. I picture our reunion and how amazing it will feel to fall back into your arms. I can see the evening spread out in front of me. You'll tell me everything that was wrong with Eden and I'll be able to release all my insecurity and jealousy. You'll promise to make it up to me, and I trust that, initially, you really will. I will be adored, and nothing will be too much. I can picture the presents and the dates and the grovelling apologies. You'll probably write me a song, even.

Tonight we can go to yours and have sex, and I know it won't be like Sheffield. It will be loving and tender and amazing, like it was in the start. If you rub out all the bad stuff, all the stuff that has almost destroyed me, and focus on what you and me could be like in the upcoming weeks – man, could we make the world jealous. We burn and we soar and we make each other feel alive and so many pathetic people will never get a taste of what love can be, and what life can be like if you have a love like ours.

That's not love, Amelie.

A mother bashes into me with her double buggy and doesn't apologize. I shake my head, trying to rouse myself from this daze. I know where you'll be waiting for me. You'll be on the sofas. You always managed to get the best table anywhere. I know the moment I walk in you'll scoop me up and kiss me in front of everyone. You'll whisper you knew I'd come, that you are so sorry. Everyone will look on jealously. Word will get around college. You've always loved a stage.

That's not love, Amelie.

Can I walk away from all that? Isn't it *madness* to walk away from all that? Who would sacrifice the chance at that kind of love? Even though my gut is saying something. And the something my gut is saying is: *It won't last.* I know it won't. You will not be able to sustain it. I will mess up again somehow. Someone shiny and new will come along, because I am never shiny enough for long enough.

Yet – despite this – I'm walking towards BoJangles. I'm walking towards you.

What is love?

Maybe it's something else. Maybe it's not what we've been told it is. Maybe it's boring words like *security* and *safety, warmth* and *growth*. Maybe it's the comfort of knowing someone really well and them knowing you back. Maybe it's kisses where you sometimes bump noses but you can laugh it off? Maybe it's never getting butterflies because you always know where you stand? Maybe it's not passion, but caution? Shouldn't you be cautious? If you're going to go through the emotional stripping necessary to give your heart to another? To let them hold it beating in the palms of their hands, both of you knowing they can close their fingers at any time and squash it to mush? Shouldn't you feel *safe* with that person, rather than delirious with passion or insecurity or...a trauma bond? Maybe love – real love – is mellow. A slow-cooking stew only just simmering on the hob, but if you leave it long enough the flavour deepens and deepens. Maybe it's your favourite song being played on a really low volume, but it doesn't matter because you know the words and melody so well you can sing it in your head.

I've had one love and I've had another type of love. I've experienced both and one made me warm and safe, and the other has led me to therapy and isolation...

Yet, Reese? I don't *care*. I'm coming for you! I'm coming. I'm so sorry I doubted us, baby.

I pick up into a run. What if you're not there? What if you've changed your mind? The nerves kick-start, the butterflies flap their wings and start a storm across the sea.

I can't walk away from us. The thought makes me burst into tears. I can't walk away from you. I'm so sorry I even thought about it.

I love you, Reese. I love you, I love you, I love you! I'm coming for you. For us. I'm on my way. I'm running. I love you, I lo—

"Amelie?"

I'm being grabbed and stopped. Someone's taken my arm and jolted me to a halt. I whiplash backwards and look up to see who's dared stop me from my sprint back towards you.

"Hannah?"

She's holding my arm, worry engraved all over her face.

"Amelie? What's wrong?"

Why is she delaying me? I have to go! I have to find you! And be with you, and probably destroy myself in the process, but I'm kind of certain it will all be worth it…

"I have to go." I pull away from her. "I'm late for something."

She doesn't let me go though. She steps in front of me, blocking my path, staring, horrified, at my crying face. "Amelie. It can wait. What's wrong? Why are you crying?"

"Please, let me go. Please, I'm late for a…"

She shakes her head. "Whatever you're late for, Amelie, it isn't worth it." She, ever so gently, puts her hand on my shoulder. "I know we've not spoken in quite a while, but why don't we go for a walk or something? Talk?"

I'm at war with myself, every part of my body caught up

with these two conflicting urges. The urge to see you and feel that release – but oh, the cost, the cost, the cost… And the urge to stay and fight and know that Joan is right – what you and I have *isn't* love. It was never love. It was an illusion – one that eroded me from the inside out and robbed me of myself and everything I ever loved, leaving me a husk that's only just begun to try and put herself back together. The urge to self-destruct at the hands of a boy, or the urge to try and restore myself at the hands of a girl, a friend, who is asking me if I'm okay.

I blink and gasp and start crying harder. I must look crazy. People try to get past on the pavement, and tut and grumble, but Hannah doesn't care. She's not taking her hand off my shoulder. She's not repulsed by my crying. If anything, she looks deeply upset that I'm crying at all. Even though I was such a twat to her.

"Amelie. You're scaring me. Please? Come on. We can get a coffee in the park. My treat."

I don't want to lose you, Reese. I don't want to walk away from us. But I can't pretend none of it happened. That none of the bad stuff and the awful stuff and the truly horrifying stuff didn't happen.

That's not love, Amelie.

And, I…

I…

I let go of you.

I sigh, and release the toxic idea of us into the bright-blue sky.

The grief hits harder than I ever thought possible. I disintegrate into such spectacular hysterics that Hannah leads me to a bench, sits me down, and tells me to breathe, but *I cannot I cannot I cannot*. It's over. It *has* to be over. And even though you've hurt me so much – in ways I'm not sure I'll ever recover from – it hurts so much to let you go. Hannah's hand doesn't stop rubbing my back, she doesn't stop whispering reassurances. She stays with me until the tears reach their natural stopping point, as they're always able to do, no matter how hard you're crying.

"Amelie?" she asks, when my river of tears has temporarily been dammed. "What's going on?"

I look up through my red-raw eyes. I snuffle up my snot. I wipe the grief from my face. And I have one last realization.

This is the first time I've cried in public and someone has noticed and has truly cared.

The first person who has seen me and has thought to stop and ask if I'm okay – because, whenever someone cries in full view of the public, they're clearly not okay.

I open my mouth.

And I start to tell her.

Platform Thirteen, Clapham Junction Train Station

People around me wilt in the heat.

The sun bounces off the railway tracks and passengers fight for the tiny patches of shade as they wait for their trains to arrive with welcome air-conditioning. I'm sat here, slurping on a plastic cup of iced coffee, in my new dress covered in sunflowers. Even I will admit that it's too hot for a cardigan today.

This is the last place, Reese. The final spot on my memory map, before I send it off to the museum. You may've noticed there's been quite a gap between this final call and my previous spots. Winter took off its jumper to reveal spring, and spring dropped off its blossom to let summer have a turn, and here we are. In the baking heat, with nobody's deodorant quite strong enough. I'm going to bid you adieu to the sweet tang of a stranger's BO.

Fitting, really.

I don't really want to go into why I was last here and last crying, and how very awful it was. At the time, it was one of the worst nights of my life. You and Eden got offered a gig, just the two of you, at the Underdog, and you were both all the more insufferable because the gig was, like, totally in London. Yes, in London? Didn't I tell you it was in London? Clapham, as you're asking. Nobody really asked you, but it didn't stop either of you from telling us all about it all the time. And, I mean, *of course*, I wasn't welcome to come, being your girlfriend and all.

"You'd be too distracting," you'd told me – not even bothering to look at me or say sorry or even touch me that day. "The other gig went really well and I think it's because I was much more relaxed. And I know you're all psycho about me and Eden getting off with each other. That's not fair on either of us, to have to deal with you on our big day."

Because you were a right twat-end, weren't you, Reese? Total fucking ball-ache of a human being. I mean, what a crazy psycho I was, thinking you were going to leave me for her, when all you did was go and LEAVE ME FOR HER! OH I WAS SO FREAKING CRAZY, WASN'T I? FOR ACCURATELY GUESSING WHAT THE HELL WAS GOING ON THE WHOLE DAMN TIME? CRAZY, CRAZY AMELIE, WITH HER TOTALLY NORMAL GRIP ON REALITY!!!

Whoops. Sorry.

Joan says the grieving process does include all the clichéd stages that we think of – denial, bargaining, anger, etc. I think we can both agree I may be lurking in anger at the moment.

What am I grieving for? you ask. *For the break-up?* No, Reese, breaking up with you is the best thing that's ever happened to me. Although that's somewhat counterbalanced by the fact meeting you was the worst thing that's ever happened to me. So, am I grieving for you? No. Not really. Maybe, for a while, I had to grieve for the *idea* of you. I had to accept that the good bits in you weren't real, not really. They were only ever a trap. A spider's web, to lure me in and get me entangled, so you could bind me and then suck me dry, before you moved on to your next fly. So, you ask again: *Who are you grieving for, Amelie?*

And, I'll tell you, Reese.

I'm grieving for me.

I'm grieving for the me I was before I met you. The me who trusted people. The me who trusted that love was a good thing. The me who had friends and a life, and was respected for being true to herself. That girl is gone. You killed her. I'm starting to grow her back, of course, but she will never be the same.

"That's one of the things that's going to be the hardest to accept," Joan said. "That you can't turn back the clock. What happened with this boy happened. It's part of who you are now. I know it's unfair and I know it's hard, but what's important now is you know what to look out for, so that it never happens again."

I'm grieving for the girl I was before you mesmerized me and idolized me and made us both feel like our love would move mountains. I'm mourning the girl I was before you started grinding me down and making me believe everything I was was wrong. I'm mourning the girl who had friends that you gradually, carefully – ever so subtly, so I can never really prove you did it at all – forced me to get rid of. I'm grieving the girl you manipulated into sex and then brutally raped while she was crying. The girl who still has nightmares, and got referred to specialist trauma recovery therapy to try and help come to terms with what you did to my body. I'm grieving for my parents, who still can't believe such a thing could happen to their own girl, not when they'd tried so very hard to protect me from boys like you. I'm grieving the loss of all of our innocence. None of us will be the same again after you. Not me, or Mum, or Dad, or Alfie.

Let's finish this story then, shall we?

\ \

I wasn't allowed to come to the gig but, like the maniac Reese had made me, I decided to follow him. I knew, if he or his friends caught me, I'd never be able to deny I wasn't crazy. Not when I was full-on stalking my own boyfriend, who'd promised me he could be trusted. I dressed all in black because, if you're going to be a loon who actually starts stalking people, you may as well go the whole hog. I tied my hair back. I looked up what time his gig was and calculated what time they'd be getting there to set up, to ensure we didn't accidentally end up on the same train.

"Off out somewhere?" Mum asked, hope in her voice when she saw me tie the belt on my coat.

"Yes, just going to a gig." I tucked my ponytail into my scarf.

She sagged in relief. "That's great! You've not played in a while. Your dad's delighted you're not keeping us up all night, but it's good you've got a gig tonight."

I shook my head. "It's not my gig, it's Reese's. In London."

I tried to ignore how her face changed when I brought up his name. "Oh. Reese's. Well, have fun."

I shook uncontrollably on the train up. My hands could hardly hold my phone. I felt like everyone on the carriage could sense what I was doing and they were watching me suspiciously.

You are crazy, I told myself. *Look how totally crazy you are. Look at what the hell you are doing, Amelie. No wonder Reese is going off you. You are completely nuts.*

Yet my gut told me to stay on the train, and my gut told me to get off at Clapham Junction and navigate my way up St John's Road, dodging all the clumps of smokers spilling out of pubs, onto the pavement. I arrived too early. Their set didn't start for another forty minutes and I couldn't risk anyone seeing me. So I found a little alleyway and just stood in it, taking out my phone every thirty seconds to see how much time had passed. Telling myself, *you are crazy, you are so crazy, you are going to go in there and see it's perfectly innocent and then you will probably kill yourself because you will have proven how totally insane you are.*

Eventually, by the time my lips were actually blue from the cold, it was almost time for their slot. He'd be backstage, getting ready with her, and it was safe to stake out my best crazy-stalker-psycho-girlfriend stalking spot at the back, in case his old band had come.

I quietly pushed my way through the throngs of smokers outside, ordered a lime and soda water, just so I'd have something to do with my shaking hands, and then wedged myself near the back. The crowd around me were chatty and disinterested, hardly taking any notice of the stage. It was very different from how he'd described the venue when he'd been boasting about it and telling me I wasn't welcome and that I wasn't allowed to have an emotional response to that fact. "It's such an incredible venue. The crowd is so focused, really into their music, you know?"

But, from what I could tell, this wasn't the case. The group of blokes next to me were egging each other on to down Jägerbombs and telling their mate Mikey to "stop being a pussy". A group of girls to the other side of me appeared to be lost in a shouted discussion about the emotional availability of one of their boyfriends. "I just FEEL like he's into it, even though, he, like, doesn't ACT like he's into it? Do you know what I mean?" one yelled, while the others all nodded and sipped through their straws and glanced over at Mikey the Pussy and then pretended they hadn't. I started to feel worried for Reese. You can sense within the first ten seconds of a gig if the crowd is going to be on your side. From out here, things weren't looking too great. And even though I was hurt and humiliated at the not being invited, I still loved Reese and wanted the best for him.

It went dark. Nobody whooped or cheered as he and Eden walked onstage. In fact, one of the girls just grumbled about the lights going out. There was a smattering of minor applause as I watched the brim of his hat move across the stage to stand at the mike. I watched Eden in the darkness and a stab of wet, hot hatred bubbled up. The lights blasted on again. Reese took the mike in his hand. "Hey, everyone, thanks for having us. We're Dimmer Switch."

They launched into their first song, both of them harmonizing perfectly. I could feel the sizzle of their chemistry from way back where I was standing. I felt like, if they were to reach out and touch one another, you'd see an actual electric spark flicker between their fingers. He stared at her during each song, exactly how he used to stare at me. I felt like I was watching a re-enactment of our night at the Cube. Eden stared right back. In fact, it was clear to all involved that the two of them were in their own little bubble – the audience needn't even be there. Which was just as well, because they weren't exactly riveted to the stage. Mikey was still being called a pussy, and one of Mikey's friends approached one of the girls and asked their opinion on Mikey's pussiness. No one seemed to give a flying damn about Reese and Eden, the little singing duo, and their songs, and the fact it was clear they'd fallen in love with one another.

No one apart from me.

Me, who, at this point, held on to the wall like it had handlebars. I tried to regulate my breathing and told myself I was just being crazy and paranoid, yet again, like he said. But song after song, their chemistry increased (though the quality of their set really did not). I wasn't crying. Not yet. I was in too much shock. Too sick. Actually physically sick. The searing jealousy was like being injected with high-strength nausea directly into my heart. *"GET AWAY FROM HIM!"* I wanted to scream at Eden. *"GET AWAY GET AWAY GET AWAY!"* But instead I just stood and watched, and felt my insides collapse into insecurity and terribleness and grief.

You're just imagining it, you're just imagining it, you're just imagining it, I muttered to myself, begging it to be true, so keen to believe him. I wanted his lies about me to be true. It was less painful to accept I was a nutjob than that Reese loved someone else.

The set was drawing to a close, and I knew I should leave. I was risking my last scrap of dignity by staying and maybe being spotted, but my feet felt superglued to the floor. I couldn't not stay and see this played out in its entirety. Reese strummed the last chord and the crowd clapped politely. He nodded and said, "Thank you, thank you. You've been amazing – thank you," like he was at Wembley or something...

Then it happened.

Time slowed, as it tends to do in the precise moment that hearts are broken. He looked at Eden and smiled, and Eden looked back and smiled, and then...then, they both leaned forward on stage, and they...they...

They...

...

...

...

kissed each other.

I can't remember much else, to be honest. If you ask me what happened between that kiss – the sort of kiss where it's obvious they've kissed many times before – and getting to this platform at Clapham Junction, I can't tell you. There's a blank. At least half an hour is missing from my life. I don't remember leaving, or walking back, or even getting through the station turnstiles. I just remember coming around here, on platform thirteen, just as the next train was cancelled.

"Southern Rail are sorry for the delay this will cause to your journey."

There was a forty-minute wait till the next train, and nothing else for me to do but huddle into a ball on an uncomfortable chair in the shitty waiting room and fall apart completely. I've never cried harder – I shook the chair from my sobbing. It was like I'd fallen into a vortex of grief. Every part of my body hurt, like each of my muscles had been twisted into a ball and then punched multiple times. I could hardly breathe. I was hiccupping and making strange gasps and, of course, nobody came over to ask if I was okay. Why would they, when it was so much more convenient to ignore the hysterical girl sobbing in the corner?

I close my eyes here, on the same platform, and feel the sun on my eyelids. When I was last here, I was a mess. I thought I was broken beyond repair. I thought my world had collapsed. When the train eventually did pull in, I could hardly walk as I staggered onto it. I, of course, messaged you, dignity full-blown out the window, and told you I knew. That I'd seen you. I called you names. I called Eden worse names. Because we always make the girls the villains rather than the victims. You told me I was crazy. You told me you'd never loved me, not really.

You told everyone at college what a stalking psycho I was. I mean, I did go a bit crazy after that. I turned up outside your house, screaming and crying and wailing and asking what I'd done, and why you'd done this to me, and please please please take me back, and apologizing for all the things I'd done wrong just by being myself and trying to love you enough. You'd stared at me in cold disgust and told me I was pathetic, and no wonder you had fallen for Eden.

That isn't love.

What we had wasn't love, Reese.

That's what I've learned. By retracing these steps, by

listening to my gut again, by following the trail of my tears, by admitting I needed help.

It wasn't love in the slightest.

It was abuse.

Abuse.

"But he never hit me," I said to Joan, when she got that big word out of its box and made it into a necklace for me to wear. "He never once hit me, or strangled me, or threatened me in any way."

For so long I felt I couldn't put that necklace on, I couldn't own that word. Abuse is when they kick you and hold you against the wall by your throat. Abuse is when you cower in the corner, waiting for them to strike you. Abuse is broken ribs and black eyes and pretending to your friends that you've fallen down the stairs. Abuse isn't what you did to me, Reese, *surely?*

And Joan smiled warmly and pulled out her trusty box of tissues and said a few things that took a while to dissolve in.

Abuse is also when your personality is attacked, not just your body. Abuse is feeling like you constantly have to walk on eggshells around the person you're supposed to love. Abuse is being cut off from your friends, even if you could never prove it was their idea you did it. Abuse is being made to feel you're going crazy. Abuse is being lured in with grand promises and wild declarations of love that can never be sustained. Abuse is being pushed into doing sexual things you're not comfortable with. That is also called rape, another word that has taken me some time to feel belongs to me. Abuse is intentionally humiliating you. Abuse is constantly blaming *you* for everything, and never *them*.

"The trauma it causes is just the same as if he had hit you," Joan told me, pulling out another tissue. "Trauma is trauma. Your brain and body don't differentiate between physical and emotional abuse. They only respond to attack. Attack that you didn't deserve, Amelie. Nobody deserves to be treated the way this boy treated you."

It's taken me months of counselling to accept that you abused me and I am traumatized because of it. It's taken hours upon hours of specialist therapy, hundreds of miles, and bucketloads upon bucketloads of tears.

You abused me and it left me traumatized.

There is something wrong with you, not me.

I was just unlucky. As is every girl who stumbles into your net.

But I've managed to break away and break free, and grow myself back.

It really is a hot day. The pavement almost crackles, ice melts into my syrupy coffee within moments, everyone's fanning their faces with whatever makeshift equipment they can. Nobody's sitting on my sunny bench on this platform. I can feel my nose prickle with the itch of sunburn. I should get into the shade, but not yet. There are still two things I need to do.

The specialist trauma lady I was referred to, Sandy, taught me a technique. One to distance my feelings towards you and towards it and the whole mess that was meeting you. We did it in her office. She'd put me into a deep relaxation and repeat the same technique over and over until I didn't shake and clam up and start sobbing uncontrollably whenever I thought of what you've done to me.

"*Imagine you're in a cinema,*" Sandy said. "*You've got the whole cinema to yourself. It's dark and warm and safe.*"

I close my eyes, here, on the bench, on the platform where I cried. The stifling heat fades away, the sun dims. I see myself sat in an empty cinema, the screen blank. I'm in the dark, waiting for the film to start. I'm a million miles away from London.

"*Now, think of a time, before the trauma started, where you felt safe. Truly safe,*" Sandy would say next. "*That is where the film will start.*"

Reese, I'm sitting here with my eyes closed, and I'm thinking I felt a whole lot safer before I met you. So this film is going to start with Sheffield. With my arms around Alfie, and with friends who love me, on the north side of the chimneys that bellow smoke out into the sky. I let the feeling of safety engulf me before I move on to the next step.

"*Now, a black-and-white film is about to start of your traumatic experience. But, before we press play, I want you to float out of your body and up into the tiny projectionist's room, right at the back and at the top of the cinema,*" Sandy prompted.

Reese, I'm floating up. I can see two versions of myself now. In my head, I can see Amelie on the screen, safe and smiling in Sheffield. And I can see Amelie sat in the cinema, waiting for the film about to start.

"Now, this is the hard bit. The film starts to play. Watch you watching yourself…"

And the film starts. I watch me watch the film of you and me.

It's still hard, Reese. Not as hard as it was, but it's still very damn difficult. I still want to reach inside the screen and yank myself out and drag myself away from it, but I can't. I watch my first day of college and I watch myself crying on the bench because I miss Alfie. I watch myself cry onstage in the college refectory, and meet you, and be so, so dazzled by the charming boy in the hat. I watch you walk me home and take me on incredible dates, where life felt like I was living a fairy tale. I watch myself cry at the bus stop, when I realize my love for you means I'll break Alfie's heart. I watch us through all the good places and the dazzlement of being under your spell, and how I fell so, so hard – despite all the warnings and red flags. I watch you hijack my first massive gig and make it all about you and I watch myself think it was the most romantic thing ever. I watch you start to strain away when I couldn't live up to the huge hype you put on me and watch the poison creep in. I watch myself be humiliated and ignored at your house. I watch myself sob on your street. I watch myself lose my friends and lose myself and make my entire life about trying to make you happy, at the expense of my everything. I watch us walk around London and how I'm nervous and stressed and constantly trying to make you okay, us okay, *it* okay because where did it go? I watch you make me feel bad about being myself on the bridge, and I watch myself cry tears that melt off my face and drop down into the polluted water of the Thames. I watch myself get the train to Sheffield…and here…here is where I still struggle.

I gulp and lose where I am for a moment. Wanting so much to pull myself back into this hot sunny day where I am safe… But I dig my fingernails into the palm of my hands and I watch you turn up at the gig, and I watch Alfie's heart disintegrate, and I watch myself chasing you to the station and begging for forgiveness. Then I watch what happened in the hotel room. The thing that can never be undone. The thing I can never forgive you for. I watch the me who tried to blank that out, who was addicted to checking her phone, addicted to trying to be who you wanted me to be, but always getting it wrong. I watch you introduce me to Eden and use her to further make me feel wrong about myself, and I watch myself weep in the music room. And then I come here in the film. I come up to Clapham and see something I'd been told I was mental for even imagining, and I watch myself cry in the waiting room of the station, with nothing left but apparently more tears. I've always been able to find tears when it comes to you.

Then the movie comes to a stop.

I sigh. I keep my eyes closed, but reach up to brush

away the tears that have fallen.

"*Now, congratulate yourself on being brave enough to relive that,*" Sandy said.

"I am brave," I whisper to myself.

And I am. I am so, so brave. As is every girl who manages to escape someone like you with even a shred of herself left. I may have lost a lot of tears. I may've lost my trust and my dignity and my friends and my hope, but I didn't lose me. Not entirely. I was brave enough to leave just a sliver of myself that can regenerate and regrow. So many girls don't. Always, *always* be the girl who does.

"*And now, float down from the projection room, and step through the cinema screen into the film. It's now Technicolor. You will feel everything you felt. But the film is about to play backwards, really, really fast, okay?*"

Here I am, sat on a bench on a train platform. And yet, in my head, I'm floating through a cinema screen and emerging onto the same train platform, not so many months ago, when it was cold and I was broken. It's all in colour and I can feel how much it hurt, and...

"*And go! The film is rewinding – super, super fast – right back to the beginning, where you were last safe.*"

And I'm whizzing backwards in time. Back-back-back through the sticky floors of that London venue, back-back-back through the music room, back-back-back through Sheffield, back-back-back to the Golden Jubilee Bridge, back-back-back to your road, back-back-back to being onstage at the Cube, back-back-back past the good places that were actually all just a trick, back-back-back through the number thirty-seven bus stop, back-back-back through the college talent show, back-back-back to my first day of college and not telling Alfie I loved him and back-back-back up the motorway. I unpack my belongings and make my room up in Sheffield to how it was before I was forced to leave it. And Alfie is here and I do not know you exist, and I am safe. I am safe.

I am finally safe.

I open my eyes.

It's summer and it's over. It's summer and I've got my guitar on my lap. It's summer and I'm going to busk now, even if it's illegal. Even if none of these busy, sweaty people around me care. I've got my voice back, and I've got a song to sing.

I strum the opening chord, and I open my mouth. I used to get scared of performing, but I've learned there are much bigger things to be frightened of.

I smile, and I start to sing.

I've been retracing all the memories
Sketching the map of me and you
I just passed the body of my boundaries
Kicked into the road
Alongside my truth

Here are the places I've cried
Here's the bed I made in your lies
Here's the last shred of my pride
Take it all, take it all, take it all

It started on a quiet bench
And it ended, oh, right here.
I'm finding myself in my footprints
There's not much left
To grow back
But there's enough…

Here are the places I've cried
Here are all the tears that fell from my eyes
Here are the pointless times that I tried
Take it all, take it all, take it all

And here I grow
Now it's my spring, now it's my spring
And there you go
I can sing, I can sing
I've finally, finally, learned how to say no

Here are the places I've cried
Here's the bed I made in your lies
Here's the last shred of my pride
Take it all, take it all, take it all
Here are the places I've cried
Here are all the tears that fell from my eyes
Here are the pointless times that I tried
Take it all, take it all, take it all

Some people stop and listen to the song I have to sing, the story I have to tell. They nod their heads, enjoying it. A man tries to offer me money, but I smile and shake my head. Others pretend I'm not there. They are lost in the haze of their own lives and their own problems. That's okay. I'm not doing this for anyone but me.

My bag is packed at my feet.

This is goodbye, Reese. I will not see you again.

You don't deserve a goodbye, of course. But this is more for me than it is for you. I've got a room in Jessa's house, where I can finish my A levels on my side of the chimneys, and I've got parents who've agreed it's probably for the best. I've got a good friend in Hannah to hang out with when I come down to visit. I've got a university course to try and get onto, and gigs booked in at my old favourite spots. I've got a whole life to try and lead without you, and, by damn, that's a good life to have. I can never go back to the girl I was before, I can't undo the past. But I can take my journey and my scars and I can use the lessons they gave me to ensure my future path has fewer tears in it. There's a trail of salt across the country, from the tears that rolled down my cheeks, marking the path of this mess, but it ends here.

Because you know what?

I hardly ever cry any more.

The End

If you have been affected by the issues raised in this book, the following organizations can help:

Samaritans are available round the clock, every single day of the year. You can talk to them any time you like, and in your own way, about whatever's getting to you.

Call, free, any time, on 116 123

Or email jo@samaritans.org

Visit – find your nearest branch on

samaritans.org

The Mix is here to help under 25s get to grips with any challenge they face. Anywhere and anytime, online, over the phone or via social media.

Helpline: 0808 808 4994

themix.org.uk

HOLLY BOURNE

Are We All
LEMMINGS
&
SNOWFLAKES?

Everyone wants to
feel ~~special~~ normal.

Welcome to Camp Reset,
a summer camp with a difference.

A place offering a shot at normality for Olive, a girl
on the edge, and for her new friends, who are all
dealing with their own battles.

But as Olive settles in she starts to wonder –
maybe it's this messed-up world that needs fixing,
and not them. And so she comes up with a plan.

Because together, snowflakes can form avalanches...

"An honest, funny book full of heart."
Irish Sunday Independent

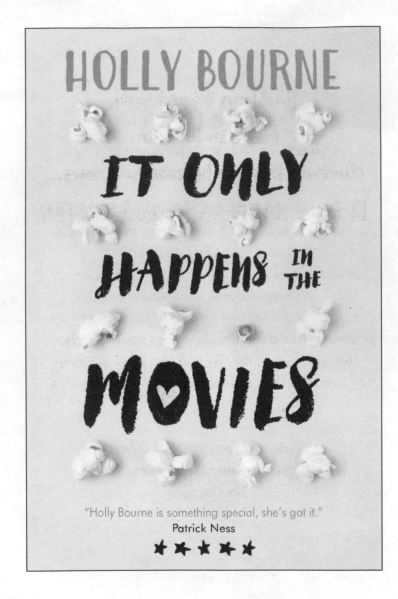

HOLLY BOURNE

IT ONLY

HAPPENS IN THE

MOVIES

"Holly Bourne is something special, she's got it."
Patrick Ness

★ ★ ★ ★ ★

Bad boys turned good,
kisses in the rain,
climbing through bedroom windows...
IT ONLY HAPPENS IN THE MOVIES

When Audrey meets Harry, it's the start of a truly
cinematic love story – or is it?

Audrey knows that Harry is every movie cliché
rolled into one. But she still chooses to let him
into her heart...

"This is Bourne at her outrageous,
courageous, necessary best."
The Guardian

Love this book? Love Usborne YA

Follow us online and sign up to the Usborne YA
newsletter for the latest YA books,
news and competitions:

usborne.com/yanewsletter

 @UsborneYA

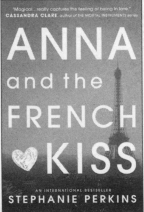